PenWorks

Publishers

Keene's Law
A PenWorks Publishers Book
All rights reserved
Copyright ©2005 by George Patte
Editing by Beth H. Evans
Cover and Graphic Design by Mark Costa

For information address:
    PenWorks Publishers, inc.
    144 Ridgecrest Road
    Ithaca, New York 14850
    www.PenWorksPublishers.com

ISBN 0-9768575-1-0

10 9 8 7 6 5 4 3 2 1

To my Dad and Mom, who first showed me the North Country in my youth. And to my wife, Mary, who has offered crucial support to me in my writing of this novel over the last six years.

KEENE'S LAW

George Notte

Contents

Prologue
September 10, 1960

*M*y view is of the Great Basin wilderness framed by distant mountain peaks. They form a rugged, half-bowl amphitheatre at the head of the valley, with native hemlock, cedar, spruce, white birch and hardwoods growing below the tree line. Granite slabs, in hues of blue and gray, stand sunlit above the amphitheater. The near-vertical granite descends to ridgelines and plateaus that cast tones of deep purple and lavender on the alpine lake and sandy beach nestled in the Basin in front of me.

I sit on the porch of the Adirondack camp, an old man rich with memories of a life spent here. As a boy I learned about the wild forest, waters, and trails on this land from my father and my mentor, Duryea. Father and Mother first brought me here in 1889 when I was four years old. My first memory is of running about the clearing where the great camp would be built in 1894, happy with the sights and smells and sounds of the mountains.

I have returned here to this great camp my family calls the Basin, to stay the night, perhaps for the last time. It has not changed in my lifetime.

The cooling autumn air sends a tingle down my spine as I think about the decision before me. Later this September day I plan to meet with my son Will, and lawyers representing the State of New York, to make the final plans. Together we'll do a last review of the deed that preserves this immense tract of wilderness forever — in perpetuity. The reasons for my visit today weigh heavily on my mind.

I followed in my father's footsteps and became a lawyer. We formed the Durant Law Firm and became known in the Adirondacks for land transactions and litigated land disputes, going back to the creation of the state forests of the Adirondacks.

But I am not sure Keene Durant would approve of what I plan for this place he so revered. This is something that I, Jack Durant, must decide. Father passed on in 1920 and left me with a thriving law practice and an ownership interest in this land—four hundred thousand acres of wilderness barely touched by any man.

But legal title to the Basin has remained surrounded by intrigue. Questions about my legal proof of ownership, the validity of an escrow deed my father held, and even the location of the Basin's boundaries, have loomed around me since my youth.

Some say the Great Basin is the most complete preserved tract of land in the Adirondack Park still in private hands. State lands surround it. Water that is cold and clean flows from high elevations and descends to its rivers and lakes. I've spent a lifetime fly-fishing these waters, watching and learning the ways of the native brook trout.

Kora Longfellow Hubreth, with whom I grew up and who still comes here, claims an interest in the Basin lands adverse to my own. For over forty years Kora and I have vacillated between being lovers and being alienated from one another over the question of ownership of these lands. Those periods of estrangement have sometimes left us near emotional ruin, and they're the reason any future plans remain suspended in uncertainty. Kora has monitored this planned land transaction of mine closely, as have the heirs of Rondeau, a backwoods hermit who once lived on a remote reach of the land and whose family I want to protect if I can.

To understand all of this, you must come to know the Basin lands and the decision my father made to complete and record the escrow deed—the deed I've kept in my office safe — which could make or break a good title on this land. I'm holding in my hands the letter Father left me the day he died, containing instructions for the deed. I've sat here on the porch for quite a while now contemplating it for the hundredth time. This letter simplified my task in some ways, but it also brought my relationship with Kora, already strained, near the breaking point.

As my father Keene once said, Kora and I were on separate life paths, and he was right. But we've been held together over decades by the tension and uncertainty centered around these Basin lands and the great camp. The years have taken us on a long and winding journey.

I learned many of my facts about the Basin and its history from hearing stories told by Duryea, Father, and others, and from reading journals, documents, correspondence, and law. At times I've had to depend on educated guesses about key events, all of which have transpired over eight decades with twists and turns and shadings of gray at times. I'll tell you what I know to be true, since certain things have been verified to my satisfaction. But be mindful that intrigue, unanswered questions, and vagueness—enemies of the lawyer—surround the Basin and its owners.

Certain dates are established by known facts or events: the State of New York, in 1885, created a forest preserve, an area of the Adirondacks inside a blue line on the map. Those state-owned lands received special protection requiring that they be maintained as wild forest. 1885 was also the year I was born, and the year in which William West Longfellow hired Keene Durant as his lawyer. The Adirondack Park was created by the legislature in 1892; two years later a change to the state constitution was proposed so that the forest preserve would remain forever wild, and voters approved the amendment.

In 1894 my father's client, William West Longfellow, delivered his escrow deed to Father with his letter of instructions, which Father still held at the time I joined his law firm in 1905.

With these known facts laid out, I will now tell you my story of the Basin, my father Keene, Longfellow and his daughter Kora, and Keene's grandson, Will. I'll start on September 1, 1894, the night of the flash fire. I wasn't in camp that night, having stayed with a friend in town. But the memory of it is as real as if I had been there.

One
September 1, 1894

I'd heard Father and Duryea tell the story so many times that I knew the facts by rote. Nonetheless, Duryea and I gathered eagerly around our hearth in the great room, my 14-year-old imagination more fascinated than ever by the story and the storyteller, my father. Keene Durant poked at the glowing embers, and began in a soft voice.

"It was the night of September first, 1894 — five years ago now, Jack, just shortly after your mother died. You were nine. Longfellow's steam engine churned along the tracks in the black night when just a hint of a freshening breeze started up. Red-hot cinders rose from the coal firebox and escaped to the cooling air. Most of the embers caught in the screen on the smokestack, but a few made it through to the boreal forest, dry from the just-ended Adirondack summer. I'd come out here at Longfellow's invitation for an inaugural visit with him and Duryea.

"The three of us — Longfellow, Duryea, and I — were asleep in this camp, less than a mile from the train. Longfellow owned the wilderness land and had seen his way clear, with his own money, to open this area to civilization and exploitation. He'd gained great wealth from his ventures in timbering and mining, and his railroad had been the force behind it. But he was about to pay for his exploits at the hands of his own creation."

At this point in Father's story, so well known to me, my mind often seized on the effects September 1, 1894, had had on those three men. They'd all been reading, and passing along to each other, John Muir's just published articles in the Overland Monthly, and his book Mountains of California. Muir had a lot to say about the wilderness and how, if not yet despoiled, it was being threatened by man. The three men were often in conversation about Muir's views of the natural world and its relationship to men and civilization. Earlier that very afternoon, they'd had a discussion while hiking to the Unnamed Mountain on the Basin lands, a conversation Duryea had on many occasions repeated to me.

Father had said, "William, this man Muir surprises me again and again. He says he goes to the mountains 'now and then for fresh life,' feeling — "

" — 'Up and away for life.'" Longfellow finished the quote.

Father had laughed with delight. "So you're actually reading him, now."

Longfellow nodded, grinning rather sheepishly. "Yes. And I think I know what he meant."

The men stopped then, as was their custom, and lowered themselves onto a fallen hemlock worn smooth by the seat of their pants. Longfellow scratched his chin.

"Muir's words have turned me upside down. He has his natural wilderness get-away out there in California, just as we have ours here. But he sees his only as a place to visit, not a place to stay and intrude upon."

They sat quietly for a while, looking at the views from one of their favorite stopping points. Keene was known as a man who held close his thoughts with most, if not with William and Duryea, and his counsel and wisdom were widely sought. Most of what he learned, he said, came in great part from his father, who had run a grain mill in Elizabethtown. There Keene had observed Ethan Durant, an early settler in the Adirondacks, give advice to farmers and businessmen on such everyday problems as finance and family. Keene learned to be practical and cunning, and to stay in things for the long haul. He loved the people here, but his independence had always set him apart a bit, something I suspect I inherited from him.

William West Longfellow was born to a prominent New York City family. Like his father he became a captain of industry, making and losing fortunes, but with a tenacity that always landed him on his feet. He was not a man to be backed into to a corner, and once his mind was made up he pushed ahead relentlessly. His marriage to Janet, also a City native, ended largely because of his mercurial business ventures, but also because William had moved Janet and their daughter Kora to the Adirondacks to oversee his timber and mining interests. Janet never adapted to the move. She was a city person, and felt stifled in the quiet solitude of the wilderness.

William liked to say that he often sat in meetings with Andrew Carnegie, who could manage a business and earn a dollar, but who'd never spent a day in the woods in his life and had no understanding of Mother Nature. William himself became quite at home here, gaining an understanding of the people and nature's bounty. More recently, with his two friends he'd begun to wonder if he was wrong to diminish nature with his industry.

Percy Duryea was self-taught. He had a steel-trap mind for learning of every kind, and displayed great intelligence, even genius, in matters of design, mechanics, and construction. Of humble French-Canadian stock, his inquisitiveness led him to read anything available. He had a steady source of materials sent to him by Father's Albany colleague, William Kelly, including a subscription to the Overland Monthly. Eventually he ordered Muir's books for himself, and began sharing them with his two compatriots, and eventually with me. As master builder for Longfellow, Duryea became inseparable from and loyal to the businessman. I'm sure that at times it was difficult for Duryea to hold his own views about the wilderness and work for the man who wanted to change it. Then again, knowing Duryea, maybe that's exactly why he stayed with Longfellow, sensing the man's profound goodness and hoping to move him in the direction of conservation. Duryea eventually developed the same close relationship with Keene and me that he had with Longfellow, though for me, he became my shining mentor and fly-fishing master, and a major factor in my outlook on life.

Together the three men had pieced together a kind of loosely stated, seat-of-the-pants philosophy heavily swayed by Muir, of course, but also born of their own experiences in the Basin. I'm sure Duryea was pleased to learn that Longfellow had memorized the Muir lines about the feeling of being in the mountains.

After a while, Duryea said, "This wilderness land is fast disappearing, gentlemen. It won't last unless we set some of it aside — as much as possible, and as soon as possible." Duryea looked straight at Longfellow with unmistakable directness.

William nodded agreement. "True. I was just reading something from the 1890 census saying that the American frontier has already disappeared."

No doubt it was in all their minds that the same thing could happen to the wilderness. They sat quietly for a while, listening to the breeze whispering in the leaves, and looking off into the distant valley, still wild and unspoiled. Suddenly William pushed to his feet.

"We need to make a pact, one based on our friendship and trust, one man to the next—a pact to stand for these mountains and our right—no, nature's right — to be left in exactly the state we see before us today."

I can imagine Duryea's quiet, satisfied smile.

Longfellow threw both arms forward, palms facing the ground. Keene and Duryea joined him in a layering of hands, one atop the other, to sanction their promise.

"This Basin," William said, "a wilderness running 16 miles in one direction," he nodded to his left, "and 40 in the other, shall remain wilderness. Forever."

They remained where they were for a while discussing the ambitious commitment they'd rather suddenly committed themselves to. Whether it was the infectious passion of John Muir or a consequence of their time together in the woods of the Adirondacks, somehow they felt a bond and a connection to history at a time when the public preserve had only recently been recognized. Their pledge was something none of them would ever turn his back to.

That's why the flash fire of 1894 was so seminal an event for them — the thing that, once it occurred, led Longfellow to give instructions on the Basin lands to his lawyer, my father, Keene Durant. Those instructions, which remained secret for years, and the pact the men made, are at the heart of my story.

Keene's voice, retelling the story of the fire as Duryea and I sat at the hearth of the Basin camp, returned my mind to the present. It wouldn't be long before he'd get to the best part, where Duryea turned up missing during the worst of the firestorm.

"The three of us were about to be awakened and learn that the forest of cedar, spruce, and hemlock, some of it one hundred fifty feet in height and a century old, was in jeopardy. Those ancient trees stood along the river and up into the alpine valley where Otter Brook meets the river. The junction was near the tracks, and the hot embers were spreading along the rails as the train moved through the Basin in the night.

"With a rising breeze an ember reached the flame point, and a dry cedar branch first smoldered and then burst into flame of dry bark and oil from the ancient giant. The flame spread quickly to other trees and undergrowth. The first 10 acres around the junction were consumed within minutes.

"The conductor sounded the first alarm and the engineer saw the combustion and knew his crew could not contain the fire. He had to report the disaster to Longfellow, under standing instructions to notify him at once of any emergencies. He knew Longfellow would be enraged." Keene looked at Duryea and me, shaking his head. "The danger had been known and understood by the rail men, but not by Longfellow, the businessman."

Father's voice rose as he described the path of the fire. Getting to his feet, his words poured out from his heart.

"The fire raced along the brook to the big bend where 3,000 acres of forest lay dry. But Mother Nature was about to play her hand. Ba-room — a thundercloud sounded overhead and the sky opened to the heaviest rain any of us had ever seen. A bolt of lightning cracked and lit the sky. Red-orange flames shot above the trees and met the gray rain.

The water ran off quickly, building to a deluge that sped toward lower land, down the slopes to the valley. The fire raced against the storm, a contest of water and fire, one trying to overcome the other. And there it stood — the future of our alpine wilderness was hanging on the outcome of the raging firestorm.

"The booming thunder and lightning had brought all of us to our feet. Instantly, we saw the high flames in the forest and the hard sideways rain, and felt the intensity of the storm. Longfellow knew his rail men would be no match for the fire. His only hope was for the rain to overpower it, or else the Basin would be destroyed.

"A strong wind moved up the valley, coming with a powerful blast and driving the fire deeper into the forest, near to where the brook crested its banks and washed sand and water over the granite floor. The fire had jumped the brook and was heading directly for camp!

"The pace of rain quickened yet again, coming in sheets. The brook spilled over even faster, and a torrent of water was forced into the forest, the wall of water hissing in the red-hot embers. It was the most amazing thing, Jack. It was as if the very heavens were involved in fighting the ravenous fire!

"With water racing toward the flames, there were great clouds of steam wherever they met. It filled my nostrils and burned my lungs.

"The brook crested again in another wave, one mighty wall. It swept through hundreds of majestic stands of trees. The great wave toppled many of them, then made a turn on the valley floor and moved still closer to camp, where Longfellow and I had begun to order men into action to fight the calamity. This great camp, just completed by Duryea, was in peril. Think of it, Jack — the very camp where we sit, directly in the path of a wall of fire!"

Duryea nodded in agreement. He remained silent as Father talked, but by the expression on his face I could almost read his mind as it replayed the twists and turns of that night.

Duryea had been the first to reach the firestorm coming toward the Basin camp, and he'd known immediately that his newly built camp was in danger. Carrying an axe in one hand and a long two-man saw in the other, he hollered for his man, Jacques, to grab a long iron pry bar, called a peevey, and follow him, as he ran out towards the fire.

But Duryea didn't know he was heading into a trap.

He raced to a point where a small tributary creek crossed the line of trees. The firestorm was approaching and swelling waters ran from the flames. Duryea knew he had to redirect the flow into the fire, and he took the only action he could think of. He yelled out to Jacques, pointing out three trees they must fell and gesturing how to drop them just right, into the creek, so that its waters would be diverted toward the flames.

But they had only minutes to accomplish this. Duryea expertly notched the first tree with a few swings of his axe. Each man, one on either end of the saw, moved in unison. They had to fell the tree in exactly the right place near the bank if it were to act as a diversion dam. Then they'd need to bring down the other two trees because one lone trunk would just be pummeled about by crashing water.

The first tree came down exactly where they wanted it. The men moved to the next tree and carried out the same maneuvers, quickly felling it too into the river. It landed exactly as Duryea had intended, and increased the dam's strength. One final tree was needed to send the creek's waters headlong into the firestorm, hopefully to turn or slow it. Duryea and Jacques were near exhaustion.

The wind suddenly rose to a roar and the line of fire picked up in intensity, threatening to jump the creek and Duryea's dam. He and Jacques began sawing at the third tree with a vengeance, making every move count. To their amazement, though, even when the notching and sawing were done, the last tree did not come down. Duryea went to its far side and saw that his axe was still wedged in the notch. He yanked on it, and suddenly the tree crashed into the spot Duryea had designed for it. But it took him to the ground with it, pinning him under a large limb. Then, to his horror, the large tree trunk shifted ever so slowly, trapping his left ankle as well. Without immediate rescue, he would either drown or be consumed in flames.

Jacques, realizing that he could do nothing without help, called out loudly, hoping to be heard over the roar of the fire and the water. He was well aware of Duryea's plight and the need for haste. The flames were almost on him, even as the waters rose and swirled around him and the dam of trees. Duryea must be extricated soon, or die."

Duryea had fought to stay conscious, knowing he must keep struggling for air. But the weight of the tree across his chest was crushing, and even the adrenaline of panic couldn't overcome the increasing loss of oxygen. He felt remote, tingly, as if he were fading. He knew he was losing the battle. Time seemed suspended.

He didn't hear Jacques shout, "I'll go for help, Duryea. Hold on!"

Jacques, glancing back as he ran, saw Duryea's eyes close. Even as he rushed off to find help, he wondered if he was too late.

Duryea lay in water rising around his hips and moving up toward his chest. He seemed to come to for a moment, and tried to give a final push against the limb. Throbbing pain shot through his chest, and just before all went dark, he had a final thought: he would go up in flames in a burning hell, only to later be washed away by water raging over the dam he himself had created.

Jacques ran, stumbling through the smoke, and calling for Keene or William. He heard no answering cries. With every moment that passed, he knew the chances for saving Duryea lessened.

Keene and William were only perhaps 50 feet from Jacques, but hidden from him by the blinding the smoke. They and a group of men had dug deep trenches they hoped the fire wouldn't leap. They were constantly aware of the firestorm on their flank, chewing its way through everything in its path. In a brief pause to wipe the sweat and soot from his eyes, Keene thought about Duryea. Where was he and what was he up to? It wasn't like him not to be right beside them, commanding the fight.

"William!" he called over the wall of sound; "I haven't seen Duryea, and I'm worried! He'd be here, if he could."

"I know!" Longfellow called back. "But I haven't seen Jacques, either. Maybe they're together!"

"I wonder if they're — "

Keene's words were interrupted by Jacques, who literally stumbled right into him.

"Monsieur Longfellow, Duryea is in danger! Come, come Monsieur Durant!"

As they hurried to follow Jacques, they heard the story of the felled tree that had pinned Duryea to what was a certain deathbed unless they managed to find him immediately in the blinding smoke. Hearing the story, Keene and William had to wonder if Duryea would manage to survive his injuries, even if they found him alive.

"I think he is over here!" Jacques shouted, suddenly darting to his left. But by the time Longfellow and Keene stopped and turned around, Jacques had disappeared into the smoke and rain.

Jacques glanced back to make sure the others were following him, and stopped short with fear. No one was behind him. He thought he heard thrashing about nearby, but the smoke and rain screened any vision more than a few feet away. Precious seconds and minutes tore by; Jacques was desperate and knew that Keene and Longfellow would be gripped by the same fear for Duryea as he was.

Jacques, nearly hoarse from calling out, suddenly thought he heard Keene calling back to him. Yes! It was Keene's voice!

"Jacques, over here! Quick! We've found Duryea!"

But the sound was deceiving and Jacques did not move directly to Keene, nor did he see or hear William. The exhausted man was now wading in near waist-deep water through hissing embers of burning, charred trees. Rain and soot soaked his clothes and his head, and his despair grew.

Keene and William were, at that moment, studying Duryea's predicament. Their friend was still trapped, and the swirling water was rising up his neck. He wasn't moving,. As they stared, stymied and desperate to help, the water inched over Duryea's head, and slowly covered him.

In that moment Keene realized that a strap around the tree trunk was also wrapped around Duryea's body. At what point in his desperation, Keene wondered, had the man thought to strap his torso to the topmost part of the trunk in hopes of saving himself? Keene felt a surge of renewed power rush into him.

Hearing splashing sounds, he and William looked up to find Jacques three feet from them.

With cries of surprise and relief, the three of them moved into the high water and began to push on the tree. But it would not move. Then Jacques came to his senses and, realizing that his and Duryea's tools couldn't be more than feet from them, climbed the bank to search for them. He directed Keene with his peevey, and with William's help he began sawing desperately, later moving to his axe to free some limbs.

It had been half a minute since Duryea had gone under. The tree shifted and water swirled. Jacques and Keene and William all groped for a hold on Duryea, but nothing came to their lunging grasps into the dark water.

Keene felt his strength ebbing. His body began to shake. But he wouldn't quit. He knew that each of them would simply have to summon more strength — from somewhere — to release Duryea and pull him out.

Light from the fire shifted and suddenly Keene saw part of the problem. Duryea was caught on a branch eight inches in diameter.

"We've got to cut that and then use the peevey as a lever!" he shouted.

They worked at a feverish pitch. William and Jacques returned to the saw, pushing and pulling through water and wood, their muscles burning with pain and fatigue. While they sawed, Keene used a thick branch to pry up the limb, trying to relieve the weight that was trapping and suffocating Duryea. Still, the tree somehow kept its prey ensnared.

Feeling as if his heart might burst with the effort, Keene summoned the last of all his strength and energy, knowing that if this didn't work, he couldn't try further and Duryea would die. Focusing all his might and being, and roaring with the effort of it, Keene slammed his weight against the lever one last time, shouting, "Now, men!" as he did so.

The tree rolled.

But Duryea was no longer right beneath them. Desperate, Keene went under the water, groping for him. In a moment he felt something — a shoulder, Duryea's shoulder. He also felt the leather strap holding Duryea to the trunk, and realized that Duryea had rolled with the tree.

He rose, sputtering, "He's here! Help me!" Sinking quickly again, Keene used his knife to cut Duryea free from the strap.

All three men grasped Duryea and pulled him away from the trunk. He rose quickly to the surface, freed from the tree. But he wasn't moving or breathing. The men pulled him from the water up to a high bank. Keene immediately laid him out and began pushing on Perry Duryea's chest with the heels of his hands, trying to force air into his lungs.

Still no movement.

Keene returned to his efforts to revive Duryea, but minutes passed without any sign of success. Despairing for his old friend, he looked into William's face and saw the same fear and despair.

Keene finally gave up and slouched, exhausted, beside Duryea's lifeless body. Moments passed and no one said a word. The fire, having met Duryea's redirected creek waters, was receding. An eerie, smoke-filled silence covered each man in his loss.

Keene pushed himself to his feet. He would pick up the body and carry it back to camp. Choking back sobs welling up from his depths, he bent down to hug his loyal, heroic friend one last time. William and Jacques stood too, but William turned away in his grief.

Then, a cough.

Keene heard the sputter and thought for a moment it was his own, but when he realized it wasn't, he dropped to his knees beside Duryea, studying him closely. Duryea's chest moved, ever so little — but it moved! Amazed and excited, the three men pulled him further up the bank, and as they did so, Duryea gave out a low, almost imperceptible groan. Keene knelt over him once again, lightly pushing on his chest until Duryea was breathing on his own. Keene lifted his friend's head, and immediately Duryea began to spit up blood and water. He coughed and gasped in pain, but he opened his eyes and sucked in a shallow but life-giving breath. Some color came back to his ashen face.

The water-soaked men, buoyed by Duryea's good fate and this astounding turn of events, carried their friend back to the camp. Duryea had broken ribs, a bruised chest and a badly bruised ankle. But he was alive, though breathing in a strained pattern. Keene heard him say, "I'll make it, Keene. Get me to a safe place and return to the fire."

And then he lapsed into a pained and fitful sleep.

I could see the remembered tension easing from Father's body. His muscles relaxed; he was winding down.

"The wall of water crested farther down the valley, Jack, sending up shrouds of white smoke in the Basin. There, the fire wall was stopped by the torrent of cool water from the miraculous cloudburst. The great camp with its magnificent virgin timber was out of danger."

Father's voice softened and I moved forward to hear better.

"Duryea saved the camp, Jack. We were saved by his genius and bravery and by an act of nature not often so kind and forgiving of man and his ways."

Father sat down, not quite finished, but satisfied by his story and its telling.

"Back at the camp, when it was all over, the men collapsed in exhaustion, but Longfellow and I sat up almost through the night. When Duryea was awake he joined us in discussing the pledge we'd made that very afternoon to preserve the Basin.

"'Duryea and Keene,' Longfellow said, 'we'll always remember this as the day we stood together and saved the Basin and this great camp. It was the first action of our new pact, and we shall continue to stand together for this wilderness.'"

Duryea admitted that his memory of Longfellow's words were a bit vague. When he'd awakened from his initial sleep William had given him a vial of laudanum along with the brandy, and he was quickly put into an even deeper sleep, one that he said was filled with searing but numbed arcs of pain shooting through his chest.

Father and William had shared another shot or two of Longfellow's best brandy and talked over what they'd just been through.

"'Keene,' William said to me," and Father raised his right hand toward me as he spoke; "'Keene, we made a sacred pledge today, but let me add to it. I swear to you that I shall never endanger this land again. The railroad will no longer run through our paradise here in the Basin. We nearly lost everything tonight, including our lives, and that's as lucky as I ever intend to be in this world.'"

Father paused, looked me straight in the eye, raising his pointed finger to command my attention. Bringing the story to a close he said, "Then Longfellow said, 'Soon, Keene, I will give you instructions about ownership and preservation of this Basin once I'm gone. You remind me in the morning, so we can review it and get it taken care of.'"

Father's story ended with those words, and one raised eyebrow, leaving me with a hard feeling in my gut.

Keene's Law

In the morning, the first light revealed about 300 acres of charred landscape, but the rest of the 400,000 acres remained intact. Keene, William and Duryea realized that their pact, to protect the wilderness from nearly inevitable development, would almost certainly put the Basin on a course of significant challenges in the future.

But those challenges, conflicted by family and law, were not resolved for decades, and devolved to me for the final decision.

Now in 1960, rocking gently on the porch overlooking the Basin, I must face those challenges set into motion that fateful day of September 1, 1894.

It was left to me to find a way to honor the solemn pledges made right here in this camp. The Basin lands recovered from the great fire, and, as Keene's son, I in time became part of the pact to keep the land wild.

But can I fulfill that promise and still preserve my relationship with Kora Longfellow, the woman I love?

Closing my eyes, I feel the warmth of the midday sun and the cool of the air. The 1894 letter to Father from Longfellow—the letter giving him escrow instructions on the Basin title — and Father's later letter to me, now lie collapsed in my hands, awaiting my final reply.

Two
Saving Title

When I was 10, Father told me the story of the tax foreclosure brought in 1885 against Longfellow. He could not pay his taxes and would lose the Basin property. Father and Duryea both told me that thereafter, the tale got more complicated. Longfellow was at a low time in his life, having just been divorced from Janet Longfellow. But around this time, the land baron read in the newspaper an account of a North Country real estate development. The story, as I pieced it together, was as follows:

Longfellow studied the report in the *Albany Times Union*, which stated that a tax sale conducted by the State had been set aside by the courts. The State Forest Commission and a court had ruled that the tax assessed on property owned by a friend of the Governor, and occupied by a few nominal "farmers," had been wrongly levied as commercial or lumbering property, resulting in a tax assessment much higher than the tax rate for farmland.

According to the court, the owner was entitled to have the tax foreclosure cancelled, and Longfellow saw a way to stop tax foreclosure on the Basin lands as well, using the same argument and a few assertions about the goings-on at his property. In fact, Longfellow did not at first farm the land in the Basin tract. He sent into the interior a timber surveying party and only a little timber was ever harvested. But the court decision was enough to give him a plan, Duryea told me, the opening he needed. He hired Alvah Dunning and Rondeau to go in and set up as homesteaders. This shrewdly gave him the legal basis to make his argument.

Carefully worded statements were crafted and sworn to by the residents who went in to build and live in shanties on the land, and who farmed, hunted, trapped, and fished on it. The State of New York fought the claim, but had no proof refuting it.

As I matured to a young man with some ability to understand, Duryea told me more about Keene's dealings with Longfellow. I learned the role Father had played in the scheme to save the Basin from being taken over by the state. Longfellow hired him to challenge the tax foreclosure and Father had asserted that the sale should be stopped because of the wrongful assessment. If he succeeded, his client's deed to 400,000 acres of Basin wilderness lost to back taxes would remain valid.

The challenge Father mounted led to a favorable conclusion. Keene succeeded in convincing the Forest Commission that the tax rate levied against the land was wrongfully levied and therefore unlawful. A court confirmed the result, canceling the foreclosure in 1885. Ever since, Keene was Longfellow's lawyer, and they became fast friends.

"I was there with Longfellow the day your father left for Albany," Duryea said. "As we stood on the platform at the railroad station, Longfellow told your father, 'Keene, clear this up and I will be forever in your debt. We can do business together.'"

It turned out to be true tenfold. The Basin title was saved, and it was Longfellow's greatest asset in those days. Keene Durant and William Longfellow went on to many years of prosperity, with Keene leading his client out of financial disasters.

"It gave Longfellow the ability to pay back taxes — a reduced rate over a number of years — and allowed Longfellow to prosper again.

"Then, after the fire of '94 I heard Longfellow tell your father, 'Keene, we need to decide what to do. I want to complete a deed on the Basin before I get much older.' I know they met again — some time in November — but Keene didn't tell me what happened." There was an ominous tone in Duryea's voice as he said this, one I came to recognize as I got older.

But the years passed and nothing happened on the deed.

Duryea said that after Longfellow's divorce, Father reviewed the Basin title for him and realized that Janet Longfellow, William's ex-wife, had never signed off on her dower interest in it. Apparently William's divorce lawyer Longfellow had overlooked that detail. This created a "cloud on title" if ever there was one, Father explained to his client.

Clearing the title seemed to remain a sore point with Keene, Duryea said. Client Longfellow dispatched lawyer Durant to find Janet Longfellow and secure a deed from her, if possible.

"Janet Longfellow cooperated and signed the deed, and Longfellow's title was then free and clear. And yet Keene was still troubled. I know the two of them — Janet and Keene — talked again, but Keene never told me what was said, though I have my ideas." And there Duryea stopped, until one evening when we sat alone. The old man had been sipping his favorite Madeira wine, and let it slip out.

"Keene did say a thing or two I think you should know, Jack. It was on their last occasion to meet, just before Janet moved away. She said she had something to say to clear the air. She told Keene how much the Basin meant to her and her daughter, Kora. She talked about the hikes Kora and Longfellow had loved to take on the Basin, and of conversations between herself and Longfellow about what should happen to the Basin. Your father was surprised by this conversation. And then… that was about it. I don't know what more was said because your father just stopped talking. He refused to say any more." The ominous tone was again there.

And Father never did say more about it to Duryea. The conversation Keene had with Janet Longfellow remained a subject of conjecture. Based on what Father later wrote to me, I believe further things were said, but that no meeting of the minds emerged.

Keene's conversation with Janet came up directly thereafter only once more, years later when he talked to her about the secret escrow deed he held to the Basin, and his plan for its future as wilderness. I know, on the other hand, that Kora Longfellow and Keene had sharp words for each other, and that Kora asserted that she had a right to the Basin. Father had to decide what was proper in light of all he knew.

By then, things had festered and worked on Kora's mind, shaping how she viewed the Basin, Father, and me. She and Keene basically stopped talking to each other, and Kora still carries a certain resentment toward us.

I knew it was up to me to confront Father on this whole confusion.

Three
The Instructions

"I've seen this beautiful window for a long time."

I laid on my featherbed in my favorite place to sit and talk with Duryea, nursing a miserable cold. The oval wood and glass mosaic framed his gentle face and round, bald head, outlined by white sideburns and a moustache that often bristled. The granite peak above the tree line, visible through the window, was cloaked with a new October snow. Tall white pines and cedars swayed in a gentle current of air, and wreaths of white powder on green boughs glistened in the midday sun. My eyes followed the scene back and upward to the sunlit horizon, where white birch stood sentinel on the converging slopes.

"It's been there a long time now, Jack," Duryea said, motioning his hand toward the window. "Since you were a little boy." His old eyes turned to mine and he grew quiet again for the moment, resisting my probing questions about Father, the Basin, and Longfellow. We both sipped the tea he'd brought up to share with me. When he did speak again it was in a low voice, just audible as I leaned toward him.

"You're asking me these questions once again, but this time we are both older, n'est-ce pas? And this time I see you are to be more stubborn." Duryea often reverted to his French- Canadian dialect when he was bothered, as he was now by my questions. But in a moment he returned to his more perfected English.

"But you are asking me to share what your mother and father knew about this place, all its history. But I do not know all of it, my young friend. And somehow it is hard to talk about it— this is for your father to say, not me. Keene knows what Longfellow, and for that matter what Janet and Kora, told him about this Great Basin. I do not. My own life, Jack, has been one of study and learning about nature and man in these mountains. That is what I know. It is all I know." Duryea got up and went downstairs.

I thought about the old man's words, and looked again on the Basin vista. I'd returned home, having finished my Albany law clerking, my studies done. The time had come for Father and me to decide what was to become of these thousands of acres of land that had great intrinsic value to us. I still hadn't mustered the directness, even at age twenty and with a license to practice law, to confront Father with my questions.

I was also home to make a decision about joining Keene's law firm. Just that morning I'd seen him leaving the Basin camp for work with a look of deep consternation on his face. If I joined the firm, I could undoubtedly take on myself some of whatever was causing him such worry.

In the afternoon, however, Duryea returned to my bedside. "I will tell you one story, Jack," he said. "Something I know to be true. And after this, I don't want any more of your questions." He pulled a chair up beside my bed, and I turned on my side to listen to him.

"A few weeks ago, at your father's request, I went to his office to build another bookshelf under the library window."

My mind's eye pictured Father seated at his desk, dressed in his three-piece charcoal worsted wool suit, a white shirt with a button-on mandarin collar, and a black grosgrain ribbon tie. The gas-fired lights would hiss quietly as he worked.

"He was typing something on his newfangled L. C. Smith typewriter, but every once in a while he would stop and pick up a document lying beside the typewriter. He'd study it as if it were something quite mysterious. At one point, and it was almost as if he had to say it aloud and so he said it to me, 'This is the deed William Longfellow entrusted to me in 1894.'"

I could almost see Keene at his desk, his blue, almond-shaped eyes closed for a moment as he thought about the remote wilderness where he had hiked and paddled as a younger man. His strong hands holding the indenture, and his athletic frame, were evidence of the physical prowess he'd developed through his years of wilderness living. I pictured him resting the document on his desk and sitting back in his chair, rocking in the contemplative melancholy that considering the deed often put him in.

"He has often reminisced about the time Longfellow came to his office in November of 1894," Duryea said. "It was two months after the flash fire, and Longfellow wanted to declare his plan for the Basin.

"'Keene,' he said, 'keep this deed here in your office safe, and follow my instructions. As you know, my desire is for the deed to be delivered to a party as yet unnamed.'

"But until a few weeks ago, that's all your father had ever said — just that Longfellow had come to the office about the deed. He always looked as if he wanted to tell me more, but he never did."

Duryea shifted in his chair, draping one leg over the other. "But there in the office, as I worked, your father began to reminisce about that day again, only this time he told me the rest of the story."

I sat up in my bed, despite my cold. The sudden shift caused a slight dizziness for me, but I hardly cared.

"He said their conversation was an exchange between trusted friends, and between lawyer and client. Longfellow signed the deed and handed it to your father, who warned William that he needed to complete his instructions right away.

"William stood up and extended his hand to your father. 'I too hope we can finish this soon, Keene. We've talked a great deal about the Basin and about John Muir's new wilderness ethic. You know my intentions. So if we cannot complete the deed, for any reason, this letter states my intent and my instructions to you. Do your very best to protect the Basin and see that it's kept as wilderness.

"'I'm a practical man, Keene,' he said. 'If the state keeps its forest lands forever wild, as proposed — and if the state acts responsibly — then this area will be preserved and it will stay wild — assuming the constitutional protection is enforced. If that's the case, then the grantee on this deed might better be the state, hard as that is for me to say after all my wrangling with it. But a state-created Adirondack Park would be protected forever—just as my private Basin should be protected from anyone who would ruin it.'

"He got quiet for a bit, but then he said, 'If the amendment is approved at the convention, and then by the voting public, so be it. I'll be ready to complete my deed.'

"And then he signed the incomplete deed and handed his letter of instructions to Keene."

Longfellow was two decades older than my father,

and Keene respected him as he would a mentor. But he must have puzzled Father greatly. Longfellow had won and lost fortunes, he'd lumbered off vast tracts of land to make his money, and yet now he wanted to preserve the Basin as wilderness — perhaps to atone for past excesses or indiscretions.

"What did Father say to all that?" I asked Duryea.

"He told Longfellow that he must complete his instructions regarding the deed right away. Decide who the land was to be transferred to. 'You have no last will and testament, for reasons of your own, and against my advice,' he said. 'Your affairs are in confidence with me, but I must have your specific instructions on this deed by tomorrow, William! The blank space for the grantee must be filled in promptly. You just never know, in life.' With that, your father witnessed Longfellow's signature on the deed."

Duryea fell silent for a while and seemed to drift off into his own thoughts. In time I nudged him on. "Was that it, then?"

Duryea shook his head. "No. Longfellow expressed his own hope that they could get it all finished up soon. The two of them sat around the library table for a while, talking more about Muir's belief that the wilderness should only be visited by man, not intruded on." Duryea paused and stared out the oval window. His eyes looked tired and thoughtful.

"And then Longfellow said something rather peculiar, given the way things turned out. He said that if for whatever reason they were unable to complete the deed, your father knew Longfellow's intentions. He wanted to follow Muir's philosophy regarding the use of the Basin and see that it was kept as wilderness. And with that, he handed your Father his letter of instructions. As you know, Longfellow in fact died without ever having completed the deed."

Duryea and I held each other's eyes for several minutes.

"Thank you for telling me this, Duryea." My head ached and I felt chilled, and I couldn't fully sort through what I'd just learned. But I was certain that Duryea had just given me some very important information.

"And now, ask me no more."

The letter Duryea told me about that afternoon at my bedside is the very letter I hold now as I sit at the Basin camp in 1960.

Keene had known the importance of the letter, and reading it again he was no doubt struck by the burden it placed upon him. It read:

> *November 20, 1894*
> *Dear Keene,*
>   *As my trusted lawyer, I am giving to you to hold the deed, signed by me today, to 400,000 acres of the Basin lands. Kindly witness it and then in time we shall decide who takes title to it. This decision shall be made by year's end, once it is determined what occurs in Saratoga at the Constitutional Convention on the fate of the state's wilderness forestlands of this Adirondack Park.*
>   *Keene, you know I have not made a last will. I trust you to complete the deed if I do not, but follow my wishes —our wishes — to preserve it.*
>
>   *William West Longfellow*

William Longfellow didn't lived to see the outcome of the 1894 convention, and he never completed the deed with a named grantee to take title. He died in his sleep on the evening of November 20, 1894. The maid found him in the morning and Keene was notified. All Longfellow's affairs were in Keene's hands, and all of them were in order except for the escrow deed. Keene had that acknowledged by the local judge of the justice court, who knew Longfellow's signature.

Keene waited for news of passage of the forever-wild clause in the state constitution. The voters approved it for all forest preserve inside the blue line, just as Longfellow had hoped. But Keene, wondering if the state would be as good as its word on the matter, still delayed in deciding what to do with William Longfellow's deed.

Lurking under the surface of Father's thoughts, I can now surmise, was this issue of title to the Basin and the quandary in which it would place both of us. No doubt Father could foresee how events could unfold and become the compelling force in our lives, as he had a lawyer's grasp of the conundrum in which the escrow deed placed us. I did not, yet.

But still more years passed and Father did not come to terms with his quandary. The boreal forest and wilderness streams remained in their unspoiled state, just as when Nessmuk, the renowned outdoor journalist, paddled them in 1883 and described the wilderness to a curious public in *Forest and Stream* magazine. The native brook trout continued to spawn each fall in the fine gravel of the cold, clean waters. The wild place did not noticeably change, and still the matter of who would claim title to the Basin remained undecided.

As for me, I grew to adulthood, and the wound I bore continued to surface in my dreams of camping in a hidden lean-to in the Basin wilderness, feeling like an intruder not an owner. After each of those dreams I could settle myself again only by walking around the darkened Basin camp, reassuring myself things would be all right. Father did not seem aware of my disturbance and I never shared it with Kora. My wound turned slowly to a scar.

I rock gently, my eyes closed in the now waning sun. My attention has turned to today's meeting with the state officials to consider and review the title that Keene and William West Longfellow had sworn to complete 66 years earlier. Keene's letter of instructions, left for me in 1920, has been carefully placed in a hidden pocket of my valise.

Necessity has required, up to this point, that I rely upon inference and informed conjecture to tell you my story. But I've come now to a point of departure, because of my personal knowledge I can now finish the tale of this magnificent landscape where I spent my life, the Durant Law Firm, which I joined, Kora Longfellow, whom I loved, the surprising outcome of the escrow deed, and the fate of the Great Basin.

Four
The Great Basin

With my meeting with Father scheduled for dinner at the end of the day, I left camp, carrying my fly rod with me, and walked alone on a get-away hike to the alpine country near the source of Otter Brook. Hiking somehow brought me a sense of both perspective and renewal, and I hoped to achieve some clarity on this hike.

At its source, high in the granite face of the mountainside, water flowed from a high pond through an insurgence, where it drained underground through quartz and mica stones and cobble before bubbling to the surface. Once surfaced, the stream fell in rapid descent over giant granite slabs of quartz, feldspars, and hornblende, and streamed around giant boulders where the fall line lessened. At the tree line, freshets joined to form a brook. Craggy and stunted hemlock grew from stress lines in the rock to shade its course as the brook dropped to the valley

Basin on its way southeasterly to join the Hudson River. I climbed above the tree line that afternoon, up to the water's bubbly source. The view was a crystal clear vision of the primordial wilderness valley bowl and its surrounding high peaks.

These high peaks had their own climate. Where I was, the granite was covered by ice five months of the year, and year-round by lichens made of yellow, gray and brown thallus that spread branch-like over the rock. The stream here fell softly into a deep pool, sounding a gentle shi-soo, shi-soo.

At this time of year, the high pool was spawning water for native brook trout. Thousands of fry hatched out in early spring, and many moved downstream to the cold, clean headwaters where their parents had migrated after their spawning. The speckled natives of these waters had lived and died here over millennia, feeding on mayflies, stoneflies, and caddisflies. The brook was known simply as The Otter, and the point at which it met the main stem of the river was called the Junction.

At the dawn of this October day I walked the brook to its source, looking into the pools in which I was accustomed to watching the fry grow to fingerlings, later to return as adults. Duryea had taught me to catch large mature brookies on the fly in every brook in the Basin, but The Otter and this pool were our favorites._

The full name for this land was the Great Basin, and it was aptly named: many brooks came off the east and south ranges, and the Basin valley at its head was carved from the granite into an ever-widening half-bowl-shaped cirque. The cirque was unequalled in the entire North Country for its unique land and water formations. Its written title of ownership under the white man traced back to a time after the Revolutionary War, when the State of New York sold much of the northern Adirondacks in a transaction known as Macomb's Purchase. These wild lands and unspoiled waters — the rivers and brooks, the trout found there, the mountains and flower-spotted alpine meadows — satisfied my senses as little else could.

The wilderness sounds always brought back to me an early memory of my mother. I had to have been quite small, for I recall lying in her lap on the porch of the great camp as she rocked me into a deep sleep with the lullaby she would sing to me in her French accent and rock me into a sound sleep. I still have an empty feeling when this memory returns, a yearning for the mother I never really knew. As a young boy without her, I transferred my love to every part of the Basin, and this connection with nature deepened to a spiritual reserve that I would call up throughout life.

My fishing on Otter Brook was not infrequently interrupted by a bear coming to the water at dawn to drink. And that's just what happened on this early morning before my dinner date with Father. A magnificent black bear, with sheen in his dark coat, appeared on the high bank of the brook where I'd seen him several times before. Usually, when he encountered me near his watering hole, he backed off, but this morning he did not. He'd come for his drink.

Somewhat unsettled, I moved away to a safer distance from him, but he paid me little mind, taking his drink and moving on. In Native American cultures a bear represented gentle strength and healing; I'd long ago adopted Duryea's superstition that the appearance of a bear signified the coming of important changes.

My line suddenly came alive as one brookie, another, and then a third took the fly deep and went to my creel. I didn't want to have my fun in only one pool, and I packed up and hiked on.

As I went, I thought more about this vast Basin wilderness and the thorny question of ownership. As I'd grown older, I'd become more certain than ever that I didn't know the full story of Father's legal standing regarding the Basin. Here I was, an adult and a trained lawyer trying to decide on my future here, but I was without essential clarity on this point.

Stopping again to fish, I let my fly play down into the pool. The water here ran gin clear and low after the run-off of early fall, and the angled early rays of the sun found the deep end of the pool. It seemed the perfect spot. Nonetheless, even after quite some time, my favorite pheasant tail, which I'd tied e as a mayfly in the nymph stage, brought no hint of the large brookie I knew lived there. I remembered Duryea's lesson on presenting the fly. Quoting one of the early masters, he'd said, "If the fly is in the range of total visibility, the trout recognizes the fly for the fraud that it is." It was irritating to think that my every movement was being watched by a large speckled trout who saw me for the fraud I was, but this big fellow had obviously learned Duryea's lesson quite well.

Eventually I told myself to get out of the stream and head back to camp, but I stood a moment longer, considering my talk with Father that evening. When I did turn in the current to leave the brook, I froze. There on top of a high bank that ran some distance along the shore, about 50 yards from me, stood the same bear I'd seen earlier. Had he come back for more water — or for me? I stood stock still, barely breathing. In a moment he lowered his great shaggy head and lapped at the water. Some part of me must have twitched, for now it was the bear's turn to freeze. He turned in my direction, but seeing me, he bolted across Otter Brook at full speed, thrashing through the water and into dense woods, running over anything in his way. Heart pounding, I headed on, grateful that I'd have another day to fly fish the brook.

The sounds of the moving waters receded as I walked briskly on and were soon replaced by the king fisher's call and the osprey's screech. Appearing in the distance, near the forest opening, was the familiar roofline of our camp. It stood at a point that commanded a view of the alpine lake and the distant mountains. The magnificent oval window at its peak shone brilliantly as the morning sun streamed into it. The very sight of the camp filled my chest with an aching love, and I moved on with a sense of purpose. I needed answers to the legal questions concerning this place. Those answers had to come from Keene, and they couldn't wait. The memory of my two encounters with the same bear that day heightened my enthusiasm for the conversation I'd have that evening with Father.

When I pushed through the lodge door, Duryea was stoking the wood-fired oven preparing a hot fire for breakfast. His kitchen was alive with cooking and the wonderful blended scents of wilderness and good food. I handed him my catch of small brookies. He smiled ever so slightly, but didn't lose any efficiency of movement, nor did he utter a word as he quickly filleted the fish and set them to cook. There was nothing unusual in his expediency; since I could remember, the kitchen had been his domain. After Mother passed on, Duryea had raised me, along with Father, and had taken up the caretaking chores for us with dispatch, efficiency, and love.

A few days earlier, as Duryea had cleaned up from lunch and I'd stood washing the dishes, he had taken me into his confidence in a way he never had during my boyhood. He'd wanted to talk about camp and the Basin. He said he loved what he created here, but that he often felt pangs of guilt about it.

"Why, Duryea?" His remark took me quite by surprise.

He'd leaned one sinewy arm against the sink where I was working. "This is my home," he said, gesturing beyond the kitchen window to the wilderness beyond. "I understand what unspoiled woods and waters are, how they are supposed to be. I have always loved the Basin. I am grateful to live here. But over the last years my thinking has changed about the proper use of this beautiful land."

It was Muir again, I could see. Muir's philosophy had left Duryea feeling convicted of a wrong committed against the land he loved.

"As it was, I didn't want to build this great camp. I told Longfellow I would only do it for him if he promised that it would be the only one built here. I could not insist on this — I was in no position to make demands on him — but we talked over a long period of time. The three of us — your father, William, and I — talked many times, and at great length, about John Muir's arguments. In time Longfellow reached a philosophical agreement with us and Muir. That's just about the same time that the great firestorm came along, which sealed his growing conviction to preserve the land — just after I'd built the camp."

Duryea absently picked up a dishtowel and set to work drying. I slowed down my pace, washing, wanting to extend this conversation and my sense of being trusted by him.

"But then Longfellow died, and now it falls to Keene, and perhaps to you, Jack, to carry on in the same tradition." Duryea finished, but stared intensely at me, so intensely that I felt his power over me and this place.

There was silence as Duryea pondered his next words.

"But in this camp, I went to every precaution." He paused again and looked around the camp. His eyes traveled up to the oval mosaic. "I located the camp away from the lake so that the waters that flow out of my kitchen, and the dirty water from the toilets, all flow in hollowed cedar laid in the ground to a settling pool, away from everything." As he did this he pointed with his index finger to the area in back of camp.

"The dirty water drains and filters through sand after passing through the settling tank. Then it is clean and does no harm — not like other camps I see near the lakes and streams that pollute with filth. I do not do this. I come from a family, my foster family, where such care was not taken, long before Longfellow took me in, gave me a roof and a bed and a job. But I save for another day that story."

Duryea returned to his wood stove and began preparations for the evening meal, and I knew his sharing was done for the day.

Longfellow had challenged Duryea to design and build a year-round wilderness lodge that would be warm, open, and light. Duryea build a structure filled with natural light coming in from high windows. Two open mezzanines, cantilevered from opposite sides of the frame on the second and third floors, left the central space of all three levels open. Distinctive chestnut stairs rose on each side of the open space to a high peak at the third level. There, he built the large oval window which faced south and east. Natural light streamed though to the great room below.

Duryea had handcrafted the oval mosaic, with twelve large parabolic panels of glass held in place by thin, strong splines of spruce on either side. At its center an 18-inch-wide by nine-inch-high oval piece of hand carved varnished spruce accepted the dowelled end of each of the twelve mullions. Each of these fanned out geometrically to an oval wood frame, perhaps ten feet in length and six feet high at its center, and were supported mid-point by a concentric oval spline angling them out to the arched frame.

The high space and magnificent oval thirty feet above the cherry and white oak floor, and solid hewn beams supporting the structure, all worked together to give the sense of being in the wilderness, but protected from it. Duryea said he'd built it as a place to watch the wilderness, as a place to sit and wonder, to read and study, about things important to one's spiritual being; and as a beacon to welcome us home. The oval mosaic nurtured a sense of well-being and satisfaction.

How many times a day did I look out that window, from up in the loft, to the range of high peaks surrounding us? For the rest of my life, any thought of the camp would bring to mind its vista as seen through the oval mosaic. Duryea created exactly what Longfellow had had in mind, and Longfellow spent only a few months here before his death, at which time my family and I settled into the Great Camp and called it home.

Duryea had continued his craft on the furnishings in camp, transforming the tables, chairs, chests, cupboards, rockers, and beds in all the rooms into folk art. He crafted all manner of things, like mirrors and coat trees, with maple, pine, spruce and chestnut. Some of the walls were clad with cedar bark that had been dried and cut into geometric shapes to form a large rectangle, giving the effect of being in the forest while yet inside.

On the outside, he'd quartered cedar logs and laid them up, using split pole battens for the gaps. But on other walls, he halved the logs, and laid them up with no gap between. Our main porch was an offset to the east side of the house, where the early light came in, and from it large doors opened onto the deck. This design allowed for sunlight to penetrate the interior without having a large porch-roof overhang block the light.

Duryea crafted the camp into a unique, warm home.

The inviting aroma of brookies in a cast iron pan, alongside a second pan with eggs and fried potatoes, began filling the camp. His typical faint smile on his face, Duryea worked his stove, while beyond the kitchen in the sunlit great room, Father sat studying a document, which, I could see, was a map.

He waved me in. Even before he began to speak, I knew that the discussion we'd planned for later that evening over dinner was going to start early.

"Jack, I want you to decide on your... our law practice. You've finished your apprenticeship, and I know a clerkship awaits you, whether here or back in Albany, or wherever. The choice is yours. William Kelly in Albany would be an excellent mentor for you, of course, as you know, having worked in his office over these last three years. But you're also welcome to stay here and form a partnership with me in a law firm that serves the entire North Country." He tapped his fingers on the arm of the deep rocking chair.

"You know times are hard here, Jack, and the pay would be little compared to Albany. But the rewards can be great if we work as a team."

He paused, and I suspect he knew that my delay was an effort to buy some time. But I felt precious little time remaining under his imposed offering.

"Make a decision, Jack. Establish your life."

That was it. He stopped there. Father had always been decisive but fair. He'd raised me to be the same, but on this matter I wasn't prepared to be as decisive as he might have liked. I had my reservations about running a family business, especially a law practice, and doing all the mundane things required in a small firm in the North Country. My eyes had been opened wide by life in the big city of Albany, the capital of the great Empire State. I'd discovered a world beyond anything I'd previously known. I was just about to make my request for more time when Duryea served up the fresh brookies, eggs, potatoes, and fried dough—neurelles, he called them. The delicious aromas were followed by Duryea's call to breakfast.

"*Asseyez-vous ici,*" Duryea commanded, and even Father knew to cease conversation and approach the dining room, for when Duryea broke into French it signaled impatience.

Breakfast never tasted better, and for a while business was forgotten for good food and easy conversation about the day's coming events among three old compatriots.

In passing, Duryea said, "Fall visitors are arriving, you know. Longfellow's daughter is due home tomorrow or the next day. "

His eyes turned to me. My heart skipped a beat at the thought of my last visit with her two summers ago, when we discovered we were compatible. We'd established a correspondence after she moved, and she'd owed me a letter for quite some time. Duryea's eyes lit in a twinkle, for I had shared with him that I was sweet on Kora. It occurred to me that perhaps the change portended by the bear's appearance was Kora's arrival. The mere thought of her was exciting!

But the business at hand pulled my attention away from Kora. I turned to Father and made a point to meet his eyes, blue eyes on blue eyes.

"Father, I will have a decision for you by tonight. Please forgive me for the time I've taken. You're right. It's time to decide. We've reviewed all the details, and now all that remains is for me to make up my mind. I'll do so by this evening." With that said, I pushed my chair away from the table and went outside.

I'd returned from Mr. Kelly's clerkship six weeks earlier. I'd spent this time back home relaxing, fishing, and hanging around Father's office, almost as though I were 16 again. But I knew I was not. On one of those afternoons, as I sat near him doing some research for him on a boundary dispute, I'd looked up and found him staring intently at me.

"Your mother would want us to be together," he said. "She said so from the moment you were born. I feel somehow obliged to her to tell you so. But I won't stand in the way of any decision you make."

I hadn't known how to respond to that information and sat quietly looking back at him.

"But don't let your mother's wishes decide this for you, Jack. Just make a sound decision." Then Keene Durant stepped from his desk to the next room, calling as he went for his secretary, Elaine, to get his files.

Father had come to the point and left it dangling ever so carefully in front of me. He didn't know then that my decision had already been made in my heart, and that now my head needed time to arrive at the same place. But I knew I couldn't leave the Basin. I'd stay with Father and work to preserve this wilderness. I'd practice law here and honor my mother's wish.

What Father didn't know was that when I was thirteen I'd read from Mother's diary, still on the bookshelf in Father's room. She'd written of her love for this place, a love, it seemed, that had been transferred to me as if through her genes. I knew that my decision, finally, would come from my soul, which always heard the wilderness calling me to live out my life here.

Even so, the decision, spiritual though it was, had to be practical as well. I pushed away from the pillar, shaking myself. I needed to do something physical, to balance out all this thinking, and decided on a vigorous row down the lake in the Austin double-ender. I sprinted to the boathouse, leaped easily into the Austin, and pushed off the dock, working the oars hard and fast.

As I rowed I felt a physical release, and decided to keep rowing all the way into town. I'd go see if that letter from Kora was going to arrive before she herself did the next day. I was also expecting a letter from William Kelly in Albany, describing the most recent pronouncements and news from state leaders concerning the future of the state's wild forestlands. The legislature created a preserve for this region and was deliberating possible changes in the forever-wild provision of the state constitution. Proposals from the logging and timber industry to allow cutting in the preserve were common, but so far none had succeeded. Mr. Kelly had promised to keep me apprised of their deliberations.

Just a week before, he'd sent me a clipping from the newspaper of the speech made by Louis Marshall, the well-known lawyer and constitutional scholar. I'd read the man's words again and again, imagining how it must have sounded, delivered to the convention in Albany:

> ... and here in New York State anyone who has intelligently observed the operations in the Adirondack forests is grieved to see how mountain top after mountain top is being denuded, how the bare rock begins to glisten through the forest cover, and it is only a question of a few years, if these propositions are read into the Constitution under a guise of reforestation of a liberal policy,

a more liberal policy in connection with forestry matters — it is only a few years, if that policy should be adopted ...before we will have to chew the bitter cud of reflection and future generations will find themselves precisely where today are found the people of China, Mesopotamia, of Syria, of Northern Africa, and in those nations where the foolish policy which is sought to be incorporated in this amendment has been observed.

Marshall concluded by saying there was no middle course with regard to the question, and the proposal to allow cutting in the forest preserve was defeated.

My own inclinations, reinforced by Duryea, Father, and William Longfellow — and by the journals of John Muir and John Burroughs — left me convinced that preservation of wilderness as a place for quiet retreat was a necessary thing, but one that was far from certain in our state. Pulling hard on the oars, I felt an almost painfully intense loyalty to this wilderness, and knew that, in my next free moments I would return to the source of Otter Creek in the high country where the wild native brookies lived, my place of refuge and renewal.

The sounds of the village greeted me as I approached the town dock, where I secured the Austin and walked leisurely to the post office. But my box was empty — nothing from Kora or Kelly. I returned to camp feeling relieved of physical tension, but oddly unsettled by Kora's silence and thinking again about my dinner meeting with Father.

Dinner that evening was set just for two. Duryea had arranged a special table with our best china and stemware, and Father and I enjoyed Duryea's tender veal, potatoes, and green beans, and the luxury of the setting.

After the meal Father sat silently, waiting. After looking at him for what seemed an eternity, I came to the point.

"Father, I am ready to join your firm on whatever terms you find agreeable."

He stood, smiling broadly. "I couldn't be more pleased! Report for work on Monday, young man!"

I stood and raised my glass to his for a toast, but we realized we held empty glasses. Duryea materialized with a bottle of champagne, filled the glasses as we chuckled, and returned to his kitchen.

"To the Durant Law Firm," I said proudly, "which has doubled in size!"

Father's eyes glistened as the stemware clinked. We sat and drank more of Duryea's fine wine and talked of our plans for the office. I thought it was neither the time nor the place to raise my questions about the Basin title, though it was very much on my mind, of course. Just the night before, my recurring dream had come again—camping on the Basin, believing I had no ownership or connection to this place—and had brought yet more urgency to my need for resolution, if one was to be found.

But for now, in this moment, it was sufficient to sit across from my father, and enjoy the prospects of our new joint venture.

Five
New Start

As planned, I spent the next morning preparing to return to the source of Otter Brook. The October sun on its southerly seasonal course would leave me plenty of time to hike the remote reach, quiet time in which I could consider the possibilities of my life and the direction in which I was headed.

One of the things I needed to think about was Kora Longfellow.

In the early afternoon I changed to my worn, comfortable duck pants, and layered on two shirts, one lighter, one of a heavier wool. Heading out, I walked the brook along the path I'd made over the years to where the water cascaded down the granite façade of the mountain. The walk warmed my body to a light and comfortable sweat.

The brook flowed gently as it started down the façade, still in sunlight, giving off a barely perceptible sound until the last vertical drop. There, the water formed a strand a foot wide, and fell with the muffled sound of a distant ocean surf to a pool at the bottom. There was a brief silence while the strand re-gathered water to fall again. I stood above the cascade, watched and listened, watched and listened, until my mind was relaxed and one with my surroundings.

From a distance of about a hundred feet, I looked down into the clear, deep pool and studied it for signs of the female squaretail that had lived there last fall when I'd last seen her on the redd. Her eggs had been carefully deposited in the clean small pebbles at the substrate. I'd watched the male brookie fertilize those eggs, turning the water milky for a moment before the female worked her tail fin back and forth to cover the spawn. The eggs would overwinter, and brook trout fry would be born right there if the ravages of the spring run-off didn't sweep them away or kill them.

Now, in autumn, I spotted four-inch fry moving about. In the deeper water there was a dark shadow, the mother, but her fry were on their own. Such was the way of nature, the way of the wild, working as it had for millennia, without interference.

At some point, my thoughts shifted away from brook trout. I moved up the steep granite face, climbing easily hand over hand up the familiar rock, warm and comforting to my touch. The sound of the brook changed as I moved away from it, then returned to my ear as the path moved closer again. I aimed to beat the sun's falling rays as they left the high granular rock. In moments its light receded to the westernmost peak, nothing but its slanted last rays still perceptible in the near twilight.

I reached my high destination, out of breath and thinking about nothing but the young woman I'd chanced to meet earlier that morning at Paul's Hotel in the village, which I frequented for news and gossip of our area. Kora Longfellow, who had been absent from the Basin for the past two years, had returned.

When we were twelve Kora and I discovered many interests in common. I don't think either of us could remember a time we hadn't been friends and constant playmates. Kora was for me as much a part of the Basin lands as the trees, the mountains, or Otter Brook. But on that particular day, something changed for me, and even though it would be months before I could articulate what it, I was governed by it from that day forward.

Duryea and I were fishing along Otter Brook, and could hear William and Kora Longfellow chatting long before they came into view along the trail. Maybe it was the way the sun hit her, maybe it was her position a few feet above me, but I found myself looking at Kora in a way I never had before. She was beautiful. For the first time in our long history, I didn't greet her.

"Jack!" Duryea nudged me gently.

"Good morning, Mr. Longfellow. Hello, Kora."

"Jack," she said, "there are trout in the pools. I've seen them just this morning! If you catch some and bring them to me, I'll cook them for you! Speckles are my favorites."

Suddenly I found my tongue. "I'll catch you some nice trout, Kora, and I'll show you how to cook them!"

She'd smiled at me, but it was as if I'd never seen her smile before. She continued down the trail with her father, and I stood, fly rod in hand, watching them go. I heard Duryea's gentle chuckle beside me.

I caught some speckled beauties and late that day I took them in my creel, in a bed of fresh grass, cooled and looking pretty, to Kora's house. She saw me coming and ran out to meet me. I proudly displayed my catch.

"Let's cook them now, on the beach!" she said, which we did, there on the sandy shore around her parent's pond. The sweet taste of brook trout had never tasted better

I don't know when I realized that Kora had been looking at me differently for quite some time, too. But I knew it was undeniably different from that point on. In one way I sorely missed the free and easy give and take of our early childhood. I felt like the proverbial stranger in a strange land in our new territory. But whatever was lost was more than made up for in the soaring feeling of love I was introduced to that summer.

That fall my belief in Kora's perfection only intensified. A new family moved into the area, the Abers. Their two children, Etienne and Susie, began attending our one-room school house, which served all the local children. Being both new and a bit backwards, I'm afraid they took a lot of unpleasantness from many of the other students. I felt bad for them, but it was Kora who stepped up to the plate for them. Every day, the Abers walked six miles in from their parents' wilderness farm, trekking the rutted wagon path, to attend school. One pleasant, cloud-free October morning as Kora and I walked toward school, she stopped at the abandoned trappers' cabin, saying she was going to wait for the Abers, and that from now on we would accompany them to school.

"They have a terribly long walk, Jack, and they're so little." Susie was seven, and Etienne was nine. "And they always look so tired and sad. Etienne said he's thinking about not coming to school anymore because the other children are so unkind."

"You must get your education," she encouraged them as we walked that morning, "so you can read and write well in English. From here on I'm going to meet you in the woods and we'll review your lessons for the day as we walk to school."

I'll admit I felt a little jealous of Kora's attentions to the children, but when I asked if I could walk with them each morning, Etienne said they'd be delighted to have my company, and Kora seemed charmed by my willingness to be the Abers' friend. And so began our daily routine of walking to the old trappers' cabin to wait for the Aber kids and accompanying them the rest of the way in.

Kora knew how to talk about things of interest to younger children — things like doll making, and picking blueberries. She described so well how delicious blueberries were that I could almost taste them, and she told the younger girls how much fun it was to take a basket to the blueberry patch at a certain clearing in the woods. We took to doing just that, and on many early summer days we set a challenge to see who could pick the most berries after school. When our youthful backs grew tired from stooping for blueberries, we'd stop and eat our fill of the sweet berry. Sometimes Kora let Susie win the challenge, just to please her; Kora never knew that I sometimes let her win, for the same reason.

Kora and I turned 13 that fall. My interest and admiration for her continued to grow. Her friendship with the Aber girls caught the other students' attention, and if they didn't warm up to Susie and Etienne, at least they stopped picking on them. I learned from Kora that one person really can make a difference in the world. That our actions always affect someone else, for good or ill.

I also learned to appreciate Kora's gift of farsightedness. As fall pushed toward winter, she arrived at our own meeting place one morning with two pairs of small snow shoes called racquettes. When we got to the trappers' cabin, she handed them to the Abers.

"The wilderness can be dangerous in the winter," she told them, "and you must be careful of the weather. Use these racquettes once the snow comes. And if anything ever happens — if you ever have trouble — take refuge right here at this old cabin. Do you know how to build a fire?"

Etienne said they did not.

"Jack will teach you, and if you're ever stuck here you can build a fire and get out of the weather."

Kora and I continued to meet the Abers each day on our racquettes at the cabin, a distance of three miles from school. I liked best the time we had before we got to the cabin, when we were still alone and could talk of things important to us.

"This home of ours is special, Jack, and I shall always love it. But I do want to get out in the world and live in other places and see other things. Don't you?"

"Why, Kora? There's no need to look somewhere else. This is the best place in the world!"

She shook her head at me and talked of other things until the Abers came along. I found myself unable to join in the conversation as freely that morning. Even then, the thought of Kora's moving away caused me a misery.

By January of that winter, Etienne and Susie were accustomed to their travels on snowshoes, and quite accomplished at it. But on a particularly cold Monday morning, as Kora and I approached the trappers' cabin, there was no sign of them. It had snowed about a foot since dawn, the time at which Etienne and Susie usually left home, and the wind had kicked up so that you couldn't see well. We waited as long as we could before going on and when we got to school we reported our concern about the Abers to Miss LaFountain.

"I don't think they would have started in these conditions, Kora, and we shouldn't worry. Their parents told me that in bad weather, they would not come in to school. Now let's proceed with our lessons."

But I could tell from the look on Kora's face that she was frightened for our friends.

"Jack," she said into my ear as we walked back toward our seats, "Etienne told me they wouldn't have to miss a day of school, now that they had racquettes."

I dropped into my seat across from her.

"I think they're out there and that they're lost and cold." Kora bit at the inside of her cheek.

I knew what was coming, and while I shared Kora's concern, I disagreed with what I knew she was thinking.

"I'm going to slip away at noon," she whispered to me. "I'm going to the area of the trappers' cabin and scout around."

I nodded slowly at her, resisting her idea, but silently.

"Are you coming?"

"I think Miss LaFountain may be right, Kora, and we shouldn't go!"

But she didn't listen, and at noon hour, without telling me, she left. When I realized she was no longer in the building, I looked outside to check the weather conditions. It was continuing to blow and snow, but the worst of it seemed to have passed, and my concerns for Kora's safety ebbed slightly. When Miss LaFountain questioned me about Kora's whereabouts, I fibbed, saying I didn't know where she was. As the other children understood that Kora had left school in a storm in search of the Aber children, they grew quiet. They were North Country children, and they knew the danger all three girls could be in. We all spent the afternoon distracted from our lessons, and looking out the windows in hopes of seeing Kora and the Abers approaching the schoolhouse. Imaginations ran wild about what might have happened to our schoolmates.

Around 3:30, Miss LaFountain finally notified the head of the school of the situation, and a search party was organized. All the children were to remain in the schoolhouse, and nearly a dozen nearby adults were to spread out in the direction of the trappers' cabin, then beyond that in the direction of the Abers' farm.

But just as Miss LaFountain herself was preparing to join the search, I looked out the front window and saw three figures slowly moving through the deep snow on racquettes. Everyone gathered at the door as it swung open and revealed a snow-covered Kora, with her hands on equally powdered Susie and Etienne on either side of her. Kora looked defiantly at Miss LaFountain, whose earlier look of anger quickly melted to one of relief.

Kora had noticed, around noon, that the worst of the blowing had stopped, at least temporarily, and she'd known she must go. With improved vision, she'd headed back toward the old trappers' cabin, and sure enough, there was smoke coming from the chimney.

"It was Etienne and Susie, and they were cold but okay. They'd done exactly what I'd told them to do if they ever got in trouble in a winter storm. I know I shouldn't have left school without telling you, Miss LaFountain, but I just had to."

Kora was roundly cheered by all her schoolmates — and by Miss LaFountain — and from then on, the Aber children, co-stars with Kora in the drama of the great rescue, found a place of honor among their schoolmates.

Word quickly spread through community of Kora's heroics. Mr. And Mrs. Aber later thanked her personally at a public gathering at school. As for me, my love for Kora — my adulation — increased tenfold for her loyalty, courage, and strong will. For most of the rest of my life, through thick and thin, and with a few exceptions, it has never wavered.

The summer we turned 16, Kora began accompanying me on some fishing trips. She'd sit on the bank and admire my form and the fish I would land. One day, to my surprise, she expressed interest in tying flies. I held up a streamer fly, explaining that it looked so much like a minnow in the water, it fooled the brook trout.

"How did you learn to tie that streamer, Jack?"

"From Duryea. It is not as hard as it might seem." I shrugged, hoping to sound wise and worldly. "Why?"

"Because I'd like to learn how to do that. They're so beautiful!"

"Duryea and I can teach you!" I said, delighted to think she might come to share my great passion for fishing.

And she did. Kora came to camp where Duryea and I had assembled materials at our bench for a simple streamer pattern. He stayed in the background, busying himself with other things, but available if he was needed. I had two vises, each holding a number 12 hook ready to use.

"Start by tying on the waxed silk thread to the hook shank with several turns — like so — then tie and wrap in the copper wire, like this, and then secure it in place. Go ahead and tie that on your hook, Kora and leave a little wire as extra to use later."

Kora did both steps effortlessly.

"Now wrap in some of these trimmed turkey feathers near the eye — as tail feathers — like this." Again, I demonstrated, and again she repeated the maneuver perfectly, displaying great dexterity. We completed the body with shorter, white chicken hackle, finished the wraps of wire, tied a whip knot at the eye of the hook to hold everything securely on the shank, and coated the knot with a sealer. I dropped her fly into our sink filled with water, and when the water rippled, the fly moved and looked like the minnows we'd often seen in Otter Brook. Kora's smile was broad, and grew broader as Duryea stepped over to admire it.

"A very nice start, young lady!" he offered. Out of Kora's line of vision, he gave me a special look, with raised eyebrows and a great grin that conveyed his pleasure and his good opinion of Kora.

Two hours later Kora had completed five patterns. She was hooked. From then on she tied her own flies, and got in the habit of leaving most of them for me, placed where I'd be sure to find them, but rarely giving them to me directly. An exception was that first lesson, when she presented me with her first streamer.

"You keep it," she said, "since you showed me how and it was so much fun!"

I kept her first streamer in my pouch, and still have it. It has never been in the water since that day; it is too dear to me to risk losing it.

After she left us that day, Duryea poked me softly in the side with his elbow. "Kora is quite a young lady, my young man, une belle jeune fille. Your father and I have noticed her. Yes, she is a wonderful person." He flashed his best Duryea, and my heart danced a little celebratory dance.

I hated to admit to it, but as she practiced, Kora's flies became better tied than mine. They approached Duryea's in quality. And so, from an early age, I grew to realize that while Kora shared many interests and loves, she was of two minds about others things that meant the world to me — like the Basin. She loved the wilderness and our time together in it, but she didn't want to stay here. The very thought of leaving the Basin confounded me. Yes, that was it: I found her confounding.

Despite this, our relationship, and our reliance on each other, flourished. What started with a shared interest in trout fishing, in time developed into a sharing of deep confidences. Over the years we exchanged notes, sometimes lengthy ones, containing our private thoughts about all manner of things. We began to read the works of Shelley and Emerson, kindred spirits to us as we grew older, and we became inseparable that final year of school, when we took to regularly hiking and canoeing through the wilderness.

That summer Kora posted a letter to me, writing, "You are special to me and I understand how you feel about life. I also love that you read literature and share it with me."

I wrote back out of my youthful idealism, expressing passionate belief that she and I were natives here, spirits of the North Country where we had the freedom to be with nature, where we could study literature unencumbered by any man's preconceived notions. We were originals, I said, and meant to be together.

But Kora's reply, her last letter before she moved away, was prescient:

> *While we have similar interests, I confess that I am eager to acquire possessions — perhaps more than you realize, Jack. This trait comes from my father, who, as you know, was a collector of fine objects from*

around the world. I may not be cut out to stay here in the Adirondacks, as you are. I know I shall at least try other things

Keep reading and thinking about things, Jack, as we have over the past years. You are a fine man, a man I admire and hold dear to my heart. I fear you also are a man from whom I must keep my distance for now, given my plan to see the world and experience new things. Father always told me, when I was a young girl, that he would see to it that I experienced all the travel and material pleasures I wished. But he failed, in large part due to his untimely death and his lack of planning for my future. I'm ashamed to say so, but I resent that.

Father taught me to be zealous of my own interests ... maybe too much so. But it is in my nature to be protective of myself, and to doubt others who might say they are acting for me, in my best interest.

I am leaving the Basin now to live with Mother in New York. I hope I find that the traits I have of Father's are balanced by my mother's nature to see the good and good will in everyone.

I accept your invitation, and will meet you Wednesday morning for a hike around the lake—my last before I leave here. Some day I hope to return and determine exactly what it is that we share. Perhaps we shall conclude that we share enduring values and interests, and will better understand the possibilities.

Kora

Duryea hadn't known at what time Kora would be arriving that morning, and I'd had no thought whatsoever that I might see her at the hotel. So her presence took me by surprise. I studied her figure as I approached the counter, where she stood with her back to me. A woman now, she turned to me as I came closer. Our gaze met and her bright, sparkling, large brown eyes seized my full attention.

Walking up the mountain, my heart beginning to work harder, I was reminded of how it had raced on seeing her. It was unlike her not to have let me know directly that she would be coming. Her periodic letters had described her current reading, mainly the classics with a special interest in poetry, and her continuing interest in the romantic poems of Shelley. But she'd said nothing about returning to the Basin, and, as I've said, it already had been a long time since I'd heard anything at all from her. Any time I didn't receive a letter from Kora, my instincts told me something was not right. I sensed something was not right now.

"Kora!" I'd said with excitement. "I didn't even know you were coming, not until Duryea said so yesterday!"

"Well, here I am, and it's nice to see you."

We held each other's eyes through an awkward pause before she asked, "Have you started with your father in his law office?"

"Not yet, but I intend to decide on that soon." I wasn't sure why I was reluctant to tell her my plan to do so. Kora seemed to sense my confusion. She put her hand lightly on mine.

"I can't talk right now, Jack, but let's meet soon. I need to bring you up to date on my life."

We made arrangements to meet at the hotel the next day, and went in separate directions.

Standing near the peak of the mountain, thoughts of Kora mingled with the brilliant reds and yellows cast by maple and oaks in a forest that stretched for miles in front of me. The white and gray of birch and beech trunks, visible in the fall sparseness, portended the coming winter. The sun played upon the mountainside in the west, casting gently-angled light on the waters of the lake five miles away.

I'd walked to the lakeshore earlier in the afternoon, while the sun was overhead. Sitting there on the beach, with no one else on the lake, I'd studied the patterns of the wind on water. A refreshing breeze made a rippled pattern, then magically erased it for a checked and dappled pattern of soft curves etched across the surface. Low clouds raced into the sun's path, dimming the light until they cleared, at which time the restored light, brilliant on the water, forced my eyes momentarily closed. Another white puffy cloud raced in, and once again a show of muted blues on the water gave way to the brilliant, unscreened sunlight on its surface.

From my perch on the mountain, looking at those same waters now from significant elevation, the silver white light was just a patch on the lake, brilliant, but not the exquisite, overpowering light from close up. From here the patch of water shimmered rather than dazzled; its subdued silver and aqua-green was surrounded by the brilliance of fall leaves still on the trees in the woods.

The last of the sun receded from sight and in the twilight I began my downward retreat, with urgency now to avoid full darkness. The sounds of the brook came back to my ear as I passed alongside it, quieter now than earlier. In the cooling air, I felt the rock and forest giving up the day's warmth; the gentle whisper of downdraft on the mountain surrounded me. Fall had come in full measure to the North Country wilderness.

Walking along the familiar footpath back to the Basin camp, thoughts of my relationship with Kora chilled me.

Thursday morning, the day we were to meet, dawned with a warm sun that would make it pleasant to be on Paul's Hotel porch. Under a delftware sky on an Indian summer morning, I set out for our meeting and arrived moments before Kora did. Paul had escorted me to the great porch and seated me in a caned high-back rocker with broad wooden arms, and I'd just settled myself when I saw Kora arrive at the door. I waved and she smiled, then came and sat beside me in another rocking chair with a shorter back and new caning, put in by Paul's crew for this season.

When I'd run into Kora in the hotel two days earlier, she'd worn calico — a hooped dress, trimmed in linsey on an Indian print of earthy tones, and fitting snuggly over her breasts. Her shining dark brown hair, falling to her square shoulders, had been tied off in back with a matching print ribbon. Today she was dressed in a more Adirondack style, lightweight wool pants and a heavy brushed cotton blouse, mixed with the New York fashion of a bright silk scarf around her neck. Her straight and strong body gave her an extraordinary presence, made the more remarkable by perfect skin, save for a tiny scar at the corner of her mouth, a remembrance from a girlhood bushwhacking trip up a nearby mountain. The local tomboy, we'd called her then, a quality she retained to some degree even now.

At the sight of her approaching, my thoughts had raced back two summers to the first time we'd made love. It had been a warm summer morning and we'd hiked through the Basin along Otter Brook, near where I occasionally saw the bear on the high bank. It was the last hike we would share before her departure for New York. Our planned route took us along the brook and around the distant lake we called Nehasane.

I held her hand as we crossed the stream, leapfrogging from one boulder to the next in small steps, laughing and trying not to get wet. At the far side I reached out to help her with her final leap to shore, but she jumped too far and landed virtually in my arms.

Face to face, our bodies met and ignited. Kora's shyness and my own receded as I kissed her lips, her neck, then her breasts through her clothing. Her hands on my shoulders were as sensual as anything I'd ever known. As her fingers moved to the buttons on my shirt, and then to my trouser braces, my eyes never left hers. My trousers slid to my ankles; Kora removed her slacks and undergarments, her blouse and camisole, revealing her lithe body and firm breasts. We stood naked for a long moment, holding one another. Trembling, I lowered Kora to the ground, into the high ferns by the bank, where silver moss, clean and sensual to the skin, made a natural bed.

Our naked bodies, warmed by sun and touching, electrified us. Our passion grew until it reached an intense culmination, and not long after that, was rekindled. Finally we lay spent in each other's arms among the ferns beside Otter Brook.

In time Kora spoke, her voice as soft as her skin. "I can't think of any place more beautiful than this, or anyone else but you, for my first time."

"Kora, we're meant to be lovers," I said, but it came out sounding more like a question, and she didn't answer. After a time of silence in my arms, she pushed away and got dressed.

Sitting over breakfast on the hotel porch, I knew I still needed to give our relationship a definition and hear Kora's. But she was content to talk about easy matters. She spoke of her mother, who had not accompanied her on this trip, and about life in New York, the theater and concerts, the many museums. We moved on through our obvious awkwardness exchanging news of the village and people we both knew. I told her I'd seen the Aber children in town a few weeks ago with their father, that they'd seemed fine and had asked after her. When I finally did tell her about my plans with Father, and hinted at the sort of future my work could ensure, Kora listened, but she didn't say much. Her face took on a distant look.

"I've just been for a walk near the big swamp," she said. "The osprey family still nests there and the male was fishing on the lake just below — a nice Adirondack morning, and right at my door." Then she said, "And you, Jack, how have you really been? Tell me more about your life."

"Kora," I protested, feeling my frustration grow, "that's my question to you! I need to know the same of you." I decided to come more to the point. "I need to know, Kora, if you've given more thought to our relationship. After all our sharing and letters of the past two years, is there is anything between us?"

Kora blushed. I'd pushed too hard.

"I'm sorry, Kora; that is a bit of a rush, isn't it? Can I just put that question on hold while we sit here and enjoy each other ... enjoy the nice day, take in the lake and mountains—just have a nice visit?" I knew I was babbling.

But Kora didn't hesitate.

"Yes, Jack, slow down. Let me tell you—tell you first how much I have missed this place during the past two years, and how —"

Mrs. Smith appeared at our table to take our order. Kora stopped speaking, and we both wondered if we'd been too loud and overheard. But Marie Smith only smiled and looked at me expectantly.

"We'll have neurelles and black tea with your fresh honey and currant jam," I said. "That is, if Kora agrees."

Kora nodded and we were again in private.

Kora continued. "There really is something very special about being in this wonderful, wild Basin, isn't there, Jack. With the forest and animals and waters everywhere, and the sounds in the woods and the smells of fall. It's truly nice to get back here for a while."

I sat silently, careful not to once again blurt out too many questions or push Kora too hard.

"But I've seen how, in some parts of this country, Jack, men are plundering the earth! It makes me ill. Will it happen here, too?"

I told her that Father, Duryea, and I shared her concern, that we didn't yet know the answer to her question, but that we were committed to protecting the Basin.

"Well, I'm concerned for these lands," she said, "and I must speak to Keene about the issue of ownership. That appears never to have been cleared up after Father's death—at least, that's what I understand. I mean to resolve that to my satisfaction, and sooner rather than later."

Kora's claim to dominion over these lands created a miserable knot in my gut. I changed the topic.

"Do you remember our canoe trip through the Basin and beyond in our Rushton canoes? That storm on the lake?" I knew that neither one of us could ever forget that adventure. Talking about it now would give our conversation a surer foothold.

"I do," she said quietly, casting her gaze upon the distant mountains.

We were each in our Rushton canoes on the lake, with high expectations for our tour through the wilderness Basin and beyond. This was before we'd made love, and it was implicitly understood that our relationship would remain, as it had always been, platonic. If Kora's parents felt any uneasiness about our going off together for a period of time, they kept their thoughts to themselves. We were 18 by then, and in the Adirondack society that meant we were adults and expected to make and live with our own decisions.

We'd just embarked from camp and had paddled to the first point beyond Otter Bay, moving away from the peaks at the head of the cirque. I looked back over my shoulder to see the great camp and its high oval window pass from view as I made for the north end of the lake where there was a carry to move us on to the next flow — something I'd done only once, and Kora never before. She followed at a distance but she handled her one-person, special-made Rushton canoe with ease, working the double-ended paddle to stay on the course I set. We chatted for a while, then a quiet rhythm set into our paddling, making even strokes in the dark deep lake water. From a rotation of the hips in our crouched mid-ship positions, power moved up to the shoulders, and out through our arms and hands to the paddles. The result was smooth, even strokes. I was transported to another place and time as we slid over the water, imagining us as voyageurs traveling to the unexplored interior, paddling into an unknown and glorious new world.

Only one squatter, Alvah Dunning, now lived in the far reaches of the area, and he was only seen once or twice a year in town. He was a mountain man, a trapper of beaver, who lived off the land. Whether we would see Dunning on this trip to the backcountry was anyone's guess. He kept to himself, but was liked as a man who'd lend a hand to any person in need.

Our course followed the flow around Cascade Peak through one flow, then into an outlet that became so small we had to carry our boats and gear a short distance. The first day passed under quiet waters and a sunset that cast a pink glow on the water. We quickly caught four brookies and pan-fried them over an open fire on the sandy beach. Turning in under a makeshift lean-to, we were serenaded by the gentle lapping cadence of water on the sandy beach. The next day would be the long reach to Eagle Point over open water.

"Be ready for anything, Kora," I said as we loaded up the canoes in the morning. "Let's get off now, though — we can stop later for something to eat."

Kora took a moment to slip a bright red silk cloth over her hair and tie it in back. "For good luck," she said, and I laughed at her.

"Come on, Little Red Riding Hood." She laughed too, and followed me to the Rushtons.

We glided in the first light on the quiet bay waters to the long, open reach of the lake. The eastern sky was lit in lavender, muted at first, then growing brighter as we paddled in unison side by side. The cloud-sprinkled sky cast amber light in almost horizontal rays on the water's surface, reflecting the darker amber of the deep lake. Only small ripples moved the water's surface. Fog had formed the night before and was still clearing away as we paddled

I cleared the point first and felt a breeze rising over the open reach. It had a certain gathering strength to it that got my attention. Straight away was Eagle Point, barely visible in the rising, foggy mist some seven miles away. The possibility of having to fight a stiff headwind crossed my mind. Glancing over my shoulder, I saw Kora working her paddle in my wake. We were as set for this as we were going to be.

For the next hour the warming sun caused the fog to lift, and we paddled up the lake, stroking right, left, right, left in unison, one stroke after the other, fluid and repetitive. Our pace was brisk.

"We've reached the halfway mark, Kora. If we keep going at this rate, we'll be in good shape!" I turned to make eye contact with her behind me, and as I did so I noticed for the first time the darkening sky in the southeast, and a rising southerly wind. The water in the south had already turned slate gray, matching the sky.

Ripples moved on the surface, perhaps a mile away at first and coming toward us. They were growing in size, approaching waves with a small froth, not quite a white cap.

"Not what we want right now, Kora. Look behind you!" We both stopped paddling and studied the wind and water in the south.

I quickly calculated the options before us. We could turn into the gathering storm and return to the leeside of the Point we'd just cleared, or we could ride out the storm downwind. Each choice came with risks. One was the possibility of being blown past Eagle Point into a yet broader reach of open water, and the other was of swamping our Rushtons with their scant freeboards, as waves washed over us astern. Looking back one more time and seeing the strength of the gathering storm, I made my decision.

"Let's ride this downwind to Eagle, Kora. Quarter to the south a bit so we don't miss the Point—rudder with your paddle—don't go beyond the Point! There's nothing there but open heavy water." I had to shout over the rising wind.

"We can handle this, Jack!" she yelled back.

"Watch the water over your stern and don't miss the Point!"

With that, we began to paddle. I could see that Kora understood exactly what she must do. Yet, alone in our canoes, each of us was on our own, and there was no turning back.

The next minute brought the storm on us. Our canoes became floating corks driven along by a wind that was near gale force and still rising as it neared us. Control of our boats became our life-or-death focus.

The southeast wind came into our port side. I ruddered to the south and west, holding it as long as I dared, until the stern swung too far, coming close to breaching the boat. Hunkering on my knees I rode low in the boat, crouched to handle the force of the wind and water raking my port side. I made one quick recovery after another, switching from using my paddle as a rudder, to employing it in short stabilizing strokes to make corrections. It was heavy work that required great skill. I wasn't sure if either Kora or I would meet the challenge of the conditions.

I struggled to keep a course that would take me into the cove at Eagle Point, still miles away and not visible now in the raging storm. I caught a glimpse of Kora in her little canoe, dealing with the conditions and making some headway, and shouted to her to follow my course. Could she hear me? I didn't know. I felt my gut wrench.

The lake was frothed in whitecaps that lashed over the boats and threw up a cold spray. Water was being taken on astern and mid-ship. My clothes were drenched through, and my strength began to ebb. I hadn't seen Kora's boat for a few minutes, and until now, had not even had a chance to look around to her, upwind of me.

Risking a glance now, my heart raced as I looked, saw nothing, and searched again. Kora was not in the piece of water she should be in, just over my left shoulder and behind me. I shifted farther back, straining to turn, and I froze, almost getting knocked over for my lack of attention to my course on the top of a cresting white cap.

Kora had been blown off course. She was about two hundred yards off my stern, farther out and too southerly, swept there by the wind. She would miss the point and be in grave danger with the rough open water downwind of her. The wind whipped the water even higher and the sky grew a dark and sober gray, although it wasn't yet noon.

I moved west and south on the downwind, using a left rudder to quarter closer to her. Kora appeared on a crest and disappeared in a trough. The top of her head remained barely visible as the red babushka came and went from my sight.

Approaching her, but still at a distance, I shouted to her. "Rudder toward me, rudder hard toward me now!" I yelled as loudly I could. Just then her canoe broached to the wind as she strained to hear me. She took in water and went lower. I saw fear in her face, and sensed that she was no longer able to control her course against the wind and the weight of water in the boat. Steadying my own craft, I looked again. I could not pick out Kora or her canoe.

I knew she would stay with her boat. But where was she? With another rudder and quarter I moved further toward where I'd last seen her. I couldn't find her. I kept moving, looking, searching for any sign of her. For an instant I thought I picked up a glint of red in the water at the crest of a wave, but my sight was clouded by mist and rain, and when I was able to see again, the red cloth was gone. I peered hard through the rain and wind, trying to hold my course and stay afloat, but feeling helpless. Desperately, I kept maneuvering for a position to help her, but how could I help her if I couldn't even locate her?

The realization hit me that, now so far south and east, I might go into the open water beyond Eagle Point myself. This was my last opportunity to move back westward, but if I did so, it would be without Kora. I knew Dunning was rumored to have a cabin in the Eagle Point area, and it occurred to me that I could get help from him if I could track him down. I looked and listened for Kora one more time... nothing.

Reluctantly, I steered my course back westward. Kora would have to try to ride it out with her boat. Perhaps she'd survive if she was able to get out of the water soon enough to avoid drowning or freezing. That thought enraged me, and adrenaline shot strength into my sapped muscles.

My spirits were shattered, beaten low, but I called upon a residue of strength to pull my way toward the Point and help. Time after time I took on water and came near swamping. I bailed to keep ballast, and the Rushton proved her seaworthiness again and again. I did weight shifts with my body, curling and leaning to counterbalance the forces hurled at me by the gale, and with each battering I could only think of Kora and her boat, now out of my vision. I made slow headway, moving toward the inside of the Point, catching sight of it and ruddering against the gale at my stern, and riding breakers toward the distant cove. Finally, I could clearly see the beach and tree line there. I put in at a rock-strewn beach in heavy surf, soaked and cold and shivering to my bones. After pulling up the Rushton, I looked for cover to get out of the wind.

I found a windbreak among hemlocks with a cache of dry wood stowed by the last soul to put-in here. Gathered in a dry nook of the hemlock was kindling to start the fire, and I attended to it. Some of the wood was dry enough to catch and soon the fire threw heat to my body as I stripped off clothes and searched my duffel for replacements. I stood next to the roaring flame, which even in the lee was driven by the forces raging in from the south. Spent physically and emotionally, an empty feeling gripped and held me. I feared that I'd lost Kora, thereby irrevocably diminishing nearly everything in this world of importance to me. I kept a constant lookout down the stormy lake for any sign of her, searching the water beyond the lee of the Point, shuddering for her fate somewhere in the immense bay.

I did not know if she was dead or alive.

Finding no sign of her in the water, I still clung to the belief that this was a quickly passing storm and I would soon be able to return to my canoe and resume my search downwind. It was now noon, but the day grew darker and the storm seemed to rage even harder. I lost visibility of the bay, where she must have been washed. My heart felt too heavy to contain.

Kora later confessed, when she was able to talk, that she knew she was a prisoner of the sudden gale the moment her canoe broached and swamped. She lost control. Her paddle stroked the water, but had no effect except to roll her to a gunwale. The wind and sea driving her down the lake grew even rougher, and after her last glimpse of me, she knew her only salvation was to stay with her boat, to use it for flotation and ride out the storm.

She struggled to right the canoe, but slowly it turned hull up. Her stowed pack came out and disappeared in the water. She shouted, and thought she heard my voice on the wind, but she couldn't see me. Clinging to the now capsized craft at mid-ship, with her arms draped over the hull, she felt her strength ebb in the cold. Her body temperature dropped and she grew numb and weak within mere minutes.

Desperate, Kora decided to lash herself to the canoe using a thwart, around which she made a loop with a painter, tying it to the stern. Taking the loop of line secured around the thwart, she pulled it over her shoulder, back under her arm, then through her belt. She lashed the end to gunwale at a spot with just enough room to feed it and secure the line. This used up most of her remaining strength.

Now she could see nothing, and was helpless to do much more. She knew she was being driven past Eagle Point into open water. Spread-eagled on the thin wood hull, she felt herself drift in and out of consciousness. As she fought to stay on the hull, she felt the air go out of her but not back in. Wind driven water washed over the hull, submerging her head and robbing her of oxygen, once and then again and again.

She went under a third time, and later told me she knew her end was near. She thought she was hallucinating and hearing a strange voice, and she assumed it was to be her last experience before drowning. But there on a wave top a few feet away was the hallucination again, and this time it was a man in a doubleended guide boat working long wood oars and looking directly at her. Kora thought, "He's shouting to me... I must stay awake. I must help myself."

Then she went under, the water washing over the hull and taking her with its force and loosening her hold. Somehow the painter line came unlashed, sending her in to the frothing water. Her body washed into the open water but the painter she'd secured pulled her alongside the Rushton for a few more seconds.

Dunning afterwards described everything from his perspective. He'd known he had to approach upwind to reach the person tangled in the painter if he were to get him — for he'd assumed it was a male — into his boat. Working both oars, he moved first downwind, then, at exactly the right moment, he pulled with one oar and pushed with the other with all his strength, pivoting the boat into a position of bow to the wind. As fast as he could, Dunning covered the 20 yards to the spot where he'd last seen the figure, now distinguishable as female, going under. But when he got to where she should be he saw nothing but a small blotch of red directly opposite on his port side, sinking into the water. He released the left oar, even knowing his boat would whip wildly in the gale as it crashed over a giant wave.

The seasoned boatman understood he was on the edge. He felt his body lift as his long sinewy arm stretched for the point of red. He lunged, hand open, ready to close on what he saw. Grabbing onto it, he knew immediately that it was a head wrapped in a cover. It was that bright red cover that had attracted Dunning's attention from the shore as he'd watched the fast approaching storm move across the water.

His strong hand began to ache, but he resolved to not let go. Using Kora as a counterweight allowed him to gain his balance in his boat, keeping him anchored low to the inwale as he leaned out of the boat.

Tenaciously, Dunning reached out with his right hand and grabbed a shoulder. Now he had her to the boat, but must still get her into it. With a lunge downward he pulled, and Kora's body rose chest high to the gunwales, just as the guide boat dropped into a trough. Her body careened and dropped into the boat at the very moment the craft broached in a wave and turned portside, directly into the force of the wind.

Dunning knew in an instant that the wind would knock the boat over unless he countered with a great force to keep it from rolling. He threw his body to the starboard gunwales and hung to a rib, then shifted to the outwale as the boat took on water and careened out of control. He regained one oar and his position on the seat. The woman had ended up in the bow, and her position and weight helped right the boat as Dunning headed it back upwind. His moves allowed just enough free board to let him ride out a series of waves and wind. He saw then that Kora's legs were still dangling over the port gunwale, and he secured her in the bottom of the boat, even as he made a down-wind quartering move to return to the cove where his rescue voyage had started.

He groped for the second oar, ruddered to regain equilibrium, secured it, and continued downwind. The guide boat, built by Dunning, with a steep sheer for stability, responded. He knew he had the course and position, even in this wind, to get back. Even as water continued to wash over his stern, he made his way. Kora lay at the bottom of his boat. She didn't move or appear to breathe, but for the moment he could do nothing other than give a kick with his leg and apply pressure to her back, using his foot as he rowed.

He remained concerned with reaching shore but paid close attention. Did he see some small movement, hear a faint cough? Not sure, he fought his way to the lee of the island. Hidden in a bay previously unknown to me were Dunning's small dock and beach. He pulled in to the sandy beach, grabbed the woman and hoisted her to his shoulders. The climb up the bluff was hard, but thinking of the warmth of the cabin helped him forge ahead. Reaching his door, he burst in and placed Kora in a slouched position on his bear skin rug in front of his pot bellied stove. Stoking the fire, he removed her outer wool shirt, which was soaking her to the skin, and covered her with two heavy woolen blankets. All the while, he kept applying pressure to her back.

Kora lay still for several moments, then moved, albeit barely discernibly. Soon she coughed, opened her eyes and looked around. She seemed startled and confused, Dunning said, but she also seemed to somehow sense she was safe.

"Ja...Ja..." she softly whispered, but Dunning did not understand. She began to breathe and then closed her eyes and fell into a deep sleep. Her last thoughts were a jumble of concern for Jack and confusion as to where she was, and who was the man attending to her.

Dunning was pretty sure he'd seen a second canoe some distance from the red-capped figure. That might have been the "Ja" Kora had tried to speak of.

The great nor'easter raged on over the lake for hours longer, but finally died as night approached. I was back on the water, fear in my heart, looking for Kora in her red babushka for the several hours before dark. But there was still no sign of her, even down the lake where the storm had taken her, and no indication of where Dunning might be in this vast wilderness. I understood, but resented, that this was the way of the wild.

Six
No Peace

"It's hard to believe," I half laughed to Kora there on the porch of Paul's Hotel, "that neither of us thought of Dunning or Osprey Island. But thank God for him."

"I know, Jack. I remem—"

" — I can't tell you how I felt when I saw smoke coming from his cabin that night. I'd gone out looking for you again, you know. I didn't mean to go ashore again until I'd found you. I'll never forget the feeling of looking up and seeing Dunning waving from the bluff, motioning me to shore.

I'd raced to shore and up the bluff, pushing past Dunning waiting in his doorway. There she was, still asleep and looking ashen. But her eyes opened, and for the first time since the whole thing had begun, I knew she'd be all right. She'd said something so softly, I couldn't hear her. But she'd used my name, so I knew she recognized me.

"Kora, what was it you said to me that night when I got to Dunning's cabin?"

Her bright eyes drifted downward and she said into the table, "I don't know, Jack. You were explaining everything as I was coming around. I was probably just trying to understand it all."

Kora had left the Basin again a few days after our return from Osprey Island, so we never really had a chance to fully process our near-disaster, and she hadn't returned to the Basin until just now, two years later. Our correspondence had continued, but even in our letters we'd shied away from talking about that storm, as if it had been too close a call and we'd be tempting fate if we revisited the event.

Kora's words returned me to the present.

"I've always felt bad about leaving so soon afterwards and never thanking Dunning in person. I'm sure you thanked him, Jack."

"With all my heart."

"Mother decided rather suddenly to leave here, which is like her, you know. She needed to get away after the divorce. She'd tried staying on here, she'd given it several years, but it was just too difficult for her. And I didn't want her going off all alone. I was torn about leaving the Basin, of course, but in the long run the move to New York has proven to be best for Mother and me."

I couldn't think of anything to say to that. I knew from her several letters that she had been giving serious thought to returning to the Basin and staying with me. Sitting near her now, I let my hopes rise that this time she was home to stay, that she'd come back to me.

As if she were reading my thoughts, she said, "Jack, I'm going back to New York with a friend. I stopped here mainly to see you." She looked away and would not meet my eyes. "I don't know when I'll come back again. I wanted to see you, wanted to tell you this, and to see Dunning. I went out to his place earlier this morning, but he wasn't there. Please tell him I tried to see him, and give him this note." She handed me an envelope with Dunning's name on it.

She finally looked at me again. "I'm sorry to spring this on you. It seems that—"

Words that at first wouldn't come finally tumbled out.

"It's okay, Kora, if that is what you must do." I stopped there briefly to make myself breathe. "Go to New York. Go to the city where the seasons change while you don't notice and where the Adirondacks aren't in your back yard." I couldn't seem to soften the acidic tone in my voice. "It's your life. You do as you please. But don't look too far for Dunning, or expect delivery of your nice note. He hasn't been seen in town since he helped you. People wonder if he'd still out there. We'll have to see what news we hear of him this fall or winter.

"I'm going to practice law here, Kora, where I love it — with my father. So I'll be here... And hope I can see you again, if you want to. But our relationship can't grow unless you let it—by spending time with me."

I tried to read her face, but it was impenetrable. I fought the urge to tell her what I hoped for, that I wanted her to be my wife and partner in our pursuit of life and family. But the timing wasn't right; she wasn't ready to hear me. But would she ever be?

"Passion between a man and a woman is important, of course, but it isn't the most important thing in a relationship. We need to think about the future, and what we really share in common. We had a childhood together, Jack, but that doesn't mean we'd be compatible as adults for the rest of our lives."

She looked off into the distance again. "We still need some time apart, as well as some time together. We'll have to figure it out as we go."

My head could agree with her, but not my heart. Yet I couldn't escape the wisdom in her words, and I was reminded that Kora was a person with great judgment. She wanted to be sure, to move more slowly, to make no quick decisions.

"This makes sense, Kora. But please, let's see each other. Keep writing to me and telling me your thoughts. Let me know where you are, what you're doing. You know where I'll be…" I was of a mind to say, but did not …waiting for you to come back to me, to come home.

She stood, leaned over, and kissed my cheek. Her scent was the same sweet balsam that I remembered from our lovemaking. Her fingers ran across my shoulders as she passed behind my chair.

"I promise to write, Jack. And I'll think about what is best." She stopped at the doorway. "I'll be back at some time. Winter's my favorite season, you know, and I'll miss being here."

There was a bounce to her step as she went down the porch steps, and that irritated me.

"My train leaves quite soon, Jack. Goodbye." She turned and started walking toward the train station. But after a few steps, she stopped and turned my way again. In a gentler voice than earlier, she said, "I'll see you at Christmas, Jack. We can snowshoe the Basin—maybe into the backcountry to find Dunning! And I want to see Duryea and study him as he cooks over that wood stove. I can't wait!"

Then she was gone, leaving me to wonder which message she'd meant for me to hold on to — that New York was where she belonged, or that she couldn't wait to get back at Christmastime?

A gentle smile tugged at my lips as I thought of Kora's beauty, which, for me, was synonymous with the Adirondacks. I remembered her in a canoe on a wilderness lake, paddling easily with her strong arms as she talked of nature, identifying things as we passed them. "Look there, Jack, there's the first shad in its white bloom, and there, just beyond, did you see the mother loon with young on her back?" Her face lit the scene as I saw her moving down the lake.

I saw her in the sunlight of fall against a white early snowfall, radiating excitement as she hiked through the evergreens. Her pace quickened as she went, her brown eyes shining with anticipation, a faint half-smile etched on her face. Kora was the essence of the North Country woman — elusive and ethereal one moment, real and hard the next.

It knew it was pointless, but I couldn't help but sit there at Paul's Hotel and ask myself, for the thousandth time, whether Kora and I would end up together. My mind went in circles, always coming back to the same uncertain place. In a while I tired of trying to figure it out, and turned my mind to other things.

I was resolved to get my law practice with Father going. I knew one of the first orders of business would be dealing with another Longfellow — William West Longfellow — about the deed to the Basin. There would certainly be a great deal to keep me busy, and I was determined to devote myself to my career, placing Kora on hold.

I rose from the rocker on the hotel porch and set off in search of Father. Get on with things, I told myself. Kora wasn't there, but my career and life were.

As I moved down the same steps Kora had used moments ago, I thrust my hand into a side jacket pocket and felt a silken object. I fingered it gently, that red babushka Kora had worn during the terrible storm. Dunning had given it to me the night of the rescue. It was perhaps silly of me, but I kept it, and Kora never asked about it. No doubt she assumed it had been lost in the water. I'd left it lying in a dresser drawer until long after she'd moved to the city. Coming across it the other day, I'd planned to return it to Kora when we met this morning, but I'd forgotten to.

Maybe at Christmas.

Seven
The Practice

"We'll make a good team, Jack!" Father declared in his bold way. "I have some work to give you right away. New clients are coming in this morning, and I want you to meet with us."

And with that welcome, the pace at the Durant law firm was set and remained brisk and vibrant as a new lawyer learned his trade. The next weeks and months flew by as I encountered one new thing after another. Father seemed satisfied with my progress, but I learned that I didn't yet have mastery, or anything close to it, over the practice of law. What I did have was a master teacher to guide me, and a father who seemed renewed and reinvigorated in his life. We settled into our routine, and I worked with my first clients with great eagerness and anticipation. Autumn gave way to winter in the Adirondacks and more snow built up each day. The Basin went in to its annual deep freeze.

Christmas of 1905 came and went, and the only word from Kora was a letter saying she could not come. Having decided to put Kora on hold, to whatever extent possible, I tried not to let my disappointment overtake me. We wrote to each other frequently, sharing our thoughts and hopes, and we told each other what we were reading and what we thought of it. We kept each other abreast of our daily lives. Yet the relationship couldn't mature, not through correspondence alone. The only hints of anything remotely romantic were her quotations from Shelley, but she never said the poems were directed at me, only that she "admired and respected the great poet as a true romantic."

We'd been exchanging letters for several months when Kora finally concluded one of hers by asking if Father and I were still enjoying the "family property." The phrase was so ambiguous, I wasn't sure what she truly meant to imply. Rather than head directly into things, I chose to simply reply that we were, that we "loved our Basin lands and camp."

My recurring dream, increasingly more nightmare-like, came back that night. I got up shaking and took my usual walk in the middle of a very dark night. My dream, a vision of a hidden lean-to where I camped as the intruder, gnawed away at the scar inside.

I marked my one-year anniversary with the Durant law firm in the fall of 1906 wondering how an entire year had gone by. My work on real estate transactions, and in assisting Father in his representation of both the town and county governments, was challenging and satisfying for a new lawyer. One of my first official tasks was to search a real estate title, which required me to pour over documents and form a judgment on the marketability of properties bought and sold by our clients. Some of the properties had questionable titles. They'd been lost for failure to pay taxes due, and the state had taken title back, subsequently selling off its interest without any warranty of title. We advised our clients of the risks in such situations. Some cancelled their transactions on the basis of our sometimes grim analysis.

Our firm represented defendants in criminal cases on occasion, which I found to be the most challenging responsibility I'd ever shouldered. The power of the state over an individual always astounded me, and it was sobering to know that a man's future rested on my ability to defend him.

I undertook the representation of a man referred to locally as "Dancing Dan McGruder" whose only offense was to dance at the hotel bar by himself — conduct the owner, Paul, and some patrons found offensive, resulting in his arrest and jailing. I pointed out to the prosecutor that McGruder's dancing might well be offensive and socially inept, but it was not criminal conduct worthy of prosecution. There was much fuss in the local press about the case. The district attorney was unyielding, and we had a jury trial, my first. When 12 peers found the defendant not guilty of any crime, I experienced a thrill I'll never forget. Dancing Dan was free, justice had been served, and I'd been part of that process. I can still hear the judge's voice: "You are free to walk from this courtroom, Mr. McGruder. These proceedings are ended." Paul was not pleased with me.

Lessons learned and wisdom gained were part of my legal career. I matured as an attorney through representing various clients and becoming savvy to some of the tricks of the trade. I began to grow cocky and thought of myself as unbeatable, even heroic, until I lost my next two cases and gained some needed perspective. My second and third anniversaries came and went in 1907 and '08 with little fanfare, but all my work remained under Keene's able guidance and counsel on my cases. I noticed, of course, that Keene handled the most serious cases, though I was being slowly brought in on them.

One day in 1908, after I had been at the firm more than three years, Keene appeared at my office door.

"I'm going to give you some interesting work, son, and a chance to learn a great deal about people while you're at it. The people coming in tomorrow have no money, Jack, but everyone has legal rights that must be honored — even if doing so means taking on the rich and powerful. Otherwise, society would quickly fall into bitterness and chaos with no resolution — a bad result and a bad mark on our system of justice, and something we have to fight to avoid.

"These folks are coming in to see what their rights are on some land. It doesn't look good if they're squatters on land owned by the State, as they put it to me in my one meeting with them. You studied real property law in your clerkship, Jack, and you've learned a lot about local real estate titles working here. You're about to use your knowledge to help Mr. And Mrs. Aber, so be ready and sharp in the morning."

"I know the Abers! Or their children, anyway."

"Indeed. From school." He lingered another moment in the doorway. "Let's do our best for this family. Their farmland is near a boundary of the Basin, and there are some very interesting legal questions in this case that could prove relevant to the Basin title. I'll see you early tomorrow."

With that, Father walked out of the office with his topcoat and beaver hat, heading for his home in the village where he often stayed. I decided to head for camp that night.

Our weathered wooden office sign, its gold leaf lettering slowly fading, creaked in the cold breeze as I shut and locked the door. Still thinking about the new case, I anticipated the walk and row to camp and the feel of the woods and water. The silence and beauty of the trip provided me with great solace.

I walked to the edge of town and selected a doubleender from our boathouse. Working the overlapped oars, one just over the other for the fifteen-minute row down the lake, would give me time to think. The Basin was in its fifth season, that time of year when winter had not quite arrived but the leaves were all down and frost was setting in, waiting to take over. Naked forest and undergrowth lay bare in this short-lived season.

At first the creaking of the working parts gave me away as I stroked down the lake, but the sound gradually lessened and seemed to work its way out. I oared in total silence except for the faint whoosh of the blades taking hold each stroke. Snow began to fall, at first big, light, slow-descending flakes, then smaller and faster ones. For a while I was still able to see the silhouettes of the forest and distant peaks for a few moments, changing their seasonal cover, now clad in winter white. But soon darkness fell, and overwhelming silence surrounded me as if I were in a cocoon and all of life had settled in for the newly arrived winter. From now until spring, I would take a horse-driven sled, or walk or snow shoe to camp, and Father would spend more time in town.

I looked over my shoulder to find the familiar oval window lit to guide me in to the beach, where I secured the boat in the boathouse and walked in to camp. Looking through the great room window into the kitchen, I saw Duryea moving about doing his chores. My nose told me he'd already cooked up a hearty meal as a welcome North Country dinner.

It was venison, cooked to perfection. I ate almost greedily, talking with Duryea as I did so about preparations for winter. After the meal we talked about how our days had gone and shared a glass of wine. My plan was to read some and turn in early, but as we finished cleaning the last of the dishes, Duryea motioned for me to sit down again.

Dressed in his favorite old brown hound's-tooth wool shirt and wool work vest, his pockets loaded with a cooking thermometer and various utensils and tools, he removed the apron from around his neck. He looked a bit older that night, with a touch of worry around his eyes that I seldom observed in him.

"I have promised in the past to tell you something important of my upbringing — as a youth, I mean." His countenance grew stern and serious, even strained, as he drew a breath. This was not the usual Duryea.

He moved to his favorite kitchen reading chair next to his neatly indexed recipes on the shelf over the sideboard, and sat. His bald head shone in the light and his thick white moustache and sideburns gave definition to his kind face.

"Perhaps it will help you understand me better."

I thought I understood Duryea, but when he said that I realized that in fact there was a great deal about him I didn't know.

"I was raised in Quebec in a foster family, Jack, after my mother and father died with my sister in a sleigh that went through the ice on the river. I was left alone at the age of 11 with no one, and only the memory of my loving family."

"I was in the sleigh also. I managed to jump free and stay afloat on some ice and finally to get to shore. I watched as my parents and sister were swept under the ice in the sleigh, along with our horse. I will always remember that last glimpse of my father alive. The horror in his eyes as they all went under the ice. Their bodies … they were not found until spring."

Now Duryea stopped and looked directly at me. Suddenly an old dam broke and he began to weep, the sight of which caused a hurt that cut me like a knife. I reached out for my older friend, rather awkwardly at first, wanting to somehow comfort him, but also realizing that I'd never been in the role of comfort-giver. I felt self-conscious as my hand found his broad shoulders, but the contact flooded me with memories of Duryea's attentions to me throughout my childhood. As one would with a distraught child — as Duryea had often done with me — I stroked and patted him. The feel of his old wool shirt under my fingers comforted me.

"I was placed in a home with a family," he said when he was ready to go on. "It was a family of loggers and every boy was expected to earn his keep. That's when I learned the ways of the woods and logging. I also learned that my foster father had no scruples about where he got his logs or how he clear cut the forest. He raped every piece of forest he ever worked and left it for dead.

"I planned to get away as soon as I could, but in the meantime, I also learned a great deal about building. Seems I had a gift for design, and God had given it to me as a way out. From the moment I'd learned to read, I'd been reading about the Adirondacks, Jack, and I made up my mind as a very young boy that this was where I would escape to. And I did, at age 15. I walked here from Quebec."

I was astounded at his story, and my admiration for Duryea, already enormous, grew even deeper. It occurred to me that if Duryea wanted me to understand him at his very depths, he'd chosen just the right story to share. A man of Duryea's strength and character didn't come from an easy upbringing, and his story brought that home to me. I listened intently as he went on, not wanting to interrupt.

"Longfellow was running his timber industry and he hired me. I came to know the man and I saw in him something of my foster father, but also something good and kind, unlike that other man. We talked often, and we learned from each other. That was another of Longfellow's fine suits. He would listen, even to a young kid he'd hired off the road. As I grew older, he grew to trust my judgment about the woods and the importance of preserving this beautiful country.

"I kept on learning, reading everything I could and observing everything around me. I told Longfellow what I could build for him — a camp in this wilderness — and I told him the conditions, which you already know. There would be only one camp, and we would preserve the wilderness forever.

"Then the great fire occurred in 1894, nearly burning the camp I'd just built and the Basin forests along with it. I know Keene talked to Longfellow around that time about this land and what should happen to it, but I don't know the outcome of their discussions, Jack. We need to know. I need to know. So I'm asking you — learn how Longfellow and your father resolved the matter of preserving the Basin. I am asking this of you because I will expect you to carry on with my work here."

His epiphany caught me by surprise. I wanted to hear more from the usually reticent Duryea, who did not disappoint.

"You know how I admire John Muir. Like him, I love the wilderness and believe that man should only be a visitor here, to wonder and think. For me, it is where God is. You are my family, Jack, and I am growing old. There are questions that keep me from sleep at night. Was I right to build this camp and strike my deal with Longfellow? Will our pact be honored, and is it true to the ideals of the wilderness?

"I think each day of these things. Jack, I ask you to join me now and to promise that you will see that my agreement with Longfellow is carried out."

I sat quietly for several moments, absorbing all that had been said. Duryea's love for nature had come to him in a way not unlike it had come to me: through loss and loneliness as children. Part of me was certain that Duryea knew he didn't have to ask me to carry the torch for him when he was gone, that I could no more turn my back on the wilderness than he'd been able to in his lifetime.

"Of course," was all I said.

"Know too, that I want to be buried on these lands in my favorite high meadow, in a plain way with no memorials."

His words chilled me. It was impossible to think of a world without Duryea in it.

"I built the camp and it is here to be dealt with, along with the Great Basin itself, Jack. The hour is late and we are both too tired to talk further now. Let us continue some time soon. But it is up to you as a lawyer, and as Keene's son, to seek out the truth about the Basin title. You must know with certainty it can be preserved. But I forewarn you," he said, and his eyes looked even older, "the resolution may involve your friend, Kora. She has a stake here too.

"And so my friend, good night to you. I love you and know you will make the right decisions as you go, though it will not be easy."

No, it wouldn't be easy. But I'd find a way, and I hoped I would follow well in Duryea's shoes, showing strength with a good measure of compassion.

"Duryea," I said, stopping at the kitchen door. "I'm sorry… for your loss of your family. The courage you've shown is the more remarkable to me now, my trusted friend." Patting him softly on his shoulder, I left the kitchen in silence, and Duryea remained sitting in his chair, a more peaceful expression on his face.

But his words hung in my mind that night before I slept. Duryea's revelations had left me feeling uneasy, and I wasn't sure why. Lying in bed I tried to read, but my concentration was poor. Fatigue, I thought, but then I realized I wasn't really interested in what I was reading. I wanted to read Muir's work for myself; I wanted learn how he'd arrived at his philosophy. As I thought of it, it occurred to me that Muir's writings were always visible on Duryea's favorite reading table.

Restless and unable to sleep — my thoughts still on Duryea and his steady presence through my life — I got out of bed and pulled from my office a treatise on New York real property law. I read and reread some provisions on land titles and the elements of proof that would be required to make a case for the new clients coming in tomorrow. Any information I collected for the Abers might also help clear things up regarding the Basin title. Of course, thought of the Basin led to further reflection on Muir, and those thoughts brought me full circle back to Duryea. Something about him had been troubling me since supper, and I finally understood that I was discomforted by his having turned to me in a moment of weakness. I didn't yet understand why.

Before drifting off, my last thought was of the plight of the Aber family and how Father and I might help them. And just before deepest sleep, there came a vision of my beautiful Kora, paddling with me across a beautiful alpine lake.

And yet, Kora was not here, and I didn't know when she would return. I considered going to New York and asking her outright whether she would return to the Basin with me. But I couldn't bring myself to do it. In her absence, and to busy myself, I had been on a few dates with local women but every date only proved that no one could replace Kora. My life was basically monastic, except the respite of a weekend here or there to let loose, usually in Glens Falls or Malone or Plattsburgh, where I knew women who only wanted pleasure and fun, which I supplied.

The next morning I got to the office even before Keene, my thoughts focused on the new clients and their case. The hour to meet came quickly enough.

Ada and Francis Aber had a toddler with them, a boy, whom Mrs. Aber identified as her grandson, who bore a strong resemblance to Etienne. If either Mr. or Mrs. Aber remembered me as having had a school connection with their children, they didn't acknowledge it.

Mrs. Aber spoke first.

"Our people have lived on that land for 50 years, Mr. Durant. Francis and I built our own house there, and we're raising our family there. And we've paid our taxes too!"

But they'd been directed to pay those taxes directly to the man who'd sold them the land, Jacques Paquette.

"And he's dead now."

Father and I exchanged glances.

"We have this paper we signed with him," she said, offering it to Father for his review.

So far, Mr. and Mrs. Aber's eye contact had been only with Father. Even though he'd introduced me as his son and partner in the firm, I had yet to take part in this conversation except to say hello.

Examining the paper closely Father said, "It's the usual installment land contract that states you'll get a deed after paying Paquette for 10 years. It says you must pay him principle and interest every year, $106 in one payment. Did you do this?"

"Yes, Monsieur Durant," Ada Aber said, reverting into her French-Canadian dialect, "but we did not always get a receipt. And before the last year's payment ..." Her voice dropped off, and she averted my father's penetrating gaze. Francis Aber filled in the void.

"Jacques Paquette suddenly died. We heard nothing from any relatives. We found out he had a niece living away and we got an address to send her a payment — I forget where to — but we did pay. This was many years ago."

Father studied their faces closely. I could read his mind and nearly gave the advice myself, but managed to keep quiet.

"I must tell you, Francis and Mrs. Aber, that it is well-known that the taxes on the Paquette parcel, including your land, were not paid. The state got the parcel for back taxes and therefore claims title to it.

From behind his chestnut desk Father leaned toward Mr. Aber, an intensity in his voice that was clear to all present. "Now to the important questions." I guessed what was coming and felt pleased that I was following Father's analysis.

He looked directly at Mr. Aber. "Did you," Father asked, "receive a deed from Pacquette?" We both knew the answer.

"No, we did not, Monsieur."

"Did you receive any paper from the state about the tax foreclosure for non-payment of taxes?"

"No, we did not."

"Did Pacquette lumber his land and sell the timber?" Here was the perhaps crucial piece of information, and Father awaited the answer.

"Yes, he did," said Aber. "He even told us he had the right to take trees."

Father examined the contract and quickly confirmed. "Yes, it's in the paper. Well, now, Francis and Mrs. Aber, let me give you some legal advice. First, we must find Pacquette's niece and ask her to sign a deed to you. Second, we must advise the state that their tax foreclosure is flawed because it proceeded on the basis that the land was timberland only, and therefore your parcel was wrongly taxed. That your land was farmed and used by your family as a residence. Also, that the state knew or should have known of your occupation. It should have been known because you lived on the land and, most importantly, I see, your agreement was recorded with the county. This is good."

Their case sounded remarkably like Longfellow's, and therefore I knew there was legal precedence for Father's argument.

"We may be able to set aside the tax sale and confirm your rights under the agreement. But we have to get the deed and show your title, and then we'll challenge the state —in court, if we must."

There was an uneasy pause before Mr. Aber spoke. "You know we don't have much money to pay you."

"We can talk about that soon—once we see what's involved. For now, we have several things to do. Go back to your homestead. My son and I will do our best for you. Do you have any questions?"

Ada Aber, her eyes glistening with hope, said, "I am

not sure we understand, Monsieur, all that you have just said, but we place our trust in you. Your son and his friend Kora have already helped us, you know, and now we ask for your help again. Please try. We will pay you in some way."

"I understand," Father said. "We'll need to meet again as soon as we have more facts to go on. We'll tell you soon what steps we should take!"

I nodded to Mrs. Aber. "Please send my good wishes to Etienne and Susie. I remember them fondly."

In return, they gave a humble bow to Father and me, and Father showed them out of the office, returning quickly.

"You know what has to be done, Jack. Draft a letter to the Forest Commission. Get the tax foreclosure papers from them. Find the niece and send her a demand for the deed—mention that the Abers faithfully paid, and that Mr. Pacquette did not get the taxes paid as he was bound to do. Any questions?"

"Just one. Can the firm afford to take this case if the Abers can't pay?" We were partners and I wanted to be consulted. I also needed to be paid at least something.

"I left that open-ended with them in our first meeting, except to say that I had to speak to you. We'll have to evaluate the situation as we go, Jack. We'll be fair with each other, as we always have been. For now, unless you say no, there isn't much more that can be said."

Keene Durant had a look of satisfaction in his weathered, handsome face as he said this.

"That's good enough for me, Father. So now I have work to do." I walked to my office knowing we had a deal, which Father promised to be a fair deal, and therefore I trusted it would be.

A favorite memory came to mind of sitting with Father on the front porch of the Basin lodge while he told me a story from his boyhood. This story always started the same way, but depending on what he wanted to stress, it didn't always contain the same precise teaching, though it was always similar.

"Jack, I was 15 years old when I went with my father for a visit to the county seat at Elizabethtown. We went to take a deed to the county clerk and have it recorded. The deed was all in order and we expected it would be a quick trip. But there was a long line at the public office, which was most unusual. And it was doubly unusual that the large man at the front of the line was giving instructions in a firm and steady voice to 10 Negroes, men of very black skin who hadn't been seen about town before.

"I remember very clearly the large white man turning toward me, facing me directly as he stared down the line of black men queued before him. When our eyes met, this large gruff-looking man's expression turned soft and he gave me a gentle smile from the corner of his mouth.

"'Men,' he said, addressing the Negroes, 'be ready with your quills and place your X on the line of the deed that I point to. The lawyer is here now!'"

"There was an urgent tone to his voice. Another man, it must have been Sam Dwyer, the local lawyer, all dressed in a fine suit, came down the line, looked for the "X" on each deed, then placed his seal and signature on it. He turned to the large man at the front, the one who'd smiled at me. Each black face studied his face very closely, Jack, concern all over their faces. Silence filled the room.

"Then the lawyer said to the man at the front, 'Mr. Smith, these indentures from you to these men are now fit to be recorded. You there in front, Lyman Epps, we shall record your indenture first. Step forward, right here to the clerk's counter!'

"And with that, Jack, each man stepped forward and the county clerk stamped first Lyman Epps' paper and then the others, taking the papers that each man was clearly reluctant to let go of, but had to so that their deeds could go on the record and prove ownership. I saw Lyman Epps' face as he filed out. He was filled with pride and self-respect, and he was clearly overcome by what had just happened.

Once the entire group had left the building, my father asked the clerk about it. She said that the indentures were from a man named Gerritt Smith, who'd given each freedman 10 acres of Adirondack land. It was the first time she'd ever heard of that taking place, anywhere. Keene nodded in agreement, but didn't say more.

"Walking outside to the courthouse square, we saw the man named Gerritt Smith, and the 10 freedmen talking in a group. I will always remember the look on the men's faces as each one expressed thanks and near disbelief that he now owned a piece of land to make a way for himself. It was a warm spring day, Jack, the first warm day of spring after a long winter. It was also a day of new beginnings, with something so right and palpable about it that I felt it in my bones. We learned from Mr. Smith that he was an abolitionist and a large landowner who had decided that it was the right thing to do.

"That's when I knew that there's goodness in people, Jack, and that I wanted to find that same goodness in myself— that I wanted to become a man who would watch out for others and treat each person fairly. I hope the same feelings grow in you. I only need to think back to those two abolitionists, Smith and his lawyer, to be inspired all over again. I see their faces every day and I live by the example they set.

"I never met John Brown, and I understand that the lawyer, Dwyer, disagreed with Brown's stand at Harper's Ferry when he led the insurrection against slavery. But look, Jack, Dwyer did help slaves by seeing to it that the deeds were properly recorded. Each man must decide to act as he can find the strength."

Keene told this story often, and in my favorite version he added more emphasis on justice and helping the downtrodden. It continued to inspire him in all his dealings with his fellows. And each time he told me the story, it had the same effect on me, too.

Returning to the present, my recollection now done, I turned to making Keene's ethics work in our new venture. I felt deeply satisfied. The Durant law firm was well established. Our partnership was a good thing for Father, for me, and for the firm. Now I would prove myself, by taking on more responsibility as a partner in the firm, starting with the Aber case — if Father allowed me to.

I thought we had a good case in Aber's situation, given the outcomes for Timothy Woodruff and William Longfellow in their very similar cases. What I didn't then know was how hard we would have to work on the case, or how long it would take and how much money. The sheer amount of time Father and I would spend on reading and re-reading the law, drafting pleadings, and preparing the case for trial was to prove astounding. I mastered every fact in the file and kept a record of every shred of evidence to help us defend against the claims of the state, which brought to bear all its weight and authority in such a case.

Father better understood what lay ahead, but for now he wasn't forecasting any result. For his part, he studied each move in the case and advised me with wisdom, a craftsman working with his apprentice, but one now possessed of sufficient experience to spread his wings a bit. It was late in 1908, and I was having a grand time of it. It had been a long time since my nightmare of myself as a cowering intruder on these lands.

Deeply involved in researching the Aber case and feeling a great deal of compassion for the injustices they'd experienced in life — and reflecting on Father's story of the colored men being given land — I again found myself thinking about Duryea's crying in my presence. Until that evening in the kitchen, I'd never seen a grown man cry. And to be truthful, it had shocked me. But now, feeling so aware of the Abers' difficulties in life, and thinking again of the miseries of slaves, it occurred to me that a man cries when he needs to release a burden he has carried a long time. Duryea had taught me that it took strength and courage to bring his grief to a trusted friend. By doing so, he'd simply proven our closeness. Friendship, he'd proved, must be filled with honesty and inner strength. I hoped I had those qualities in myself.

Because of Duryea, I embraced a new dimension of my identity. I now perceived myself, for the first time, as a giver of love and comfort and no longer just a receiver of such things. I could comfort and love as a man. Compared to Kora, I told myself I was a slow learner, thinking back to her courage and loyalty to friends. I enjoyed a memory of our school days together with the Aber children, happily picking berries in the patch at the clearing.

I stood taller now, I felt, and all the more ready and able to create a good and lasting union between Kora and myself. Nagging at me was Duryea's warning that resolving the Basin title could involve Kora and me in an entirely new relationship — that of adversaries.

Eight
Getting On

The legal work kept coming in. Father parsed out specific tasks to start with, and then whole cases to me as his confidence in my abilities grew. I made court appearances, got cases ready for trial, and worked closely with Father.

The Aber case became mine, in large part, under father's guidance. Pacquette's young niece, knowing that our clients had paid her uncle in full, agreed to sign a deed for nothing in return. I explained, and she understood, that Francis Aber had a possible claim against her uncle's estate due to his failure to pay the taxes owed on the property. He'd taken the Abers' tax money, but hadn't paid the tax due, thus creating the quandary which our firm was working hard to unravel. His niece was happy enough just to remove herself from the whole business.

The state had made a potentially fatal error by not checking the recording of the Aber land contract, where the parcel was referred to as a residence and farm. Although we raised our objection with the Forest Commission, the State's Attorney General denied our allegations. The State and its Forest Commission did not want to admit its errors and, clearly, it had the proof needed to show unpaid taxes. The question was whether we could find sufficient proof on the Abers' side to throw doubt on the validity of the tax due. We needed evidence, if it could be found, that our clients had farmed their land. A hearing was likely, and we prepared hard for it.

My initial investigations failed to turn up anyone who knew anything about the Abers' farming. But one person led to another, and finally I tracked down a purveyor who annually toured the backcountry and had visited the farm and sold the Abers some farm implements. The man was well-known to folks in the area. He went by the trade name of Doc Wellsprings and his Seven Sons, and sold most anything one could want or need, his homemade medicines, special powders, and secret potions created by the master himself. But he also sold some decent household goods, some tools, farm implements, dried goods, and more. The "Seven Sons" was attached to the name only to suggest to customers that he had a large family to feed. Actually, Doc Wellsprings worked on his own, and word was he sold equal parts what you needed and—as the pliant customer would soon discover once Doc slipped off—what one merely had a hankering and a shine for, but a gadget that rarely did what Doc claimed it would.

In May, Doc and his wagon would come through our area once again. I made a note on my calendar to get his affidavit and to determine his willingness to testify at trial, if required. If I felt hesitant on the point of his testimony, it was because Doc's speech was always accompanied by a whistle through a gap in his front teeth. He used this to his advantage, going to great lengths to introduce himself thusly: 'Wellsprings and Seven Sons is here to serve you with distinction, with savvy and at prices you can whistle at'. The result could be hilarious; folks would gather at his wagon just to chuckle at Doc's sales presentations. I knew I'd have to subpoena Doc Wellspring the minute he signed his affidavit, thus making him subject to the court's jurisdiction. But we couldn't subpoena him until our action was pending in court, which meant the pressure was on to draft our answer and cross claims against the state in a timely manner.

The calendar moved into 1909. My time was spent in our office library searching for relevant law on the wrongful taxation issue, and the liability of both the state and the Pacquette estate for the wrongs done to our clients. Law that supported our case proved hard to find; the case law for the state's position was strong and concerned us. The state didn't appear to have lost a case against squatters on public land in some time. This raised the specter for us of losing, unless we distinguished our case by offering compelling reason that, in our case, the citizen taxpayer was deserving of better. But what that compelling reason would be in The State of New York versus Francis Aber and Ada Aber was not yet apparent. I dug into the law books day after day, night after night, searching for a legal answer we could rely on.

I discerned at the outset of my research that the precedent of the Longfellow case, in which Father had prevailed some years before, was not controlling in our present case; the Longfellow case had been strictly limited to lands that were lived on and that the state had wrongly taxed as commercial timberlands. That didn't apply in the Aber's case.

The challenge in proving title against the magisterial State of New York was daunting. New York dug in its heels and asserted that it owned all land that was part of the Adirondack Park wilderness, the forever wild lands guaranteed to it in the state constitutional amendment of 1894.

As much as I cared about the issue just and only for the Abers' sake, it must be said that Father and I were doubly motivated by the knowledge that what we were learning in the Aber case could very well prove significant to our own issue with the Basin land and title, should we ever have to prove it. We were studying for two cases, not just one.

Another thing the Aber case kept bringing to mind was that I didn't yet fully understand the cloud on the title hovering over William West Longfellow's estate. The question was how and when could I get Father to candidly reveal all there was to this story.

Summer gave way to an early fall, which yielded to an even earlier winter. Christmas approached. The weather hard been harsh for quite a while, so when I awoke early one morning and found a break in the weather, I decided to get away for the day. Awake at a December dawn, the sun up at the winter solstice, I felt in my bones that it was right to get on the stream with my fly rod and some of my best-tied late-season patterns, which Duryea had taught me to tie years ago before. I'd learned, by repetition at my bench to tie the winter stonefly pattern, and I'd be ready for a hungry brook trout, even if it was a cold December day. But in just the time it took to prepare to leave the house, the temperature had begun warming to cause the little-known winter stonefly hatch to occur. Only two families of the stonefly hatch occur in the winter, and Duryea had taught me well to watch and wait for them on a warming winter day such as the one before me.

The native brook trout go through two feeding periods during the hatch. One is during the nymph stage as it emerges at the bottom, and, if the temperature warms enough for the nymphs to rise, in the cracks and crannies of ice and snow. The second is the small black insect, a pattern called the black angel, that occurs on the surface during a warming winter afternoon. It was these two that I had tied and that I wagered would bring home dinner. I'd make the better part of the day of it, relaxing on the stream, taking in the sounds and sights of the season along the Otter, in pursuit of these native sons and daughters of the waters I revered.

If I had to snowshoe into the stream, that would be all right with me. I needed time to just think, to let thoughts percolate in the fresh Adirondack air, and to plan my next moves in the Aber case, whatever that might prove to be. I also wanted to think about one other event of the season: Kora was due back home for the holidays.

I hadn't had much time to think about our relationship since last summer, which now seemed like a long time ago. I thought, as I strapped on the snowshoes and threw a pack rigged with gear onto my shoulders, that this might just be a bellwether day for figuring things out.

My raquettes would allow me to get to places along the stream where I'd have a good chance of finding a hungry native trout, even in this season. I started out just after first light on our shortest day of the year. I'd need to use the light of day wisely. My raquettes were just large enough that they would hold me up on all but the lightest and deepest powders. Today they worked well as I started my journey into the remote reaches of the Otter, the ground being covered in about 18 inches of snow. My destination was a part of the brook with a southern exposure where I knew the stonefly often hatched.

My progress was good. The trail roughly followed the course of the brook upstream to its high source, though today I would stick to a section in the alpine valley. My body warmed as I went. I was dressed in my union suit underwear, and over them I wore my woolen Malone pants. I had on three shirts, layered from thin to thick on the outer layer, with suspenders over the inner two shirts. My well-worn clothing served my body well for the movements and activity at hand.

One step followed the other. I lifted each foot just enough to clear the raquette from the snow, enjoying the sounds I made as I went, which varied from shew-shew in the powder, to scrunch in the open, wind-swept clearings where the powder had hardened. Body and soul felt as one.

My pack basket shifted only as required to adjust to my movement. Duryea had woven it to fit my frame and I hardly noticed that it was there. I became so engrossed in the sensations of the day, and the comfort they brought me, I moved well past my usual first spots to try my fly line. The ice had claimed only an occasional open riffle, but I moved past these and kept up my steady pace to the far interior.

Hemlock mixed with beech, maple, and oak, white birch and the whiter-yet snow were a marvel in the slanted rays of the morning sun, playing on the muted wintergreen and light charcoal tones. Against the blue sky and white high puffs of clouds, the sun now penetrating my back, I moved further west, further than I had been in winter in many years.

When I stopped it was late morning. I'd been on the move for more than three hours, steadily traversing down the brook to a long, low plain. A sweat had broken across my back and chest, and I stayed warm and comfortable in the 25 degree temperature. Pausing for a few moments, I loosened my outer shirt at the top buttons to allow air to circulate, appreciating the coolness against my skin.

Throughout the morning my thoughts had run from brook trout in the stream, and how I would fish for them today, to Kora. At this moment, Kora won my attention. I'd been here in this exact spot with her on so many perfect winter days, that if I closed my eyes I could almost see her in the woods beside me, hear her talking about the brook, the trout, the great woods. Glancing into the brook I could have sworn I saw her beautiful face looking back at me, her mouth breaking into a faint smile. I smiled in return, but when I did so I saw only my own reflection smiling back.

Moving on, I came to a riffle with ice formed on either side of a narrow ribbon of water, right above the spot at which it fed into the tail pool containing large, snowcapped boulders. I stopped, assembled my fly rod and reel, rigged the silk fly line and gut tippet, and tied on the size 14 black angel. Positioning myself at the top of the riffle, I stood over solid ice and snow, in line with the current, my raquettes still on my feet. Dappling the black angel into the gently moving current and over the dark water, I let it slide down under the ice-covered, slower water in the pool. I liked the feel of the braided silk line as I played it through my left hand. A hatch of small black stoneflies moved on the surface of the riffle in the midday December sun. Larvae had just molted into adults on the surface, and a large slick appeared under an emerger. It was the procoptera stonefly winter hatch that I had hoped to find!

As my stonefly imitation reached the top of the pool, just even with its rim of ice, I saw a large bronze flash where the fly had drifted. From the size of it, it had to be a very large brook trout. Moving my rod tip sideways, I felt the trout's weight and strength. On being pricked by my hook, he rushed downstream into the shelter of the pool, down into its depths, and braised against the sharp lip of ice. The silk line had become hung up on it and was threatening to tear. I dropped my rod to clear the ice snag, and that signaled the trout to make a sudden and unexpected run back toward me, into the riffle, by a large granite boulder.

I reeled in quickly to take up the line, but the squaretail powered his way to the far side of the boulder. My gut leader curled on a bare edge of boulder, then wrapped on a point of driftwood frozen in the ice. But it was saved by the trout, of all things, which erupted suddenly in a paroxysm of power and energy. Coming straight toward me he rose from the surface, jumping clear of the water, arching his body, startling and beautiful in the sunlight. I counted the bright orange rings that encircled brilliant crimson centers; the magnificent trout was so close to me that the details revealed themselves as if in slow motion.

He landed and scurried back to the boulder at an angle too severe for me to have control. My line went limp. My heart pumped adrenaline. The trout was off, I thought, or had fouled the slackened line I hadn't yet taken up. But no, he was still on. The line came abruptly back to his jaw, and I furiously reeled in the slack. He was making a second powerful run directly at me. I couldn't imagine that he could repeat his previous jump — yet there he came once again, arching at a razor angle from the water. Again I counted his speckles, noted his hooked jaw, his full body. This was the largest, most beautiful male brookie I'd ever seen.

But his second jump was telling. It was evident that his energy and power were subsiding. He rolled first on one side and then the other. But my line was still challenged to its limit. Exhausted, but still fighting for his freedom in his Otter Brook home, the trout came slowly toward me as I pulled in more line, hand over hand.

Finally, I pulled him onto my reel. He rolled to one side and came to my left hand. Still in my racquettes, I stooped awkwardly to reach him. Sliding my left hand down his back to his tail, I gripped him firmly to paralyze him. He was oxygen starved and no longer fighting, being entirely spent from the struggle. I stood and lifted all five pounds of him waist-high in the brilliant light.

He was a strain of Adirondack brookie found only in this backcountry, so the old-timers said. His sides were speckled in vivid lavender halos that hinted of indigo. Inside each halo was a dot of brightest red or orange, and the thick back was dark olive and steel blue, with curved gold bars that faded to shades of scarlet and vermilion. The telltale pink tone on the bottom fin drew my attention, and I realized I'd seldom examined a trout this closely.

The thought came to me, wholly unanticipated, that perhaps I would release the prize brookie I held with such pride. Let him return to his home, to spawn again in the fall and pass along to his offspring his unequalled strain. I held the powerful and elemental fish, knowing I could deliver his release and freedom. I had overcome his strength with mine, had outwitted his intelligence by fooling him, just for a moment.

Crouching next to the brook on the edge of the ice jutting into the pool, I placed both hands under his heavy body in the cold shallow water. My prisoner was without visible strength or motion, alarming me. But soon his gills and jaw started in unison taking in oxygen from the riffle as I worked his body slowly back and forth. I felt the life come back to him. A few seconds more, my fingertips spread so that I was barely touching my friend. The brookie moved to the riffle slowly, his back sticking out of it and disappeared into the pool. I would never forget him.

Standing again, my body shook and settled from the catch and release. This was a very good day, a day in which I'd learned another aspect of power and the peace of using it for good. I'd become a teacher and protector through an act I could repeat time and again for the wild Otter Brook trout.

I broke down my fly rod, stowed it, suddenly aware of a ravenous hunger. Back at camp Duryea would have one of his special Sunday meals prepared, but to enjoy it I first had to make the long trek back. Chewing on venison jerky and bread, I started out for the Basin camp, still pleased with myself for releasing the trout.

One pleasure reminded me of another, namely the news from Kora's latest letter: she was due back in a few days.

I was eager, but also apprehensive, thinking about her return. Somehow my relationship with her, my commitment to success in the Aber case, and my intentions of coming to some kind of terms with Father regarding the Basin title, had all rolled together in my mind, three strands of a single entity. Failure in any one would diminish the value of the other two. Victory in the Aber case would increase the probability of clearing up any title question on the Basin, which would then permit a resolution among Kora, Keene, and myself.

I gnawed on these thoughts all the way back, which took from me much of the pleasure I'd enjoyed on the walk out. I was relieved to see in the distance the sun's bright reflection in the great oval window, and smoke from Duryea's fire rising from the chimney.

But the reflection of Kora's face in the brook was still vivid in my mind.

Nine
Issue Joined

Keene Durant had decided. "I will try the Aber case," he declared, "and you'll sit second seat."

I was very disappointed. I thought I knew the case well and had enough confidence to be the trial lawyer. But I kept that opinion to myself for the time being.

Father had learned a great deal representing Longfellow against the state, reversing the local tax commission's foreclosure, and he felt he owed the Abers the full benefit of his personal experience. In my view, both cases involved a tax foreclosure by the state for failure to pay back taxes, but the similarity stopped right there. Moreover, an important new legal issue was now looming in Aber.

The state claimed that it had originally got title to all lands in the North Country after the Revolutionary War, then had sold some of the land, only to later reacquire it through various transactions. The state also made clear that the Abers' small parcel was part of a larger tract that it had reacquired years before when a timber company walked away from the land for defaulted taxes. Neither Aber nor his predecessors in title, including the deceased Paquette, had ownership, the state said in a response to the Forest Commission. This was the sort of case that took on a complexity that made the trial compelling and drew public attention in regional newspapers.

Bill McGrath, editor of the Adirondack Daily Enterprise, heard about the case from Father and put his reporter on it. The newspapers in Plattsburgh, Utica, and Watertown picked up on it because of its portrayal of a local, poor family fighting the state for their homestead, the place they'd carved from the wilderness decades ago, tilling the soil and building their home. The fact that the Abers also had children and a grandchild on the land, all making their living and doing harm to no one, made the story all the more compelling, giving it legs of its own. The humble and hardworking Abers versus the all-powerful state. The story came across like David against Goliath.

The community was behind the Abers and supported Father and me in our efforts. Many stepped forward to be quoted in the paper as saying that the Abers weren't squatters and that they deserved a better fate. Everyone knew that few people in the Abers' situation succeeded in prevailing against the state.

We regularly kept Bill McGrath apprised of how the case was developing.

The Attorney General's office initially informed me of its legal challenge in a letter from Joseph Alexander Hamilton, the assistant A.G., before he filed papers in state supreme court. Hamilton pled that the state reacquired title, superior to any other title, to certain lands that included the Aber parcel. Furthermore, he pled that no other deed to the state could be valid, under this theory, for any of the parcels that had been transferred by private hands for years. By filing in state supreme court, Hamilton removed all jurisdiction from the Forest Commission, and transferred it to a court of general jurisdiction where politics was less important than the merits of the case.

The Aber case appeared to turn on whether this parcel had been reacquired by the state in the mid 1800's. If that were the case, title would then be with the state. We hoped we could show that the parcel was outside the deed to the state. As Father said, we had a serious and full legal challenge on our hands.

"By filing in supreme court," Keene said, "the state is taking this case seriously. And I see that it's not only claiming title under the patent, but it's saying that the foreclosure in which Pacquette got title in 1883 was not valid!"

As he talked, I glanced through the state's papers again and realized that Father was correct. I'd been focusing primarily on the land title issue. Now I realized that the second tax foreclosure issue was also presented.

Father pushed up from his desk chair in the library, where we met to discuss our cases, and began to pace the office. "We have to resolve two issues, Jack. First, on this state claim to title, we must find Verplanck Colvin, the Albany surveyor, and the men in his party who did the surveying work for the state on this patent. They may become our witnesses on whether the Aber parcel, as it's described in the deed...." Father stopped mid-sentence.

"No, Jack, I have a better idea! Let's examine the land patent — the land sold by the state in Macomb's and the land it reacquired — and plot out the land tracts. I've studied Colvin's work before. He established the westerly line of the patent and the reacquired tract. He not only gave it a course with a bearing, he called out landmarks — landmarks that may not be in the Aber tract. So let's contact him, his guides and party. A jury would consider their testimony and give it great weight. We can look at whatever information it holds and gather sworn statements favorable to us — we may even move to dismiss the state's case!"

Keene caught his breath. I knew his mind would turn now to the 1883 deed to Pacquette. We'd both read the statute that set a deadline for the deed to be delivered to Pacquette if it were to be legal and binding on the state, and allow the Abers to step into Pacquette's shoes as rightful owners. Specified in the statute was the manner in which the deed delivery had to be accomplished.

"Jack—"

" — Yes, Father, I know what we must prove, and I know how to prove it We have to determine the day the deed was delivered to Pacquette so we can beat the deadline." I reached for the volume of the Tax Law of New York and continued. "The statute says, 'A deed from the Forest Commission to a grantee in any tax foreclosure proceeding shall be valid only if made and delivered on or before March first, 1883.'"

After that date, the state was sole party to prevail on title. Pacquette's deed from the Forest Commission was dated February 20, 1883. Its recording date was March 5, 1883. What we had to determine was the day it was delivered to him.

The commission had been in the habit of sending out packets to be delivered by guides or anyone else going into the woods. They had at times been haphazard in their delivery of the papers.

I said, "We need a witness who knows when Pacquette got delivery of his deed. I'll get access to his papers, talk to his niece again, and I'll go to Albany to find witnesses. His niece, don't forget, says she'll sign the deed to the Abers, which will at least clear up the chain of title to them. I'll track this down and ..." I stopped, concerned by the scowl on Father's face. He dropped into a chair.

"My God, Jack, this case is enormous."

"I know it."

"I'm thinking of the expenses alone, and we're not even being paid, except for the food the Abers take to Duryea. Furthermore, Mr. Hamilton is a greatly respected trial litigator. We can do nothing but the best legal work, or we shall lose."

Keene stroked his chin and looked directly into my eyes. "We could lose more than the case, Jack. A lot is at stake."

I wanted to assure Father that I knew we could manage the case. But I, too, was uneasy. I paused, gathering my next thoughts, and looked around our library, a space big enough to stack countless books yet have room left over to pace as one thought.

The bookshelves, of varnished hickory and running floor to ceiling, held volumes of leather-bound New York law books. From the high plaster ceiling hung the three polished-brass kerosene chandeliers that lighted the great room, each with four wicks going when in use. They cast an amber glow on the grand shelves and handcrafted moldings. Over the potbellied stove, vented to a stone chimney at the end of the room, stood a brass Lady Justice, blindfolded, her scales evenly balanced, on a large, reserved shelf, distinct from the books. I studied the even countenance of her classical features, and felt the power of the law, the responsibility it placed upon the advocate.

"We can share the burden of this case in a way that won't break us," I said. "The work we've already done will just go to waste unless we continue. And furthermore, we owe it to ourselves to get all the facts possible on the title and the use of this land. I have to go to Albany, and I can convince the state of the merits of this case and the principles at issue that affect all property owners." We held each other's gaze for several moments. So," I said, "I think we should go that far at least, don't you?"

But I had misread Father. His eyes now turned toward Lady of Justice as he studied it.

"Oh, indeed, Jack," he said in a firm but low voice. His fists were clenched, his lined face was drawn taut in steely determination. I was on edge, now.

"We can take on the state, Jack, at least for a good while, and we have to be prepared to go the distance. The state will—we know the state can—outspend us and try to outlast us. It has won or interminably tied-up many of these cases, son."

I could sense Father's building up to something.

"But we'll go at this case hard, we'll give it our hardest and best effort!" Keene got to his feet and walked the length of the large conference table, then turned back toward me. As he turned, his right hand shot out and pointed directly at me. "We'll go so hard, we'll get to the bottom of the case, we'll know the title, know all the facts, better than our opponents. We can't out-pend the state, but by God, we can outwork it and its lawyers. That is what this case comes down to, Jack — mastering every bit of it. It means everything to the Aber family and they deserve to have their land title cleared."

But he wasn't done. "This case means more than just the Abers, though. It's crucial to the law of real estate in this region, and even more to the future of the North Country wilderness. We're going to stand up for it. We can show Attorney General Hamilton that he's wrong. We can win, Jack, and we must win—win on the merits of our case, merits I believe are there and which we must prove."

He slowly turned and went again to the end of the table, but this time he didn't turn to face me. I remained where I was, silenced by this passionate summation to the jury not yet picked. I'd never seen my father attack a case with such a combination of vehemence, legal acumen, and emotion. This was Keene Durant at his best; this was why I'd come to practice law with him. His strong hand came to rest on the law book lying at the end of the oak library table.

"Let's find when this deed was 'made and delivered,' as the statute requires." Father looked squarely in my eyes. "Give me your best legal thinking on presenting this case in court," he said. "Map it out in writing from start to finish. State the facts that we know support us. It'll be apparent what facts we're lacking or are weak on, and we'll deal with those. I'll review what you put together and brush it up, and we'll submit the best trial brief this court has ever seen. The law we develop on this by trial will be unassailable.

"The state reacquired title to a large tract, and we can't change that, but we can prove their land isn't any part of what the Abers got. Facts and law will support us, it appears, on the deed delivery and on the intent to convey title. It had better, at least. The state will sink us if it prevails there."

I rose from my chair. "We both have a passion for this case, Father. We can win it. I'll prepare a draft of a trial brief and we can review my work at week's end."

"Good, Jack! Friday morning first thing we'll map out this case, point by point, based on your memo. Give me your absolute best. We'll need it."

Father extended both of his hands even before he was done talking, and I grasped them in a gesture of solidarity, father and son, law partner to law partner. Our grasp melted into a warm bear hug.

From the front office came a familiar voice. "Keene, please come here and answer my questions now," Elaine, Father's secretary called out.

Father, teacher and mentor, lawyer and advocate, turned and strode immediately from the library.

The rest of the week was spent in the library working on every aspect of the case. I started with the law so we would know everything we would be required to prove. I read the statutes and case laws, pulled out the elements, and boiled down the holdings of many courts to the basics as Father had taught me, a skill honed further by my mentor, William Kelly. I wrote out in longhand the legal memo supporting our positions, giving it to Elaine to type as I went.

I was pleased; it flowed dispassionately, evenly, and I saw the case coming together at a fast pace. The Abers would get their day in court, and the state would be served our answer and cross-claims. All the law and fact issues would be set up for a jury, as it was clear that a jury of North Country peers should decide our clients' fate. Hopefully the jury's decision would speak volumes to the state about our clients' title, and surrounding titles as well, including title to the Basin lands.

My study brought me to the conclusion — though I didn't include this in my trial memo — that the Basin title was inextricably tied to the land patent boundary, and perhaps also to the description of the reacquired state tract, for much of its eastern boundary where the Otter came down off the high peak at the head of the valley. I was certain Father expected me to raise this issue with him, and I would do so when we met again later in the week.

I had to learn what steps Father had taken to protect Longfellow's wishes for that title, which was still unresolved and to which Kora, as sole heir, held the controlling interest.

On Thursday I reviewed my memo, answer and counterclaims against the state, denying the substance of the state's claims, and pleading the Abers' claims of a good title. I argued that the title was delivered on a timely basis to their grantor, Paquette, from the Forest Commission under the then existing system in the tax law. I drafted demands for any maps or deeds the state relied on, and for the identity of witnesses the state had on the title, witnesses who may have had knowledge of the factual basis for including the Aber piece in the land patent, or about the reacquired state-owned tract. Our case made it clear that we considered the state's claims false and inaccurate.

As expected, the state put in a general demurral on our counterclaims, signifying its position that there was no merit to our pleading that the Abers held good title. Issue was joined.

As I worked, I remembered what Father had said on Monday. It had caught my ear when he referred to "the facts and law that support us in the case." Never before had a case become so personal as to merit the words us or our case. It had always been the clients' case, their case, but not ours. Previously, the pronouns had distanced us from the case at hand.

In the Aber case, that professional separation wasn't there. I didn't know the full extent of the quandary Father found himself in, but I would find out soon enough.

I reflected on my clients, friends, and colleagues, and on times I'd had with them discussing issues of the day. Among my acquaintances in the North Country, I counted as friends and allies fishing guides, teachers at the school, local merchants, and in particular, Bill McGrath, the editor of the *Adirondack Daily Enterprise.*

Bill and I had had many discussions about this wilderness and its future. He was my senior by perhaps fifteen years, thoughtful, and at bottom reasonable, I thought. He'd steadfastly expressed his concerns over the increasing power of the state in our region, as it had become the major landowner here over the years since the turn of the century. I understood his position, but pointed out that the local people from our region, some we'd both grown up with, were not the best caretakers of our wild resources. Some of our timber companies, controlled by outside interests with no concern for our well-being, were sometimes run by Adirondackers interested only in making a profit. Some men in the woods hunted and fished as if the species were infinite, killing off for all time the big cats and wolves, the moose, and even reducing my revered brook trout population. I'd said this to Bill on many occasions, and for years he had a ready response.

"Jack, these men, men like Longfellow, provide jobs with the timber industry and with the railroads brought in here. We were isolated from the world before these men brought in change and jobs. There is much to admire in that, don't you think?"

I acknowledged his perspective, but could not agree with it.

"Where was their responsibility, Bill, when they raped the forest, leaving it with nothing standing for thousands of acres? Their behavior led to the forever wild amendment to the state constitution in 1894, but it took others from outside the area to do that for us, as well as men from this area. And that forever wild amendment was approved overwhelmingly by the voters, Bill," I reminded him.

Bill usually got in the final word. "Jack," he'd admonish, "you can't draw a circle around the Adirondacks and say nothing will go on here, that these lands are declared saved by the almighty state for the benefit of the rich who control so much of it! What about our rights, Jack? As a lawyer, you of all people can't believe we should turn over anything to the state. Read my editorial next week, I'll tell my readers how I feel about this. I stand for the little guy who wants his land for his own uses, Jack. You'll see."

Bill made his point with me and with his readers, who had become even more adamant over the years that the state must stay out. Somewhere, I thought, there must be found a long-term answer to how the Adirondacks could be preserved and thoughtfully developed.

The desire to control our own destiny, unfettered by outside interests, was valid to a degree, I mused, but it was unrealistic. How many areas of the world were immune from outside forces? None that I knew of. Better to deal realistically with these forces and with the feelings of our populace, and to come to some consensus in a forum where everyone has a say.

And yet the next week when I read Bill's editorial in the Adirondack Daily Enterprise, his position was smoothed with a sense of reasonableness about what should happen here. He wrote that the state was not wrong in its desire to challenge outright squatters and to have plans in place that would result in benefits for everyone. Maybe, I thought, our rabid conversations and sharp exchanges had some effect on both of us.

The ultimate irony, of course, was my defense of the Abers against the abuse of power of the state, a position the Enterprise would find supportable.

I needed to tell Bill about the Aber case and get his perspective on our position and his thoughts about what a jury of our peers would likely do with the case. Over the years we'd become fast friends, and I thought Bill would be my ally in this case and on other issues affecting the North Country, now and in the future.

Keene and I chose the time, and made McGrath aware of the Aber case. Bill put his best reporter on the story. His initial column told of the Abers' plight, portraying a poor local family fighting the state for its homestead, a place the Abers had carved out of the wilderness decades ago, where they'd tilled the soil and built their home. Humble and hardworking, they came across as David fighting Goliath, a very accurate portrayal.

The article told of three generations on the land: the elder generation; their two children, whom I fondly remembered and who still helped their parents at harvest; and a grandchild who was born on the farm and who seemed a native North Country farmer even at his young age. Their story had an appeal of its own, one the community got behind, and citizens freely gave with financial help to defray the expenses of the litigation.

Many also stepped forward to offer their opinions that the Abers were not squatters and deserved a better fate. It was known far and wide that few in the Abers' position succeeded in prevailing against the state, but their case had a certain ring of authenticity to it. It was up to us as the lawyers to bring that out, and the outcome of the case seemed to hinge on who could produce the best proof on Abers' deed, the surveys of the surrounding land done by the renowned surveyor, Colvin, and the title Abers received in the deed from Paquette. The pressure in public opinion was squarely upon the lawyers in the case.

Keene had said the future of the North Country hung on the outcome of this case. Was that stretching a point? Did the penumbra cast by *The State of New York versus Aber* cast such a large shadow?

Ten
Lands Reserved

The story of Macomb's Purchase was well known in the Adirondacks. In 1792, Alexander Macomb bought 3,934,849 acres of wilderness from New York State. The sale brought eight pence per acre to the state, which, with the new federal union, had appropriated the land from the British after the Revolutionary War.

Titles to private local lands derived mainly from this purchase and from subsequent deeds from Macomb or his successor, William Constable, to individuals, or, in many cases, to timber companies, which cut down the virgin forest. The state, after the patent to Macomb, had later reacquired title to large tracts of vaguely described lands that Father and I surmised were adjacent to the Abers' and the Basin lands, or were nearby. In title searches for these properties, diligence was required to perfect a good and marketable title acceptable to a buyer at fair market value.

To further complicate matters, various tax foreclosures in the early days had resulted in tax deeds going to individuals who bought land at tax sale. This practice changed in 1883 when title went only to the state, per the mandates of the state's tax law. It was this title chain and change in law that we confronted in the Aber case.

The state had long claimed reacquired title to certain lands from the tracts in Macomb's Purchase, and rumor in the legal community was that a large part of that land might be in the Basin lands that Longfellow had died owning. I'd learned from my years of searching local titles that there was a question about the exact location of state lands near the Abers' and the Basin lands, but local legal opinion and conjecture was that the state could not prove that its title included either the Basin lands or the adjacent Aber parcel.

The problem was that the deed to the state's reacquired tract used language describing natural geographic features that could apply equally to the Basin lands and to other lands in the region unquestionably owned and controlled by the state.

The particular boundary line at issue was the state's westerly line in its tract of reacquired land. That line ran in a north-south direction, and defined a large area of land "...lying east of the brook flowing south from the peak of the unnamed mountain, and running a distance of five miles, more or less, along the center line of the brook to the ancient Indian hunting path leading to Lake Champlain."

This troubling description, according to Father, was general enough that the description fit any number of unnamed mountains and brooks descending to an old Indian hunting path. The features referred to could have been in three or four entirely different locations. The distance from the peak to the intersection with the hunting path, given as about five miles, described at least two locations.

Keene's Law

Verplanck Colvin, the renowned state-commissioned surveyor from Albany, had been hired to piece together many components of the Adirondack puzzle. He had spoken out against the timber interests since he believed their practice of clear cutting spelled doom for the region and its waterways, which would dry up or be eroded away without the cover of the great northern forests. Colvin's work, a topo-survey of the wilderness, was well-known and respected by everyone around the state. If he'd located the westerly line of this parcel within the Basin lands, we would have a difficult time proving that the Abers' land was not within any state boundaries.

My trip to Albany to find Colvin and any relevant documents took on added significance. I would go to the state capital, figuring it held the key piece of evidence in locating Colvin's original maps, journals and notes. I would determine whether the state's parcel was ascertainable with enough certainty to withstand court scrutiny, which would let me determine what it meant for our case.

The train in the moonlit night cast immense shadows over the Hudson River. Traveling along its banks from North Creek to Glens Falls and on to Albany, the trip began to seem interminable, and I occupied my thoughts with possible challenges to the validity of Colvin's maps. Some of them were implausible, on the far edge of credulity, but others seemed credible, given the topography of the area and the immense room for error in mapmaking in the 1870s and '80s. It crossed my mind that I might end up having to attack the survey work of the highly respected Colvin, perhaps on the witness stand in a court of law. But first I would review his work, meet the man, and form my own conclusions.

I disembarked at the City of Albany Grand Central, not far from the law office of William Kelly, where I'd clerked. I decided to go straight there since dawn had now given way to early morning, and I knew Kelly's office would be open. My body felt the effects of the long trip as I walked the few blocks up Pine Street, near the courthouse, then over to Steuben Street to Kelly's office.

To a North Country boy, the city was always a surprise, containing lives so different from my own. I enjoyed watching people as they moved along toward their work at a shop, factory, or wharf, or headed home after a long night of toil to one of the upper-story flats in the many row houses in this neighborhood. Those going home in the evenings had an exhausted, strained look to their faces. Some appeared younger than 14 years old, confirming my father's suspicions of child labor in the markets of our capital city. A heavy price was paid for having a job in the city, at least to my country eyes. I understood better why the Populists' platform of reforms against child labor and support for labor unions had followers across the state and country.

The brick or brownstone row houses facing Steuben Street had been built 40 years before, their trim drab and in need of paint. Each one rose three or four stories, with prominent cantilevered bay windows. Their facades stood in an even row and close to the sidewalk. Each had a front stoop with wide, hand-laid stone steps rising steeply to the first floor, and a basement entry below the steps leading to a shop or business. Commerce spilled over into residences in this busy area.

Arriving at Kelly's office, I looked up to the large window of his library and saw William's warm, smiling face. He'd been expecting me and greeted me with a wave to come directly in.

"Jack Durant, don't you look prosperous," he beamed. He shook my hand and motioned to three large stacks of material on the table. Kelly had a way of getting right to business.

"There you are, Jack. I've assembled all the documents and maps I've come by over these many decades of practice. Even some of Colvin's notes are there — he must have used them to compile his reports to the legislature. There are even a few early drafts of his work. I've not heard from him or seen him in some time, but you'll no doubt recall seeing him come here to work. I let him use my room and resources. He still lives here in Albany."

William Kelly's round, amiable face, surrounded large hazel eyes that twinkled out of his pince-nez spectacles. He drew his hands to his portly frame as his look turned serious.

"But I don't believe Colvin is well, Jack. Erastus Corning tells me that he took a fall and hasn't been the same since. Forgetful, they say. And I have to agree. Only Monday afternoon I saw him hobbling by this office on a cane. You know how he always stopped to say hello, but Monday, he didn't stop in. He didn't even look my direction."

I was disturbed by Kelly's news. If Colvin was not himself, not in his right mind, it could mean his maps and reports by themselves would be viewed as dispositive evidence in the pending case. I had traveled to Albany to get evidence directly from Colvin. But it sounded as if I might have to rely on his filed surveys and reports, and not have the benefit of his direct testimony in court. I didn't know where that left our case.

My consternation must have shown on my face, as Kelly gave me a look of understanding.

"Before we talk any further about your case, Jack, I'll leave you alone to review these stacks. That'll take you a while. Call me when you are ready to talk. And when you go back home, tell that North Country father of yours that he's overdue for a visit to his old and trusted friend!"

"Yes, William, I shall. He sends his best wishes to you."

William Kelly and Keene Durant went back many years, with a long history of loyal friendship and of helping each other out in cases whenever asked. They had many great stories between them.

"William," I said, "thank you for making me feel at home."

He turned to leave me to my task, saying, "I'll be in my office, Jack, working on Erastus Corning's bid for mayor. Always something from city hall to keep me hopping!"

I turned to the stacks on Kelly's conference table, feeling as comfortable working here as I did at my own desk, having labored here over the law books on his shelves for many hours during my clerkship. Opening my leather valise laden with the Aber papers from our file, my focus turned to the search of Colvin's maps and notes, memos, and journals, many handwritten in the same clear style.

At first I picked up each document in order, reading old deeds that Macomb, and later William Constable, had conveyed from the immense purchase, including their lengthy legal descriptions. After an hour's reading, I began to see the scope of the project in front of me and I hit on a new approach and strategy.

For the next hour I skimmed through the papers, getting an overview of what was there. Flipping through the first stack, then the second, I was astounded by the depth of materials, the maps, and rough sketches — some unfinished, and others finished and signed by Colvin. Some of the maps and sketches were of plots far distant from the Abers or the Basin lands, and none were directly on point. With each stack there was one of Colvin's journal entries with his thoughts pertinent to each segment of the survey as he went.

My time was limited, and after two more hours I began to grow anxious and to feel hurried. Only the third stack was left for me to examine, and so far nothing helpful had turned up. Finally, turning to the last collection of books, and thumbing through one after another, I found a treasure trove of maps. Familiar Basin landmarks were clearly identifiable on them.

What I'd found were Colvin's maps, his journal entries. Drafts of reports to the legislature, about land owned by the state, confirmed that the Basin and the Aber parcel were once part of Macomb's purchase, almost 100 years before Colvin's work.

I studied two maps in particular and felt a chill run down my spine as I read the one entitled Topo-Survey of Lands Owned by the State of New York in Macomb's Purchase. It showed several so-called Great Tracts and the Remainder area described and conveyed out in Macomb's Patent. Part of this land had been reacquired by the state, and it was this piece of the forest preserve that Colvin was mapping.

The state maintained that the lands it had reacquired appeared to be over 300,000 acres, but it admitted that vague legal descriptions cast some doubt on the boundaries, and therefore on its claim to so large a tract. Colvin's notes made a direct reference to the state's westerly line "lying east of the brook flowing south from the peak of the unnamed mountain, and running a distance of five miles, more or less, along the center line of the brook to the ancient Indian hunting path leading to Lake Champlain."

Next to this recitation, in pencil, was a notation in Colvin's now familiar handwriting. "Area to east of this line not located with precision, appears to be area to east of the brook and mountain now known as Hays and Debar."

I knew the location of that brook and mountain. They were not part of the Aber parcel and were not in the Basin lands where Duryea had built the camp — although the lands may have met and shared a boundary in one remote corner.

Studying further, it became apparent that Colvin thought the area owned by the state was well east and north of the Abers' and the Basin camp. In the earlier map, he had located it where Hays Brook flowed down Debar Mountain, an area in which no camps or residences now existed because, over the years, the state had secured it and kept squatters out. If my cursory analysis held up, I might be looking at compelling evidence that could defeat the state's second claim — and perhaps also the first claim — stated in its papers.

But when I set that map down and picked up the next piece of material, it seemed as if I stopped breathing. Staring me in the face was a second map, Colvin's own sketch, perfectly mapping the Basin lands. It showed the small Aber parcel under the name Pacquette, the lake and flow, the brook running from the unnamed mountain, now known as Baldface, and the old Indian hunting path. And finally, at the bottom, was this note, perhaps devastating to the state's case: "Not the same parcel now owned by state from Macomb's; Longfellow boundary shared with state. See Debar topo-survey."

Colvin had neatly dated his note and map for February 26, 1883, and signed it. As usual, in his workmanlike manner, he'd apparently done a subsequent report to the legislature in which he'd indicated that this sketch did not depict the parcel the state owned, thus confirming his journal entry of February 26, 1883, helpful to our case, that "both parcels (the Debar Mountain parcel and this unnamed mountain parcel) have the brook flowing south from the peak...and running a distance of five miles, more or less, along the center line of the brook...."

What troubled me deeply was the fact that the document in my hand was an original topo-survey. It may never have been sent to the state legislature, due to oversight or error, and yet it was critical evidence in support of our case. My challenge, I knew immediately, would be to get it into evidence at the trial.

Sitting there with the proof that Colvin's final opinion in the second map and his notation supported our side, I found myself playing out conflicting scenarios — and sweating in my discomfort. Which evidence from Colvin would be deemed most compelling and have the best chance of being proven in a court of law?

To understand Colvin's work, both maps would have to be considered. Any vagueness in his maps could be clarified by testimony called parol evidence from a qualified witness who, if permitted by the court, could explain the ambiguity.

The sketch on the second map, the Debar mountain area, which was helpful to our case, was dated a day later than the first map, which was dated February 25, 1883. Thus, Colvin's first report may not have been accurate since it appeared not to have been updated to reflect his final opinion, contained on the sketch that located the state land to the east of both the Basin and the Abers' parcel.

In fact, it appeared that the west boundary of the state land, which followed the brook flowing off Debar Mountain, formed the Basin's east boundary. This meant clear title not only for Aber, but also for the Basin! I grew excited by this revelation and my mind raced to determine my next steps.

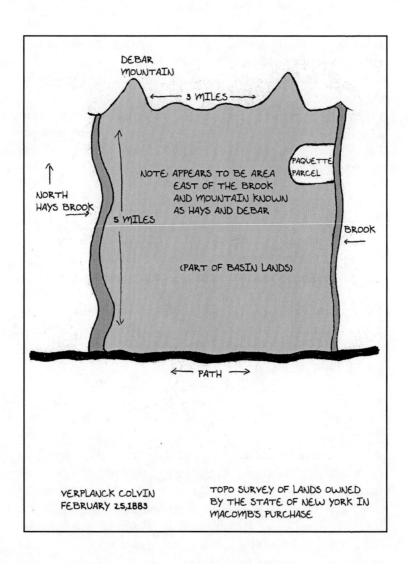

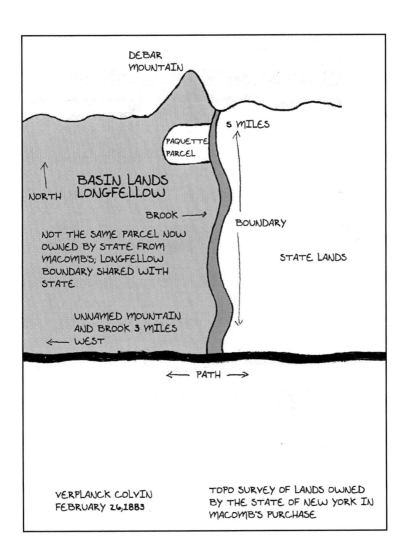

DEBAR MOUNTAIN

PAQUETTE PARCEL

5 MILES

BASIN LANDS LONGFELLOW

NORTH

BROOK →

BOUNDARY

STATE LANDS

NOT THE SAME PARCEL NOW OWNED BY STATE FROM MACOMB'S; LONGFELLOW BOUNDARY SHARED WITH STATE

UNNAMED MOUNTAIN AND BROOK 3 MILES ← WEST

← PATH →

VERPLANCK COLVIN FEBRUARY 26,1883

TOPO SURVEY OF LANDS OWNED BY THE STATE OF NEW YORK IN MACOMB'S PURCHASE

But I needed to follow up with Colvin himself. I gathered the documents, told Kelly I was off, and went down Steuben Street in search of Colvin's home and office at 121 Steuben. Reading each building number as I went, I knew that with each step I was getting closer to finding parol that would either explain our case or render it hopeless.

One twenty one Steuben Street was a row house. At the top of the stoop, at eye level, was a varnished board depicting a map of the Adirondack area, marking the blue line boundary and showing many familiar features in hues of green, blue, and brown. Inscribed at the top in heavy black India ink and trimmed in gold leaf was printed "Verplanck Colvin, Surveyor. A brass doorknocker in the shape of a compass was mounted below it on a wooden door. Taking a deep breath I rapped three times, and was rewarded by sounds from within.

Listening to the sounds of a slow-moving person coming across a wood floor on a cane, I reminded myself that despite the progress I was making, this meeting could define the entire course and direction of the litigation. I would have to ask to see Colvin's final published maps and reports, and ask him many point-blank questions—not the least of which was about his final determinations on the reserved parcel location. Such inquiry, of course, would depend on Colvin's being in any shape to give me valid information.

My thoughts were interrupted by the slow opening of the door, revealing, at first, only a large workspace filled by natural light from the high windows. Stacked papers and oversized maps, rolled up, were stored in every nook and space, on every shelf on every wall I could see. Seconds later, part of a face appeared from behind the partly open door, but at such an angle that only his head leaned out from his protected position behind the door. The face was older, very changed by time, and there was a vacant look in his eyes. Not exactly the same person I'd seen years before around Albany and in Kelly's office, yet clearly the same man. That changed figure now stood in front of me, his door fully open, saying nothing.

"Good afternoon! Mr. Colvin?"

He did not answer.

"Mr. Colvin," I repeated, "Could I speak with you about some of your survey work in the Adirondacks?" Coming right to the point would, I thought, be the best way to test his memory.

"I read your reports and had just a few questions. Could you take a minute and speak—"

I stopped, seeing no comprehension registering on Colvin's dim face. His pointed chin, growing a heavy stubble of white beard, gave him an even emptier look. His eyes seemed not to focus. We stood a moment, neither of us speaking. I tried again.

"Mr. Colvin ..." Suddenly, with his name, the elderly figure broke into slow, deliberate speech.

"My name is Verplanck Colvin. I am a surveyor. How can I help you?" His gaze went past me.

"Could you look at a map for me?" I decided to strike while the fire seemed hot. "In fact, I have two maps here." I held up the two rolled oversized maps, the one of Debar and the other of Unnamed Mountain.

Colvin motioned me to a high well-worn pine worktable. It was designed podium-style, to be used for standing and studying documents such as the maps I now unrolled and placed side by side in front of us. Colvin's eyes brightened as his attention was drawn to his work.

Studying each map, first Debar, then Unnamed Mountain, he appeared to read his notations. I did not interrupt his concentration. His visage grew dark and troubled and he stopped reading, but did not look at me. He seemed somehow frustrated or confused by what was in front of him. The time had come to ask the question I'd come to present.

"Mr. Colvin, can you tell me which of these maps accurately defines the lands originally transferred to the state in the Macomb deed?"

I felt my lips go dry. My question seemed to register with the great surveyor, and I studied his face as he paused. His mouth started to move, but no sound came out at first. Then, slowly, the edges of his lined face grew taut as his lips, now pursed and trembling, emitted one sound and then another. The first sound was trom, followed by a pause, and then lee. Then he put the sounds together. "Trom-lee," he said in his soft voice. Then he said it again, one last time, and more clearly. "Tromlee."

He appeared exhausted as he moved toward a stuffed chair. I helped steady him as he lowered his frail body into the seat. He said nothing but looked at me with sad eyes that began to close.

Yes, I thought, Kelly was right: something significant had happened to this man to so severely limit him in so relatively little time. Perhaps a mild stroke, I hazarded to guess.

Colvin's eyes dropped closed, and just as fast he was asleep, breathing slowly and steadily. Studying his gentle features, I saw a large almost-healed scar, partially hidden by his gray hair, evidence of a wound of some kind suffered at his scalp line. I wondered if the injury had come from the fall Kelly had mentioned, and if the wound to his head had been significant enough to alter the man this way. If so, he might never fully recover, given his age and overall condition. I covered the sleeping man with a blanket and rolled up my maps.

I stood another moment looking respectfully around the room. It was testament to Colvin's work, the place where he'd labored for decades on his monumental North Country surveys. A great body of history, surveying, and knowledge was contained in this room. But it was dormant now. I looked at Colvin one last time, then quietly took my leave.

Closing his door behind me, and descending the steps back to Steuben Street, I suddenly realized that by tromlee Colvin had meant Trembley, the well-known guide in the Basin area, a man Kora and I had met years ago at Nate's Pond when we guided John Burroughs. Surely Colvin's work party on the Debar and Unnamed Mountain survey jobs could be ascertained and located. Colvin had remembered Trembley's name in association with this work party, probably because it was known that Colvin had needed the assistance of local guides in doing his work. I added seeking out Trembley and asking him about his experience in the Colvin work party to my list of things to do. Trembley, I recalled, was still in good health and renowned for his knowledge of the area and his excellent memory.

Trial preparation filtered quickly, one thing to the next, in my mind. How best to prepare and attack was the lawyer's task in front of me. Colvin's work would be a key, I knew, as no other proof seemed to exist on Macomb's deed and the reacquisition of the state parcel.

Prominent in my trial strategy would be what the adversary—the esteemed state—knew about Colvin's work product. Was Attorney General Hamilton aware of the discrepancy in the two maps and what Colvin stated in his reports? Most importantly, was Hamilton aware of Colvin's uncertainty in placing the westerly line of the state-owned tract? Hamilton and our firm had exchanged only basic correspondence: a copy of the deed in Macomb's Purchase and subsequent deeds to various parties; the subsequent deed to the defaulting timber company and deed to the state. The only disclosure response by Hamilton made about the proof in the state's case was his production of Colvin's earlier, and I believed inaccurate, map. It was noteworthy that Hamilton produced no other Colvin maps, given that we had demanded all relevant evidentiary documents.

I had to find out what Hamilton knew, using a means that had worked for many in my trade — an impromptu visit to the man, unorthodox as that might be. A surprise visit at the state capitol building, the dropping of an oblique reference to my investigation and the available maps of the area, might induce him to inadvertently reveal some of the important trial strategy that he had planned.

Keene Durant would not approve. But he wasn't here in Albany with me, and the opportunity was too tempting to resist. Here I was, a young lawyer on a case with the state. I could introduce myself, look him in the eye, tell him I would have further information on the case, further demands on him, and generally grouse around a bit to size him up, man to man. I'd let him know the defense meant to mount a challenge and that we intended to be thorough in its preparation. The danger, I knew, was that it could backfire on me and be seen as imprudent and unwise.

I walked a quick pace up State Street hill to the capitol building. I found Joseph Hamilton's name on the elaborate gilded directory and proceeded to the Justice Department and the Attorney General's office on the second floor. High paneled mahogany doors with large glass panes swung open to reveal ornate moldings, woodwork finely carved with raised rosettes, cast life-size frescoes of Socrates and

Lincoln, and stately, elegant furnishings. A far cry from our office, I thought, as I studied the high raised-tin ceiling displaying angels swooning in classical style. Suspended from center-ceiling was an immense but delicate brass lady of justice perfectly positioned to give notice to all that, indeed, here was the fount of law, reason, and civility. There was no sign of another person, but before me was a finely scrolled, shining varnished wood counter stacked high with legal papers and manuscripts. My overpowering awe threatened my will to carry out my surprise visit. I shook my shoulders to regain my composure.

I turned toward the sound of footsteps approaching from the long stately corridor leading to the interior of the office. A distinguished looking gentleman entered the room and when we were face to face, I spoke first.

"I'm Jack Durant. I'd like to see Mr. Joseph Hamilton."

The man's eyes looked evenly into mine as he paused to size up a young man whose dress was clearly less stylish than his own. His even gaze turned to a look of superiority as he extended his hand to me.

"Joseph Alexander Hamilton," he said in a deep baritone voice. "You may have your visit. Follow me."

I worked to keep my face even.

He preceded me down a high corridor with rich oak and inlaid cherry floors, our footsteps echoing sonorously as we went. I was led to a corner office at the end of the passage. Hamilton's office was spacious, with large corner windows that looked in either direction over the city of Albany for some distance. As we'd walked, I'd continued to regroup so that I was ready to engage Hamilton in a conversation and get the crucial answers. Hamilton, standing behind his massive oak desk and staring out a window, turned to face me. He did not ask me to sit down.

"I know the firm of Keene Durant and you, I trust, are his son, no doubt inquiring about the Aber case. How could I help you?" This was uttered not as a question, really, but more as a statement.

I was taken off guard by his pinpointing so easily my identity and the purpose of my visit.

"I thought you might give me a few minutes," I said, clear that helping me was not his aim. "I've been unable to locate the public maps of Macomb's Purchase. They must be available somewhere in this city." That wasn't an outright falsehood.

Hamilton looked away, giving me a chance to study his fine woolen suit and silk bow tie, his matching Chamberlain vest, and the thick moustache that set off his shaved face and refined features. His eyes were dark and piercing, and his temples were touched with gray. The epitome of elegance, really. But, given the amount of time he was taking before answering me, I surmised that my direct question had thrown him a bit off-balance.

I plunged in further without waiting for his answer.

"My supporting information to the state's claims requests maps that I assumed are within your domain, either here in this office, or certainly within the state's possession somewhere. I mean, of course, any maps of the tract you claim the state reacquired. If they exist, surely you're willing to share the information with me, so —" I wasn't able to finish my sentence. Hamilton had heard enough.

"Mr. Durant, Albany is full of information in the public domain that isn't under my aegis. Your case is but one of the many I supervise. So here's my response to you. If there were such documents that I planned to rely on, and if they were under my control, rest assured I would have provided them to you. Title to the state parcel is adequately and legally shown in the Macomb patent and in the subsequent deed to the state, not to mention the state's occupation and control from time immemorial." Hamilton paused briefly before saying dismissively, "And of course, Colvin filed his survey and report for the reserved parcel—the survey I provided to your firm."

If Hamilton was being honest, he would be relying on the deed and the known Colvin map that had been filed. It was possible that he didn't know about, or wish to take into account, other documents such as the second map. My response, I decided, would be as forthright, and as veiled, as his. I searched for the right words.

"Very well. I certainly take you at your word, Mr. Hamilton. It will be for the jury to interpret the deed and determine the Abers' defense, and the jury will be from our county, where the Abers are well respected. It appears we are both comfortable with that."

Hamilton shot back words I shall not forget.

"Durant, the state will not abide any person or interest despoiling more of these Adirondack lands than have already been despoiled by lumber companies and squatters like your clients. The state intends to fully protect its title to this magnificent tract of wilderness." He stopped, looking satisfied that his rebuttal placed him on high ground.

I hoped my shock didn't show on my face at that moment, as I realized that the state had come full circle: in my lifetime, it had given away land so that timber and mining interests could despoil and rape it; and now the state had come to be its protector. This was something almost no one in 1894 believed, save perhaps Longfellow, who wanted to wait and see if forever wild lands guaranteed in the state constitution would indeed be honored. I had to admit that Hamilton, the state's lawyer, appeared to be making his point that forever wild was to be honored.

I collected myself. My rejoinder was taken from Keene Durant's teachings over a lifetime.

"Courts decide these disputes, not you and I, thankfully! And I believe the jury and the court will declare that the Abers are not squatters on state land. Good day, Mr. Hamilton."

I turned and walked through my adversary's office door, down the gilded corridor, out the tall paneled mahogany entry doors with high glass, momentarily feeling full of myself. But as my mind played out the trial of State of New York v. Aber, a landmark case in the making, a little inner voice began to quibble with me. It said I probably had the better of the proof, but questioned which side had the weight of justice with it — and the legal skills to prove its case.

I walked briskly now, feeling more doubt than self-confidence about the destiny of the Basin. As I departed Albany, I realized I'd been so preoccupied I'd forgotten to say goodbye to Kelly.

Eleven
Awakening Robin

S elf-assured or full of doubt, my preparation for Aber must go on.

I had to assume that Colvin's trom-lee referred to Trembley. Trembley was a Basin guide for those wealthy city folk we called "sports," who liked to visit the Basin as if touring some primitive outback. Trembley led parties into the wilderness by canoe and guided all manner of hunting and fishing expeditions. He had led the well-known naturalist and writer, John Burroughs, author of one of my favorite books, *Wake-Robin*, when Burroughs wanted to tour Nate's Pond. It had also been rumored over the years that Trembley got his start working for the Colvin survey party.

I thought back to the summer when I'd first met the man — the summer of Kora's and my trip in the Rushton canoes, when Dunning had rescued Kora. After she'd recovered from the experience, we'd pushed on into the wilderness south of the Basin. We'd paddled all day, and toward evening we searched the rugged shore of Nate's

Pond for a campsite. In the distance I noticed a glow in the dusky sky, and as we drew closer I could see a large beach fire burning, and the silhouette of a man sitting, then moving about on foot and feeding the fire.

Suddenly I sensed motion on the darkening water surface, and the voice of a man calling from what I soon identified as a canoe.

"*Mon Dieu*, eet ees daark," he exclaimed. "Why you here? *Venez, venez*—to camp!" he said in a hospitable tone.

Having somehow determined we were no threat, the man motioned us in, almost commanding us to follow, with a wave of a rather short arm connected to a stout frame. Kora and I were tired from a long haul and carry earlier and were ready for rest. It looked as if this camp would be our destination for the night.

As we paddled closer, we saw a nice site. There was a well-established lean-to, a second, smaller fire for cooking, several canvas tarps for weather protection, gear neatly stored, and canoes overturned on their thwarts on a sandy spot on the beach. The stout man in his canoe waved us in ahead of him, and as we glided into the sand and heard the familiar sound of sand-on-wood-hull, the solitary figure at the fire stood and watched us disembark. It was a beautiful and unforgettable Adirondack evening, the last twilight, with just enough light for me to make out a bearded face in the dancing light.

"Is this going to be all right, Jack?" Kora whispered.

I had no time for a response.

"Trembley," the bearded man called out. "Who's with you?" He peered in our direction from a distance of 30 feet into the night.

"By the grace of God, a woman!" the bearded man exclaimed as Kora came into the fire's light. His tone grew warmer. "Welcome! Come in!"

He held out a hand to Kora as we approached. She paused before accepting his hand, which he seemed to offer in a gentle and friendly enough manner. I'd identified Trembley quickly, since even then I'd heard of his reputation as a guide. But the identity of the bearded man eluded me. Perhaps, I thought, he was a wealthy industry magnate from the city, but then decided he didn't fit that image.

"Jack Durant," I said. Trembley, still in his canoe, nodded his head. I stepped toward the bearded man, who turned to me.

"John Burroughs," he said.

"And I'm Kora Longfellow."

A warm smile came over his face and Burroughs said, "Won't you join us? It's almost dark and you need a campsite. We have one ready made, eh Monsieur Trembley!"

Trembley now leapt lithely from his canoe and came quickly to the fireside. "We have food, too. *Mangez, mangez,* Mademoiselle Kora, Jack!"

This made me feel at home, and I could see from Kora's smile that she too was feeling comfortable. We sat by the now fading larger fire, its embers glowing a deep orange. The last light of that June evening shimmered and hung in the clear air. Features of the faces that, from a short distance had been indistinct, became clear by the firelight. Food, delicious and hot, was placed in front of us and we ate silently, anxious to get our fill before engaging in conversation. Our new companions seemed to understand, and joined us in finishing off the fresh pan-fried brook trout, followed by a seasoned French stew made with venison.

Between courses, Kora explained, "We're exploring a part of the wilderness we're not very familiar with. But we're not far from home. We do this a lot — explore and camp. We love this place." She finished enthusiastically, surprising me with her easy talk among strangers much older and more experienced than either of us.

Burroughs nodded approval of Kora.

It suddenly dawned on me that this was the John Burroughs, the man who'd written and become well-known for his contemplations on wilderness. I'd read him extensively, comparing his and John Muir's conflicting philosophies about the relationship of man to the wilderness. Then I remembered reading a local news story that said Burroughs was coming to the Adirondacks, but, of course, I'd had no idea I would come across him.

Burroughs ate with enjoyment, and our new compatibility settled over us as we shared a meal on the sandy beach of the Adirondack pond. Finishing his last piece of freshly made bread and trout, Burroughs' face grew full, and as he chewed he appeared to be thinking.

"I'm from the Catskill region, myself," he finally said. "This is my first visit to your Adirondacks and your state forests. But I've known wilderness all my life. I've bushwhacked my way through without maps or compass, just to see what I would find." He nodded at his companion. "Trembley agreed to bring me in here. I've begun to write about wilderness and its importance to people, its importance as a place to escape, to fish, hunt, and paddle a canoe. A place to build a house for your family."

That was where his thinking veered sharply from Muir's, who would say man had no business building anything in the wilderness. As far as Muir was concerned, we should visit, then get out of it.

While Burroughs stopped to ponder his next words, I studied his features. Middle-aged, some gray in his beard, and long straight hair, his face was lined from a life in the outdoors. His bright eyes suddenly moved from the embers of the fire to Kora. Flashing a bright quick smile, Burroughs continued:

"But you must understand me, Miss Kora, Jack, Trembley! We have to learn to live in a place like this. Your people have settled this area. It's your home. You are fortunate people. And you're entitled to use the land and resources, but you must renew them, too, preserve them. As civilized people we have to learn new rules, new thinking. We must learn all about Mother Nature, eh?"

Burroughs pushed lithely to a standing position, appearing tall, spare and strong.

"It's clear you love this place," he said, looking now directly down at me where I sat on the sand. "But will it be here for your children and grandchildren? Can the lumber companies and mining interests live by the standards I just talked about in a place like this? John Muir says it's not possible, but I disagree. I believe that Trembley's son will have his chance to be a guide and to live in this wilderness."

Burroughs stopped. "I lecture," he said, "but it is well-meaning. We cannot draw a circle around the Adirondacks and say people must not live here. Even the state, with its forever wild forests, can't claim that you have to get out or that no one should live here.

"Don't think for a moment the state has learned to manage these lands. There are individual owners who know better than the state how to manage the wilderness. No, I'm talking about the wealthy land barons, men who have opened up this area and made it useable—so that any man can homestead here, find a job, till the land, and live in wild surroundings. And that is not necessarily right; it is just the way it is!"

I bit my tongue at the sentiment expressed by Burroughs, but Kora didn't. I'd glanced at her at Burroughs' reference to the wealthy land barons, and had known right then that she wouldn't remain silent much longer. As Burroughs fed a log to the fire, Kora burst out with a response.

"Mr. Burroughs, my father was a land baron. He opened up some of the wilderness here, he lumbered off the land and worked mines. He didn't necessarily feel that the Basin should be preserved forever wild — a position you and I might agree on. But it's something that has to be studied closely before a decision is made."

Burroughs nodded in agreement, but his face expressed astonishment at Kora's candor. Although her own perspective coincided with Burroughs', she'd had the temerity to speak up and defend her father to Burroughs.

For myself, I was too confused to add anything to the conversation, and Trembley, who'd maintained a thoughtful pose for quite some time, apparently ran short on patience.

"*Eh bien*, we arise early to move on, Monsieur Burroughs," he said. "More lovelee wilderness *á voir* — to see, to see! But I tell each of you that my people will not stand for anyone telling us what we can and cannot do to make our way for our families on this land. Ze state — eet must know this, but if the bas-tards in Albany don't, they weel."

He stood and, after poking the fire and throwing a Yule log on it he turned to us. "Good night to you, Kora, Jack. Good night, Monsieur Burroughs. I am turning in to my can-vass."

Trembley walked away into the night. A loon gave out his tremolant laugh, followed by a cry, unusual in its rapid succession of tones. Perhaps it was speaking to its mate; perhaps to us. We said our good-nights, the conversation over and our compatibility now tinged with uneasiness.

The next morning Kora and I awoke at dawn. Trembley was already fishing from his canoe with his fly rod. We soon waved good-bye and paddled off to the outlet of Nate's Pond, ready to explore new areas. I didn't see Burroughs, but his words about the wilderness and John Muir, and Kora's exchange with him on wilderness, were fresh in my mind.

We were not far down the pond when I had to speak.

"Kora, Mr. Burroughs thinks it acceptable to homestead and open up the wilderness to people living here. I don't agree, and John Muir wouldn't, either. I could see it made you uncomfortable to listen to his views, but ..."

"Jack Durant! Don't you presume to know what makes me uncomfortable!" she said in raised voice. "I listened closely to the great man. And I happen to think my father actually favored development of this wilderness—you know what he did with his timber and mining interests. And at the same time, he wanted to preserve it, in much the same way Mr. Burroughs describes, so that everyone could use these lands."

"I apologize for presuming to read your mind on your views."

I was even more puzzled than I'd been last evening around the fire. Kora didn't seem aware of her father's agreement with Keene and Duryea to preserve the Basin as forever wild. She herself seemed to be more in agreement with Burroughs. The more I learned about her thoughts and about her apparent lack of knowledge about her father's wishes, the more I came to worry that she and I would not agree on the future of the Basin.

Only time would reveal if we would grow closer or farther apart on how the Basin should be used by us now, and by others in future generations.

Returning from Albany I passed some hours on the train reflecting on that discussion at Nate's Pond. The words of Burroughs, Kora, and Trembley had always remained with me. I wrestled again with thoughts about these lands, about the people who lived here with me, and how the state's claims and rights—along with individual claims and rights—were to be resolved. And how wilderness was to be preserved.

Veering northwest and leaving the Hudson behind, now skirting the high peaks of one mountain range after another, I knew I must confront Trembley. I must coax from him everything he could remember about when he guided Colvin in February 1883. He'd been there when Colvin sketched the reacquired state parcel. He had walked the state's disputed westerly boundary line. Ultimately, I would ask Trembley to be a witness in our case.

I assumed he'd be reluctant to take the stand in a courtroom. He was not a man who liked authority, or bent easily to it. My request would necessarily place him in the state's edifice, as a witness in the hall of justice governed by codes and sworn oaths that he wanted nothing to do with. What Trembley would reveal, and whether he had the will to help us, were questions that troubled me.

Dusk fell as we entered the last mountain valley, chugging me back to Duryea, Keene Durant, and the office. I was bursting with news to share.

Twelve
Trembley

I knew Trembley would be in the woods guiding a group of sports hunting for bear and deer. The only question, at this time of year, was precisely where to locate him. Known as an explorer, he really was more of a roamer and rambler, going through the wilderness with no set plans except to hunt and trap, and keep moving.

I asked a few questions at the hotel in town and soon learned that Trembley was guiding a party of sports hunting bear in the upper reaches of Otter Creek. They'd been out for several days and nothing had been heard from them, which probably meant that no bear had yet been taken. The best way to find Trembley, I decided, was to cross the lake and then bushwhack in to search for him.

I knew better than to interrupt him at work with his sports, but there might be a break in the hunt when I could speak to him about his work with Colvin. The timing of my visit might prove fortuitous in that we'd be in the very area Colvin had surveyed, within sight of the Unnamed

Mountain peak in question. Kelly had loaned me the maps on linen paper that Colvin had left in his Albany office, including the one he hadn't filed with the state. I rolled those up tight and made preparations for what might be an extended trip in the woods.

It was late spring, the very season in which no respectable guide or hunter would kill a sow and leave her cubs alone to await certain death. The party would be hunting an adult male bear and, intent on its hunt, it wouldn't be on the alert for a single person in the woods. I would need to take extra precaution in finding and approaching the party. My first choice was to locate them in their base camp while no hunt was under way.

The row to the far point of the lake in my doubleender was smooth and silent. Wilderness drew me in, as it always did, and civilization faded away to the sounds and smells of the water and the woods. I beached my boat at a sandy cove and moved inland, knowing the likely areas for a base camp and for the hunt. The hunted bear always struck me as incongruous: it was at the top of the food chain in the wild, yet the hunter sought it for the trophy, for the mounted or stuffed head or body or the bear rug, all commonly displayed in Adirondack camps as symbols of the wild. Why would man remove this beast from the wild place where it lived to display its body on the hunter's wall or floor? Any bear I'd ever seen looked better in the woods.

One tactic of a bear hunt was to push an adult bear toward the rock cliffs on the west side of the unnamed mountain, where it would be trapped and shot dead. If that was the case today, I'd be approaching from their backside during their push, and their focus would be away from me and toward the granite cliffs. I walked at a good pace in the woods, passed the party's base camp, and covered several miles in two hours.

I picked up the old Indian hunting path as it coursed north and west at a point in the woods. This was the very path referred to in the reserved parcel and in the Aber deed. It had been some years since I'd traveled it, well-worn from hundreds of years of use by hunting parties of warriors from Lake Champlain to the east. It had seen many sights unfold, but perhaps none as surprising as what suddenly occurred in quick succession in front of me.

From my left, I heard a rush and loud rustle plowing through dense undergrowth. I caught sight of a bear moving rapidly through a small clearing, followed closely by two cubs. They were moving in the direction I had come from, toward me, and not toward the rock cliff and face of unnamed mountain.

I was now caught in the middle of a rapidly changing hunt, one that would put the hunted on a keen edge, especially a sow with her cubs. It astonished me that a mother or her young would be the object of any hunting party led by Trembley, for he was fierce in his protection of game of any species rearing young.

Two hundred yards beyond the clearing, another flash of rapid movement and color caught my eye. It was a hunter in bright red, sunlight glinting off the barrel of his rifle.

The sow momentarily stopped at the edge of the clearing to test the air. My presence behind the push was probably not known to the hunting party, but the bear had undoubtedly detected my scent on the breeze. A sow that felt trapped could suddenly turn mean. I was not armed, nor did I have any desire to kill a sow nursing two cubs.

Even now, I can replay the scene as it unfolded in rapid order: the hunter sees the sow in the clearing, raises his rifle and takes aim. At the same moment, from behind the hunter's right shoulder, comes a different flash of color and shape: the signature guide hat, each one unique in color and finish, and this one displaying high partridge feathers and bright yellow headband. Under the guide hat I recognize a familiar face, gruff and weather-beaten, with a hawk-like nose and sunken jaws with no front teeth.

It's Trembley, no doubt surveying the scene in front of him and quickly assessing the situation: his sport, the sow and cubs, all in the same sight line and covering a distance of perhaps 150 yards. I hear others in the party coming closer, but I can't see them. The sow rises on her hind legs, her body bold and powerful, her shining coat massive, her face enraged like that of a warrior backed into a corner with anxious young at her side.

"Monsieur Sport, drop your barrel, thees ees ze mama—we no shoot," Trembley shouts.

The sport either doesn't hear or chooses not to respond to the order. Trembley runs toward his charge, who is about to shoot and thus breach the code of the north woods. Dropping his rifle and crouching low, Trembly races, catlike, covering thirty yards of rocky terrain in seconds, a sinew of power and energy.

The rifle sounds at the same instant that Trembley, having reached his sport, launches through the air, his arms outstretched to tackle the trophy hunter. The sport crashes down under Trembley's weight and the sow, terrified by the rifle's report, turns and races directly at me. Her cubs cannot keep pace with her.

Quickly the sow closes the ground between us. For a moment, she disappears behind the esker that rises between us, and I move instinctively to higher ground, off the path, frantically considering my options.

Suddenly mama bear is upon me, running full speed. She sees me now for the first time, and her eyes grow as wide with surprise and fear as mine. At a distance of ten feet, and despite my horror, I still can't help but feel strange awe at her massive head, white teeth, her dark eyes surrounded in amber. At two feet I feel her warm moist breath, now dead center upon me.

Suddenly the sow swerves to her left in a lightning-quick pivot at the exact moment that I lunge to my left. Her right shoulder lifts me head first into the air and down the far side of the esker, near where I had stood.

Trembley later told me that the sow kept going, probably hearing her cubs were just behind her, snorting hard as they raced in her tracks past where my prone, splayed body lay on the ground. One cub, he said, ran full speed right over me as he raced after his mother. He'd heard the sow and cubs' thrashing sounds, as they disappeared into the dense growth, for several minutes. Clearly terrified, at least they were otherwise no worse the wear for the foolishness of the sport.

I'd come to, wheezing to get air into my lungs, to the sounds of a chewing-out the likes of which few have heard or seen in these woods.

"*Monsieur*, you know *bien* - well, veree well! We no shoot ze mama. How many time I tell you this today, you bastaard! *Vous* meezerble son of a beetch from ze cité. I have votre rifle, Monsieur — a rifle you weel not take with you, eh! You beat your ass to ze camp *maintenant*, eh. Your hunt is *finis avec moi*, you fooking son of a beech!"

Trembley, his eyes wild, had the man by the throat. His powerful hands tightened against the sport's throat and shirt collar and the man's color began to fade for lack of oxygen. Suddenly Trembley released his grip from the sport's throat, but he shoved him hard down the esker in the direction of the path.

By then the rest of the party had caught up. The sport's friends stood in a quiet group some distance apart, not saying a word.

"Geet you ass to ze camp and geet out. Geet out thees day, you and your *amis*!" he ordered, gesturing to the entire party of four men.

The other men picked up their fellow sport in a gruff manner and slowly moved down the path. They had a long trek ahead of them back to their base camp on Otter Creek, miles away. "Find your way," the guide shouted. "Be out before ze dark falls thees night!"

The group disappeared into the woods. Trembley turned toward me, as I lay there still dazed. My entire body ached from the violent contact with the charging 300 pound bear and the rocky surface. The pain, especially to my chest where the cub had run over me, was just setting in.

"*Mon Dieu, Monsieur*! Monsieur Durant, Jacque Durant! Are you okay, *Monsieur*?"

"I think so. Yeah. I'm okay."

Trembley helped me to my feet, studying me carefully as I tested out my strength. We sat together on a large rock, exchanging our perspectives on the experience we'd just been through.

"You are very fortunate Monsieur Durant. *Mais qu'es que c'est*? Whaat ees eet bring you into my woods *aujourd'hui*, today, today?" he asked, and at the same time his eyes scanned the ground, coming to rest on the maps that had been scattered during my joust with the bear.

He gathered up two of them and scanned across them in a manner bespeaking a trained explorer or cartographer. Then he shocked me with recognition.

"Ah, Monsieur Colveen's map of ze mont avec no name that we find and put here," he said as he pointed to the map. "*Oui, je souvient — comment —* years and years ago."

I could only shake my head and grin at the strangeness of this day. I'd just been knocked senseless in my efforts to find the man who was looking quizzical and asking me questions about the Colvin maps.

"Monsieur Trembley," I said, "I came out here today because I need your assistance. I picked up the crucial map. "The state is claiming title to these lands, the lands where the Abers live and perhaps the lands where … we are. Here," I decided to make no reference to the title of William West Longfellow.

"*Oui, oui,* I know these lands well, Jack, and you call me just Trembley, eh? "Jack, thees map, eet show eet. I was here with Colveen, and he was in a big hurry when we get ici," he said, pointing to the unnamed mountain.

"Here, I see the unnamed mountain, the hunting path nearby to us. *Oui,* we are here now." He pointed to the place where we stood, near where a small brook intersected the path, as described in the reserved parcel. "Jack, the state — eet not own here and I tell you *pourquoi,*" Trembley said. "*Monsieur* Colveen and I, we walk thees land. I no read well, mais he read to me ze paper, how you say — ze deed — and we trace it out. I remember he question me about one part." Here Trembley paused, looking deep in thought.

"Trembley," I said, "it's the note on the margin. It says this boundary 'is a shared boundary with Longfellow,' and I must know why he concluded this."

Trembley looked at the map, studying it for several seconds, then looking at the distant peak of unnamed mountain. He looked to the map again, and then was ready to respond.

"*Je me souviens,* Jack, *maintenant* I remember Colveen — he theenk thees was ze state boundary — see here what you read to me. And I now see his writing and I study eet and see it is about cinq mile from the peak to the path where it meets ze brook. We had pace off ze distance, set up his sextant from near here to—how you say—shoot ze sextant from here to ze peak. Colveen, he use hees compass, hees level and he do ze figure pour ze deestance. Eet was fife mile, Jack, but I no agree *avec* Colvin dat ze boundary, and theen, ze fool, Rondeau, he was there, he no agree avec Colveen either." He looked around, expecting to see Rondeau, Trembley's shadow, his self-appointed scout, somewhere on the perimeter.

"Sometheeng was no right. No right because ze problem was, Jack, it no close on ze north and ze south to make the land ze deed say ees there. Colveen and me, we both *savoir.* We try, *mais non,* eet no form ze shape for the state land, eh bien, a beeg—how you say, rectang in ze wild!" Trembley stopped, scratched his head through the worn feathered hat, seeming ready to continue.

"So, Jack, Colveen, he was stuck unteel I say, '*Monsieur,* eet ees not thees mountain *cinq* mile away in ze deed. Eet ees ze next reedge over, ze next *montagne* at ze top they refer to. *Vien,* I show you', I say to heem. And I show heem, I show eet was ze next one, ze Mont nom de Debar, that ees in ze right place. Thees change *tout, tout,* and Colveen, he ees happy!

"We went—Colveen, hees man and me, to ze path where we see Debar about three miles east from thees place ici. We see Monsieur Pacquette there too, I tell you later. *Mais* Colveen, he take his instruments *encore.* He shoot up to Debar at ze peak. He make a sight line path all ze way, *eh bien?* And, he find that point ees ze right point to make ze rectang be ze right shape! *Oui, oui,* eet was right *avec* ze corners—we *savons pour* ze state."

Again Trembley stopped, proud of his memory of these events, and flashed a broad, toothless grin.

Looking down at the map once again, he read aloud slowly, studying each word of Colvin's note about the land sharing a boundary with Longfellow.

"And then, Colveen he make an 'x' at ze spot on ze map and I see heem *écrive* his note. He take ze second map and draw ze right boundary on eet, *oui*, thees map ici." Trembley checked out my second map, which still lay open on the ground, '*Oui, voila* ze map!' Colveen say, '*Merci, Trembley, merci* for assistance.'

"Then he move on weeth me to ze next state land. That was *finis* for thees land, Jack. Mais not before Colveen, he see Monsieur Paquette and he hand heem a beeg paper in an envelope and say, 'Here is your deed, Mr. Paquette, that I deliver from Albany. You may be thankful for eet. It should be recorded.' Paquette walk away with ze paper after thanking Colveen. Colveen stay with hees work on ze survey, toujours, he work hard. And thees ees as much as *je sais*, Jacque."

I assessed quickly my evidence and reviewed two sketches I'd made of the area, one showing Colvin's incorrect first version in which he had started at Baldface Mountain believing it was Debar Mountain, and one showing it as I thought Colvin intended in the end. It was clear from that second map that the westerly boundary of the reacquired state land formed the easterly boundary of the Basin. And it did so at a point and running on a course that coincided with the position of Aber on his claims to ownership, and with our longtime occupation of the Basin lands. This was in accord with a line running from Debar to the path near the brook as called for in the state's deed.

The position of our client, as well as title to the wilderness of the Basin, was protected if my proof was valid. The proof appeared strong, I could report to Father. But validity in my mind might be different from what I could prove in a court of law.

"Say, *pourquoi, mon ami*, you ask me about thees?"

It occurred to me that Trembley had put in quite a day himself. He'd dispensed with a mindless bear hunter, remembered with seeming clarity events of years ago, and correctly, I thought, interpreted Colvin's work, all with an intuitive sense about getting it right. I searched for the words to tell Trembley that he was a key witness who now would be subject to subpoena in our case. I did not have to answer him.

Trembley stated bluntly, "Jack Durant, *tu sais bien* I do not go to your court. My court ees ze forest. I tell what I know. Now you use eet, *mais...*" And now Trembley rose from the crouch he had placed himself in to read the map.

"I do not go to court, do not *répondez* to your, how you say, soopeena! I try thees one time and ze judge, he no friend of mine, the D ah A, he no friend of Trembley. I no like ze rules, ze rules in ze law, Jack. *Je n'aime pas.* I do not go there, monsieur. *Jamais, jamais. Comprenez?*" he demanded, his voice rising to a crescendo and leaving no doubt this was his final decision. For emphasis, he added, "*Boisez m'âne!*"

I would have to produce his story in court, somehow, but in what way presently eluded me.

He offered his hand to help me up from my sitting position and I got to my feet and gathered up my maps. Stowing them in my pack, I moved down the trail behind Trembley, down the ancient hunting path of Mohawk and Huron warriors. I followed another warrior, too, in Trembley, one who did not testify in a court of law.

I would have sworn that lurking on the perimeter, in the shadows just out of clear sight, was the shape of a man who seemed to be following us. The shape resembled one old Rondeau. I suspected that Trembley, too, knew he was there.

The trek home was a long walk followed by a long paddle. My body ached from the run-in with the bear, my chest felt compressed where the cub had run me over, and my shoulder carried a deep bruise.

I arrived back at camp near dinner hour with a searing headache. Through the windows I could see Duryea, working in the kitchen over his wood stove, preparing our meal. In the reading room, the westerly room of the camp, Father appeared to be studying a map, one that had the familiar look of a topographical map of the Basin.

I looked up at the fine oval window in the peak. It caught the last of the day's sun, setting now in the southwest. The familiar light brought me needed comfort. I would wait for the next day when I was rested to recount my full story.

"Greetings!" I called out. "What's for dinner?"

Thirteen
The Vault

It had been bothering me for some time: I was a lawyer and I should be able to figure out with certainty who owned title to the Basin. Yet I had not been able to do so.

After dinner I went to my room and thought more about the matter. Longfellow had title when he died, thanks to Father's success with the Forest Commission. Thereafter, Father had paid taxes over the many years since Longfellow's death.

"The tax levy is in again, Elaine," Father would announce. "Make sure we have this paid on time!" And that would be the last mention of it until the next bill was due.   But I didn't know in whose name the levy was issued. Father never said. I knew that the letter of instructions had been issued by Longfellow. I assumed those instructions had been followed, and that a deed disposing of the title had been properly executed. My assumption was based, in large part, on the fact that my family had had occupation of the Basin for decades. We'd settled at the camp that Duryea had built for Longfellow and we'd maintained dominion over it ever since.

One early evening I looked up from my desk in the office and discovered that I was the last person there. I'd been working on the Aber case, preparing it based on my visits with Colvin and Trembley, and I must have been so engrossed as to miss Father's and Elaine's departures.

It was time to quit for the day. I decided to store part of the Aber file in our vault, located in a small storage facility behind a secure locked door. The vault was for storage of important papers, and the Colvin maps certainly qualified.

The skeleton key smoothly turned the lock on the heavy door guarding the vault and allowed me access. I lit the kerosene lamps in the hall and the library, which cast enough light to see inside.

There in its steel clad frame stood the vault. I quickly worked the tumblers right and left, then opened the creaky, heavy door. The vault was nearly filled to capacity. I would have to move some of the files to gain more storage space.

I began moving some documents in the upper left corner, wondering if I could make enough room for the maps, and whether storing them in here would meet with father's housekeeping approval. He was fastidious in his organization and care of every aspect of the office.

The neatly stacked documents I picked up to move were deeds, I realized, and they were bound into packets of various sizes. The second packet I lifted caught my eye immediately: on the back cover of a neatly folded document were the words William West Longfellow.

The compulsion to read further overcame the fact that Keene Durant had not given explicit consent for me to do so, though I had an implied authority to do so as a partner. As I took the packet of papers apart, it became apparent that several deeds were lined up in chronological order, the most recent being the one with Longfellow's name typed on it.

My heart began to hammer in my chest.

Longfellow was the grantor named on page one, and there was a blank space for the grantee, followed by a long legal description of a parcel of 400,000 acres. It was signed by Longfellow, but did not bear the seal of the county clerk to indicate that it had been recorded. The notary acknowledgment clause, which was filled in, confirmed that the deed had been executed on November 20, 1894, and signed by the local judge.

Was this the incomplete deed, the escrow deed, still held by my father more than twenty years after Longfellow's death? And why was there no named grantee as the titleholder? I folded the deed into its former place in the group of deeds and carefully put it back into its place. As I did so a loose, handwritten paper floated to the floor.

It was dated November 20, 1894.

I read it, barely breathing. It was a letter of instructions from Longfellow to Father. Here was Keene Durant's secret — the one Duryea had told me about, but which I'd never seen. Longfellow's instructions were to hold the deed in escrow until he decided who should have title.

But that meant that Father wasn't the titleholder to the Basin lands! Not even his payment of taxes would be enough to prove otherwise.

I was shocked. How could Father have failed to take care of this matter so important to our family?

My mind raced with question after question. Without answers, I moved the papers to a separate compartment drawer in the vault, marking well where I placed them. My hands were trembling, and I felt my cheeks flush. The enormity of this recent information nearly paled beside the task that lay ahead of me: I would have to confront Father about this. I had to confront him with evidence that appeared to challenge the very integrity his life was founded on.

My hands were still shaking as I stored the Aber file next to the Longfellow papers. Father probably had a perfectly good explanation and resolution for this, as he had for everything. I decided not to bring the matter up at home that evening, but to get to the office early tomorrow morning and speak to him there.

But then I realized that I wasn't prepared to have this conversation with Father. Not yet. I wanted to get back to camp and think about the best way to proceed with the information. The ethics of the situation came raining down on me. How would this conversation affect Father and me? What were our legal and moral obligations on the deed in escrow? What had Longfellow meant by his instructions that Keene "follow my wishes on this most important transaction," and to "decide who takes title to it...once it is determined what occurs in Saratoga at the constitutional convention...on the fate...of this Adirondack Park"?

Having no solutions, only more questions than when I'd opened the vault, I carefully finished storing the Colvin maps. I pulled against the steel door and it opened slowly, with a creak. The entire weight of the vault's contents now seemed to be on my shoulders as well as on Keene Durant's.

The vault door creaked shut with my push and engaged its lock. I gave the vault tumblers an extra twirl for good measure.

At dinner there were plenty of other things to catch up and review with Father and Duryea. I would tell them about William Kelly in Albany, my visit to Verplanck Colvin, and about my decision to visit Joseph Alexander Hamilton at the Attorney General's office. I decided not to mention Trembley right away. Or my run-in with the hunters and the bear and her cubs.

Naturally, talk eventually turned to a review of the Aber case. My stomach clenched, but I felt that my thoughts were precise and that I kept conversation focused on our best defense: the Colvin maps showing that the state was mistaken in its position claiming ownership. Father's review was also precise and helpful, and seemed to dovetail with my analysis.

But when I told Father of my visit to our adversary's office in Albany, he answered with silence and a lack of eye contact. He stared at the dinner table, showing his disdain, I thought, for my tactic.

Dinner was over quickly, and after making plans to meet with Father early the next morning in the office, I decided to retire.

As I walked out of the dining room, Duryea said, "Jack, here is some salve for that bruise on your shoulder. I noticed it when you took off your coat, and you are grimacing even now." He handed me a small tin of salve. "And put this ice pack on it to numb the area and keep the swelling down."

I followed his instructions, with the usual good result come morning.

Morning found me entering the office quite early, and there already at the library table was Father, hard at work. A quick exchange of pleasantries assured me that he didn't sense anything about my discovery of the escrow deed and my desire to discuss it

Instead, he started right in on the Aber case.

"We both know Trembley has a keen memory that might tend to come down against claims of the state. Our job will simply be to keep his credibility high with the jury, a jury that will not favor the state to begin with. We know our neighbors take a dim view on the state's acquisition of the forestlands. We don't need to overplay our strength."

"Unfortunately," I said, dreading telling him this, "Trembley says he won't testify in a court of law." I told Father the details of Trembley's and my conversation yesterday in the woods.

"Oh, I've heard this sort of thing from him before, Jack, but if the stakes are pointed out and if he realizes the state is reaching beyond its rightful powers - and one day may order him around - I think he'll help us. I'll go see him personally and make these points. And I'll have a subpoena in my pocket ready to serve on him, just in case."

I feared Father was wrong in his assertion, but all I said at the moment was, "Beware of bears."

I needed to move on to the subject of the escrow deed. If our roles were reversed, Father would be direct in questioning me on any matter whatsoever, and I must return the courtesy. Besides, it was my nature to get to the point.

I did pause for a moment, however, to appreciate the irony before me. Longfellow had managed to snatch his land back from state ownership. Title to his land was now linked to my own claim of entitlement to the Basin, my homeland, which the state was once again trying to take from us. And the defenses in the Aber case might once again defeat the same claims by the state.

"Father," I finally said, "last evening when I finished with the Aber file for the day, I decided to store it safely in the vault because it contains irreplaceable evidence from Colvin."

I paused, looking directly at him, to let my words settle for a moment. His brows immediately creased, and I could read in his eyes that he knew what was coming.

"Last night," I continued, "storing the file for the first time, I had to move other files and documents to create room for the Aber material, and I saw papers on William West Longfellow. I didn't know about his instructions to you, Father. I didn't know you held an escrow deed awaiting further instructions from him. And I certainly didn't know that the unrecorded deed was for our Basin, Father — our camp, the wild mountain and streams — our home!"

I'd said enough — perhaps too much, given the now-defiant set of Keene Durant's jaw. But my purpose had been accomplished.

"Jack Durant, you stop right there. You were a very young boy, Jack. Your mother had just died, and I was devastated. Longfellow had become my best client and a trusted friend. He asked me to hold that deed. Some years before, as you know, I'd cleared the tax foreclosure sale with the state. I told you this, or rather, Duryea told you this—and he did so at my request.

"Until you became a lawyer, I could not share all of the facts with you, as indeed, I can't with Duryea. He's astute enough that he has probably surmised the facts, but he hasn't heard them from me. But you're my partner now, Jack. And my flesh and blood. You must understand me, and bear with me."

Keene Durant, the lawyer, paused, gathering his arguments. Feeling now like an intruder, I waited for the rest of his story.

"You must, remember that William died quite suddenly the night after he delivered that incomplete deed, along with his letter of instructions, to me. From that day on, I've wrestled with what's the right thing to do. When he divorced Janet, that left only Kora as the possible heir to the title, and of course I've known of your relationship with her. I've thought about where you'd be caught in this triangle."

Keene stood and walked to one of the library shelves, as if he needed a slight distance from me. "I mentioned this situation in a very general way in a letter to Kora after her father's death. I told her that her father died with certain assets, including Basin real estate, which I described as a large tract, and said that she should contact me regarding disposition of all his assets."

Keene moved back toward the library table again.

"We accomplished the administration of his estate to a point, and I indicated to Kora that the real estate would be more complicated because of her father's wishes. I asked her to follow up with me, but she never did. Perhaps I put it to her in too strong a manner, Jack, I don't know. I reminded her of my request only once when she was last here at Christmas, but she didn't react kindly to the reminder. She walked away from me without a word, and I've heard nothing from her since, no response, no instructions. And there, Jack, in the vault, sits that deed, and it puts me, and now you, in a vulnerable position."

Keene paused, then, and I assumed he was formulating his next thoughts, some plan of action in which I would now be inevitably involved.

"I've paid taxes on the Basin over the last 20 years, Jack. It's a burden I've carried. I've intended to bring this up to you, Jack, and probably to Kora, too. She isn't aware of my payments, and she cannot make the payments herself. Something has to be done about this, something that's fair and legal.

"On that point, of course, I've done some research. You read Longfellow's letter, so you know that it gives me instructions that were not completed in his lifetime. On the narrow grounds of the law strictly read, I have no ability to complete the deed! In that situation, Kora would inherit the property through administration of her father's estate. She'd become sole owner. But if she can't pay the taxes, then the land we both love would get sold to timber companies, to developers, or, God knows, maybe even the state."

He dropped himself into a chair at the table and was quiet for a while.

"So what comes next?" I asked.

He nodded his head at the validity of my question.

"We should speak on a business basis to Kora," he said. "She has some decisions to make. We have some decisions to make, too. One of those, Jack, is a moral decision. I have my client's written instructions and I'm his administrator. I have power under the law." Keene held my eyes. "But we're talking about what's right morally."

I sat in silence, my mind racing.

"I could ask a court of law for instructions — instructions permitting me to complete the deed Longfellow made, save for naming the grantee. It's a signed document and I took it to Judge Lagrew for his acknowledgment right after Longfellow executed it. I could complete it consistent with the instructions in his letter to me, and consistent with our many conversations in which he clearly stated that the Basin was not to be sold, but that some person or entity should preserve it in its wild state. But I know what he wanted, Jack, and it was not to leave it to Kora."

I didn't say anything, remembering my own discomfort at Kora's sympathy with John Burroughs. At least now it was clear to me that she'd spoken with Burroughs that night on Nate's Pond without any knowledge of her father's final wishes for the Basin.

Keene went on. "But I have a great reluctance to take the issue before a court. Under legal and equitable principles, I fear a court could not interpret Longfellow's intent, since he was not sufficiently clear in naming a grantee. Longfellow suggested only a general proposition for which the court could not substitute its judgment. And you understand the problem we have with the Dead Man Statute, Jack."

I nodded. The Dead Man Statute, carried from the common law, would prevent Father from giving testimony on Longfellow's intent. Dead men do not speak, and the law doesn't encourage living witness to the decedent's words under circumstances in which the testimony might be taken against the decedent's pecuniary interest.

I concurred with father's legal analysis. We were close to having clear enough instructions, but they weren't clear enough to meet legal evidentiary standards. Keene voiced the same conclusion I'd come to in my own mind.

"We couldn't prevail — not with just the written evidence. And my testimony is unlikely to be deemed admissible. Think hard about this, Jack. I know in my heart what Longfellow wanted. And I know how to accomplish it."

Father's words hung in the air. The import of our discussion came down upon me like a heavy weight. I took a deep breath.

"I've wrestled with this situation for some years now, Jack. It has been gnawing away at me, little by little, like a corrosive." He studied me hard before going on. "There's almost no chance in the world that a court would approve of it, but it's our decision to make. No one would be harmed by it, and it's consistent with what William wanted for the wilderness he wanted preserved."

Keene's blue eyes lit up, then, and a wry, warm smile of satisfaction spread to the corners of his mouth.

He rose to his feet, the soft light of the kerosene lamps complementing his even features.

"We can save this wilderness, with Kora's cooperation. Talk to her, Jack. Tell her that I have the escrow deed, and that it should be completed and recorded as William's deed to his daughter, Kora, and to you, Jack. The understanding should be that taxes will be paid, that you are equal tenants in common on the property, and that the land should not be sold unless it is consistent with William's wish to preserve it. And that maybe, in time, it could go to some entity to preserve it in perpetuity. Think of it!"

I was, of course. I was thinking of how Father's proposal could benefit all the Basin people who were committed to using it in the right way for their own peace and enjoyment. I thought about the generations to come who could be raised here the way I'd been raised by Father and Duryea — could have the wilderness in their blood. I thought about the calm the wilderness can bring, the quiet murmur of the streams, the falling of the water as it descends from the mountain pond. I thought about being part of preserving such serenity forever.

Keene knew I agreed with him. He continued with his plan.

"The deed, if Kora agrees to this, may be questioned. I'll have to give witness to it if it is. And I'm prepared to do that, even this many years after William's death, because he took this action in my presence during his life."

He sat down beside me again. "I'm not prepared to let Kora alone decide the fate of this land. I hope she agrees with this. To put the land through probate would not be in keeping with William's wishes. I'm deeply torn, Jack. But I've decided I'm prepared to take the risk to our reputation and do the right thing. I hope you are, too."

I worried that Kora might feel betrayed by her father. She had very little except the small nest egg William had left her after payment of his debts and a large divorce settlement left for Janet. I said as much to Keene, and he agreed.

"More importantly, she has never answered my invitations to inquire about the real estate," he said. "You can deal with her on that that now, Jack, in the right way. But make sure she understands that if both Kora and you hold title, I'll have no interest in it and will make no claim for reimbursement of taxes paid."

Keene Durant, caught for years in a moral and legal quandary, had answered in a way that surprised me, in part because it did not strictly comport with the law. Yet he had come to a moral solution. He'd done battle with this demon for years, and his solution was not without risk to himself — and now, to me.

The thought of resolving matters with Kora seemed remote and hard to grasp. Without question, the thing had to be confronted head-on with her, but the prospect left me feeling uncertain and unsettled. She remained, in my heart, my lover, but she herself had moved on to other things I knew nothing about. I didn't even know when she planned to come back to talk more about the possibilities of our life together.

"Well, Jack," Father interrupted my thoughts, "there you have it. The Basin, real property law, and ethics, all rolled into one case in which we have a personal interest — to say nothing of the Abers' interest — in the outcome. Do you want to take the risks? It could haunt us if things go wrong. And things could go very wrong."

I tried to give father a concise response.

"There are two people I must see, Father. One is Trembley, who has to be convinced of the rightness of appearing in court. I'll visit him again and let you know if I need the weight you might be able to bring to bear on him.

I want to be sure he'll support the title on the Basin and on the Abers' use and occupancy. If he will, in all likelihood we can prevail in the latter case and have a strong case made in the former. If Trembley won't come forward, perhaps Rondeau, who was also there, will.

"Then I need to see Kora. She loves the Basin as we do, and now I understand some of her hesitancy in dealing with us in the past. She's been torn in all this. And she may want to talk to her mother about things — and Janet may not look favorably upon this plan."

I could see that mention of Janet made Keene uncomfortable.

"Father, is there anything else I should know? Anything else I should understand about any of this, anything whatsoever bearing…."

Keene cut me off.

"No. There's nothing I can think of that affects this matter. William gave me last instructions and that is what we're obliged to act on. Anything said to me by anyone else in the family is not dispositive." Keene's features turned hard, something I'd never seen on his face before.

"We must act soon, Jack. I'm depending on you."

I thought on Keene's words for a moment, aware that he wanted my reassurance. I felt uneasy, but I didn't see any other choice.

"We'll see where we are after I visit with Kora and the witnesses. I think Kora will see the wisdom of your approach. And if she's told the whole story and understands the risks we're taking, she may agree to it."

I decided to give Keene a warning, one I hadn't initially meant to give, but which now seemed necessary.

"I'll tell her the unvarnished truth, but only after I'm certain she understands our situation and is sympathetic with it. Our disclosures must be directly yet carefully made."

It would be essential to handle this in such a way that both protected our own integrity and honored her father's wishes and the faith he'd placed in Keene Durant. I couldn't shake my fear, lest a complaint be made against us for filing a deed to any party for the Basin, which was under the signature of William West Longfellow. I knew Father felt the same fear. But it was a risk I was ready to take with him.

Father and I sat silently staring in opposite directions: he at the lady of justice, at her evenly balanced scales; I looked out the window where the distant McIntyre Range was just visible. Finally our eyes came to rest on each other from opposite sides of the library table.

I stood up. "I'll do everything in my power to make this come out the way it should, Father. And I won't move on anything until I've gone over it first with you, every step of the way."

He stood and looked evenly into my eyes. He reached out and placed his strong hand upon my shoulder, squeezing it affectionately. "Thank you, Jack Durant."

He turned and walked from the library to face the day's work. As he left, he declared to Elaine his usual order to work.

"Elaine, bring my files for the day. Let us begin!"

I walked to the office vault, opened it, and withdrew a part of the Aber file, the part I needed now for finishing the trial preparation, the part Father and I knew was crucial for my meetings with Trembley and Kora.

I glanced down at the documents in the vault and saw once again the escrow deed and Longfellow's letter, looking aged and weathered. I sensed its time here was limited, that it was a step closer to being recorded, with named grantees, in the not-too-distant future. But first it would be subject to careful scrutiny by others who might question or challenge its authenticity. Some of those challengers, I knew, may not yet even be identified. They might emerge from the detritus still settling from the chaos created by the maker of the deed.

Fourteen
Kora's Return

Duryea greeted me at camp in his warm and familiar way, yet there was an obvious look of concern in his eyes.

"Jack, go and see your Father. He is disturbed over something. I will have dinner soon, *eh bien*," he said, his eyes directing me to Keene, who was sitting in his reading room at the south end of the Basin camp.

The natural light flowing into the large, open room from the oval mosaic and the high windows was receding quickly on this late summer afternoon. Keene looked up as I approached, and a look of relief passed across his face. He stood up.

"Jack, while I was in town, I heard from members of the hunting party some of what happened to you in the woods. Are you sure you're all right?"

Running through the details of the encounter with the bear, the cub, the sport, and Trembley as best I could, I reassured him I was okay, though sore. I showed him the imprint of the cub's paw on my still bruised chest, but then redirected the conversation to the hopeful fact that the Aber parcel and the Basin lands did not appear to be on state land.

"We can deal with Trembley and with Rondeau, too, when the time comes for the appearance of either man at trial. You've done some work, my son. There's other business to talk over. But now, let us enjoy Duryea's good cooking and maybe even uncork a bottle of our best red wine to go with our venison."

He suddenly diverted his eyes from me. "Tomorrow, your day may be planned for you."

There was an uneasiness in his voice. I sensed I would soon hear the reason Duryea had sent me to father in the first place.

Keene's next words wrenched my mind, evenly dividing it between excitement and anxiety. "Kora Longfellow returned today, Jack. She stopped to see me at the office and came right to the point. She asked what I'd meant by the letter and by my request that she come to see me." Father's eyes avoided mine and his words became more measured. My heart raced.

"I decided to tell her only the most important developments regarding ownership of the Basin, and the Aber and the Basin title, in a kind of nutshell, to see how she reacted to our situation. I made clear her father had left some unfinished business on the Basin property.

"At first she just listened, nodding in agreement. I explained a little about our proposal on the unfinished deed and how we think it should be recorded so that …how did I put it? 'So that our interests are each protected.' I left it at that.

"By that point, Kora seemed perplexed, so I stopped. I said you'd be glad to explain further, that you had your own ideas on the situation. She was hard to read. Elusive, I would say."

Keene now looked at me for a reaction, but I was not prepared to give it just yet. It seemed that business was pressing in on personal matters.

"She wants to meet you tomorrow to talk. And she specified that she wants to meet here, Jack. First thing in the morning."

Still I said nothing, unable to put my thoughts into a coherent response.

Father finally said, "Okay, Jack, perhaps later. Let's go enjoy a good meal—we'll sit and talk with Duryea. Always good advice in case of doubt." As we moved toward Duryea's attractive table, he added, "But one of us must now share with Kora the letter her father wrote, giving me the escrow instructions on the basin deed, and my decision and duty to honor it. I suggest it be you, Jack. You show it to her and get her understanding, if you can."

We moved to the dining table where so many happy times had been shared. But my gut was telling me that, once again, events beyond my control were about to determine my fate.

During dinner I kept up small talk with Father and Duryea, but racing through my mind were many questions about Kora. Was she attempting to drive a wedge between Father and me? I wondered if our relationship would be destroyed by disagreement over the Basin, and if Father's pointed talk with her had been the wrong tactic. I couldn't help wondering if things would ever be right between Kora and me.

After dinner, I went to my room, ready to collapse. Undressing, I saw in the mirror the imprint on my chest of a bear cub paw. I turned off the light and got into bed. Lying there in the dark I retraced my steps from Albany to the bear hunt in the woods, to my discussions with Father over the last two days. It had been a week to remember.

Sleep came slowly, and when it did come, it brought fitful dreams of Kora, and in each dream she was angry.

I awoke with a start, the notion of Kora as co-owner of the Basin interrupting my sleep. The thought didn't sit well at all with me. Pushing aside the shade beside my bed, I saw that it was already dawn, the early first light in the eastern sky muted by clouds and a mist hanging in the cool air. Distant thunder rolled across the Basin, portending, perhaps, the day ahead of me.

A sudden rap at the open front door startled me from my bed. I threw on clothes as fast as I could and hurried down the stairs toward the impatient and persistent rapping.

There stood Kora in a full-length rain slicker, looking stern. It had been over a year since I'd last seen her, and I greeted her as best I could.

"Come in, Kora, come in! I didn't realize you meant this early, and I'm not quite ready. Would you like coffee?" She made no response. "How are you?" I pushed on. "It's so good to see you!"

Duryea had obviously got up before me. I smelled coffee brewing in the summer kitchen, but he was nowhere to be seen. I swore the man had a sixth sense.

Kora had come in the door, but she had not removed her slicker. "Black coffee," she said. "I awoke at three this morning, thinking of my talk yesterday with your father."

I went to the wood stove and poured two cups of strong coffee, handed Kora one and motioned for her to sit at the dining table, where I unfurled some papers I wanted to show her, including the Colvin maps of the Basin area. Kora did not accept my invitation to sit, but gulped coffee, looking intently at me. Not a good start, I thought.

Kora looked older now — still beautiful, but something was indefinably different. As I moved closer to offer to take her slicker, I thought I smelled alcohol emanating from her, though she didn't appear to be intoxicated. She seemed aware of my surmise as I studied her, and abruptly brought me back to the present moment.

"Yes, Jack, I did drink myself to sleep last night, and no, I do not have a drinking problem. Let me come right to the point. Your father told me about the property, this Basin land, which my father died owning. I deeply resent the fact that Keene Durant never came out and told me all this before yesterday. Your father's suggestion — that this deed he holds should now be recorded — is an outrage, Jack. Who does he think he is — for that matter, who do you think you are? This wilderness belonged to my father and I'm his sole heir. Do you both take me for a fool? I'm the owner of this property. My father told me as a young girl that I would one day own it. And you! You can never tell me different, lawyer-friend! I'm quite prepared to stand up to both of you."

Kora stopped for a moment, seemingly in full control of herself, and I awaited her next volley, knowing she did not want to hear from me just yet. So much, I thought, for Keene's entrée into uncharted territory, and for telling Kora of our plan to record the escrow deed in both our names as a resolution to the dilemma.

It was all out on the table, now, and Kora was making the long-awaited response to Father's letter. My only hope now was to establish trust with her, to convince her that our plan would work for our mutual interests. I'd do any fence-mending needed, if possible. But Kora didn't have fence-mending on her mind this morning.

"Yesterday, I consulted a lawyer about this situation. He was surprised by your father's conduct, to say the least.

He advised me that, as my father's sole heir, I'm entitled to this deed. Furthermore, he could sue Keene Durant and you in court to order delivery of the deed to me. So don't think for a moment that I don't know what I'm talking about. I'm so upset by this turn of events, I almost don't care what you have to say, Jack. I never thought this would come to pass, putting us at odds like this over what we both love. It's upsetting and disgusting to me, and I'm offended. I am so hurt…very hurt by this!"

Kora's voice dropped to a low whisper. Her body seemed to grow limp. Placing the cup of coffee on the table with a deliberate motion, she sat down.

I began, slowly at first, explaining things to Kora, especially about her father's instructions that Keene should hold the deed. Keene hadn't shown Kora her father's letter of instructions. It was time, I decided, and I held it in my hand for emphasis.

"Kora, have you seen this? It's in your father's hand—a letter to Keene Durant written the day he died. It forms the basis for everything my father has done. You and I were both young then, Kora, too young to understand your father and his life — what had happened to him to change his thinking on wilderness, for example. He didn't die a wealthy man, but he was free from debt by then, and this land was his main asset, other than what you received from his estate."

I could see Kora staring at the letter in my hand with great curiosity. It might be the one thing to give her pause in bringing legal action against Father or me. But my next disclosure would not be easy on her.

"Kora, look at this letter. It does not mention you."

I firmly placed the letter in front of her on the table, keeping my fingers on its edge. Her eyes worked the single page quickly, after which I again picked it up and held it.

"As you see, this letter states your father's desire to have the land preserved and it says that he would decide, consistent with that, who would get the land. Of course, he didn't decide, but his intention was plainly that the land be preserved, especially once it was made clear in 1894 that the Adirondacks would stay forever wild under the state constitution. Your father designated my father to complete the deed."

Kora seemed to be crediting my words, but I could not be sure.

"Once you became an adult, my father advised you to talk to him, but you didn't respond until yesterday. He didn't have a fair opportunity to explain everything, but he wants me to do so today, and he wants me to show you this letter. I've intended for some time to review it with you, but you've been gone — and I had no idea you'd return just now.

"So now is the time, Kora. And we have to be realistic. Father and I know you have an important … the most important stake in the Basin lands and camp. But over the last years my father has paid thousands of dollars in taxes on the Basin property. Many years ago the camp was built by Duryea, and I have lived here my entire life. So we have a great deal at stake here, too. But do you really think that Keene or I would treat you unfairly? We know you love this place as much as we do!"

Kora didn't say anything, but I could see in her eyes that she didn't really think we would try to cheat her.

"Now I must be direct and specific with you, Kora. Father and I believe that this property should be deeded to you and to me as equal owners. That way we'll have equal say in what happens to it. And together we should have the resources to pay the taxes and keep the place in good shape. We won't sell the Basin or any part of it. We shall remain true to your father's wishes."

I knew by the receptive look in her eyes that I'd had caught Kora's interest. I sensed that this might be my best chance to strike an agreement with her.

"Any court reviewing this would impress restrictions upon the land, Kora, and would tie your hands. Father's and my plan ends any need for court supervision. But it's only together that we can make this work I know it's true, Kora — that we can make my proposal work. Don't you agree?"

I got her answer abruptly. She rose from her chair.

"I've heard quite enough, Jack. You shall hear from my lawyer, you and your father. I'm leaving this place today, but I intend to return here as the owner, Jack, the sole rightful owner of these lands — now that you've explained so eloquently why I'm the owner, restrictions or not! Furthermore, my father, and later my mother, both stated that I should inherit this land. It was their wish."

She hadn't heard me out, hadn't understood. And now it seemed too late to say more. I stood to see her out. Her face was ashen, though blotched from crying. She walked toward the door.

"Do not leave now, Kora!" Father's voice filled the room and reverberated through the large open camp.

"Kora Longfellow, I could not help but hear this conversation. You're not understanding the reasonable compromise that's being offered! I beg you simply to understand my position. Please hear me out, before you leave this camp and the lands that may well divide us."

Keene moved in from the dim light of the next room, giving form to his voice. Thunder rolled softly in the distance; then an eerie silence commanded the room. Keene stepped forward directly toward Kora, who turned to face him. She was standing between father and me.

"Kora, I will not surrender that deed to you. It was not your father's wish. It would not be fair to the Durant family. Those considerations, especially his mandate to leave the Basin as wilderness, are paramount, Kora. If a court has to decide this, so be it. Go home and think about our words and our proposal. It's fair to you and to Jack. We're offering a plan that will establish things in a way we each can learn to live with. You do hear me, don't you, Kora?"

Kora's piercing dark eyes turned first to me, filled with hurt, and then shot back toward father. He would later tell me that she'd given him a look filled with disdain, even hate, in her strained and taut features.

She turned and raced through the door into the closing storm. I felt a freshening current of wind and moved toward the now open door to look for Kora. Her figure had already vanished into the mist, fog, and thunderstorm that now had moved in to the Basin with a vengeance.

It was the last time I was to see Kora until 1918. She wrote to me sporadically, which I chose to mean that she still cared for me, and she continued to share with me what literature she was reading, what she was doing and thinking. But missing were her innermost thoughts from her diary. She shared much of her mind, but none of her heart. And she made no further reference to the Basin lands and our conflict over them.

I remained certain that I still loved her and wanted her to be my life's mate, and I told her so in my letters. I started my own journal and made frequent entries in it about how I was feeling about things in general and Kora in particular. Having collected my thoughts, I then reminded her of the things we'd shared through our love of the wilderness and good literature; of our voyage when we were 19 into the country beyond the Basin and her rescue by Dunning; our sharing of love in the high ferns along

Otter Creek, and my admiration for her courage, beauty and intelligence. Expressing my love helped to console my spirits. But I held on to the letter for two weeks before finally posting it, knowing it had to be shared.

It was the summer of 1910. We hunkered down in our North Country hideaway not knowing what Kora would do next, or if we would find ourselves answering a court summons demanding her ownership and possession of the Basin. The world was an angry place, according to the news, which reported one country, then another, bickering and blustering. Talk of war was all around.

Kora's mood fit the world's. She was at war. For the first time I feared that she might do something she would come to regret, something that would render our relationship over and gone, beyond our control, and impossible to repair.

Fifteen
The Ruling

A heavy heart did not make my work easy. Kora was gone. The deed to the Basin had not been settled, and was the cause of a rift between us. Unexpectedly, it even threatened to cause a rift between Father and me. We talked less frequently, and the reason was my hurt and tattered heart and soul, which in low moments I blamed on his failure to come to an understanding with Kora. And yet I knew I was just as much to blame and that we would have to work it out somehow.

Part of me even agreed that Kora had her point — she was her father's rightful heir under the law — and she was entitled to the deed. Yet, Father had a point, too: it was his obligation to carry out William West Longfellow's intent to protect the wilderness. And the Durant family also had an interest to protect. I now comprehended the stake of each party in a fuller way, and knew that no simple answers were likely to appear.

As I prepared for the Aber trial, my review reminded me that we had not clearly explained to Kora the title problems facing the Basin. The Aber case was being talked about publicly, so it was likely that Kora, or a lawyer acting on her behalf, was aware of it and was awaiting its result to clarify Kora's position. Judge Heath's decision in the Aber case on my use of the Colvin survey maps, and the notations made by Colvin about the boundary, would no doubt be carefully noted by another attorney.

Our office was one of the first in the region to have telephones installed. Each day Father and I, along with Elaine, watched the mail and waited for a call, bringing word from a lawyer retained by Kora.

But months went by and still nothing came in. We didn't even know Kora's exact address, beyond our assumption that she'd returned to New York, perhaps to live with her mother. Fortunately, we didn't have a great deal of extra time to spend worrying about her, given the crush of events and trial preparation, including our compliance with the judge's ruling on my evidence.

Judge Heath had crafted a long-awaited decision and order that left me an opportunity, with a foundation witness, to win the day. The order was carefully worded at the request of the state's lawyer, the savvy Mr. Hamilton, after I disclosed the maps as evidence and my intention to use them at trial.

Both we and the state had submitted written papers making our best case on the arcane law of evidence on this point. Heath had duly considered the matter and, after months of deliberation, issued his decision, and signed an order that my map was not admissible. But the prior map, the one Colvin had filed with his report to the state legislature, was admissible. And that was the very map that, in my opinion, had incorrectly and prematurely determined the boundary.

The last line of the decretal paragraph in the court's order was perhaps my salvation: it allowed me to produce a witness who had been present when Colvin spoke and wrote on the second map, the one of Unnamed Mountain, which I found in Kelly's Albany office. I felt certain that that evidence could seal the victory. Both sides conceded, and the court agreed, that Colvin was in poor health and incompetent to take the stand as a witness.

The words in the order, "The court shall not foreclose admitting the Colvin map with proper foundation testimony from a witness," did not go unnoticed. The production of Moises Rondeau — official Adirondack hermit, shadow of, and thorn-in-the-side to Trembley — as the foundation witness took on added significance. If he had seen Colvin make notations on the map, and had contemporaneously heard him declare where the boundary to the state land was located, I had every confidence we could win the case. But the court's trial ruling would determine the outcome on this specific issue, and perhaps also be determinative on the outcome of the case. Neither side could feel smug going in to the trial.

That testimony, together with the proof that might be forthcoming from Rondeau about the deed delivery to Pacquette in the woods on February 26, 1883, would be enough to convince the jury on the ultimate issue of ownership. We had the deed from Pacquette's niece, which was now recorded, paving the way for Aber to now show that his title was valid, too. Could we close the chain of evidence and show that Colvin had changed his mind after realizing his mistake? Would I also have to produce the unwilling and hostile Trembley by "soopeena," to win my case?

If I could get Rondeau on board and properly prepared as a witness, despite his hermit-like qualities, I could do without Trembley.

Rondeau was known to live in a lodge pole dwelling he'd constructed on the Basin lands, where he weathered out long winters in a remote area of Cold River that few had visited. I found him there by following Father and Duryea's directions. I'd packed my fly rod, and stopped along the way in a glade apt to produce a nice stringer of brookies, some of which were intended as booty for Rondeau.

"Yes," he said when I found him at his camp, "the past winter was quiet, as I prefer, and now we have spring!" He looked up at me without fanfare, even though I may have been the first person he had seen the entire year of 1911.

He thanked me for the stringer of gutted-out trout, which brought a grin to his face. The man really was not a fullfledged hermit, I'd decided, as he enjoyed occasional aspects of society too much.

"*Merci, Monsieur. Oui,* I know your guide, Trembley, who I often accompany in the woods, you know — just behind, just around—when he has the sports here. I make sure all is okay in the woods, you know? Trembley does not like that I do this, but that is his worry. My worry is the wilderness.

"And I remember your Colvin. He pay me to work. *Mon Dieu,* we knock over high trees just so his sextant, theodolite, and compass can shoot his course on the land he survey." Rondeau spoke in his mix of language and accent, which varied, depending on his mood.

He was conversing with me as if he was accustomed to social intercourse, which I found strange. It occurred to me that the man had something up his sleeve. As I explained the trial strategy in as few words as possible, Rondeau nodded frequently, appearing to understand the situation as I presented it.

"Yes," he said when I was done. "I might come to court. "I shall testify for you if things are right." He spoke in a tone that had changed in intensity.

"Things should be right," I said.

"Yes," Rondeau shot back. "Things should be right for me and for you. Right for me that I should stay here, eh? For if these lands are not state lands, then they are yours, or the Abers', eh!"

He had correctly sized up his squatter status on the land, which he knew to be a losing proposition should the state prevail in its action. He seemed to feel that now he was dealing from strength and could better his standing.

"I need your help, *Monsieur, eh bien.* I live out my life here. I am not young, but I live out my life here, you understand?"

"Yes, I understand." I still felt a little wary of this cunning hermit. A small grin crossed a corner of his mouth as I proceeded.

"But you must tell me: do you remember Pacquette coming to see Colvin to get his deed?"

"Perhaps I do," he said cautiously. "I was there with Colvin in the woods and … a man came to see him and, yes, he hand him something. Yes, it might have been a deed from Albany or someplace, a deed from who, I am not sure. Colvin, he say something to the man about this. And so…."

"Rondeau, did Pacquette take his deed?"

"Pacquette took the deed, Monsieur Jack. And now where is my deed for my land here, where I have lived for so many years?"

Rondeau's expression wasn't one of great hope, as if he knew my answer would be a counter to his opener, that I would call his bluff in our little poker game. But I was ready to cut my deal, one that would recognize his continued possession of the Rondeau homestead.

"Rondeau, I'm not able to give you a deed. But I am able to give you my word. As you say, you want to live out your days here in the woods on the bank of this river. I will honor your wish and will insist on this outcome with any others who may have a say. This is my pledge to you, Rondeau, for this place you call home."

He didn't answer. There was only silence. Smoke from his little stove rose from his lodge pole, making a small hiss in the tiny room where we sat. Rondeau, cross-legged on the floor, his beard gray and shaggy, was a survivor, a small, spry but aging man of the wilderness who understood how to live alone in this forest and mountains, and took it as his right to go on living here, knowing he could not live with others. He was too cantankerous, too independent for that, a quality of the north woodsman, to be sure.

Occasionally, even the most hardpan of us could be got to, of course; soft hearts beat beneath the veneer. Take Rondeau, I thought, as I studied the figure in front of me. He was known to come to town to socialize in his limited way, and to share his thoughts at the local hotel and roadhouse on those visits. He could, on those occasions, be found in a corner of the tavern holding forth with a crony or two, adding a certain local flavor, making commentary about those around him or in the news and philosophizing until the alcohol numbed him and the bartender carried him upstairs for the night. He always shunned the sports, even castigated them, especially in front of Trembley, irritating Trembley when he met sports there at the bar before heading in to the woods with them.

Despite castigating the sports, he sometimes followed quietly behind them, acting as a kind of rearward scout for Trembley under some sort of understanding the two men had come to on a barstool some years before. It was an agreement Trembley had been heard to say he regretted, but one that Rondeau, for reasons not fully understood, would never give up.

It wasn't uncommon for Trembley, at his end of the bar, to pick on Rondeau's donkey, Zeke. Zeke, Rondeau's beast of burden for getting provisions to his camp, had become one of Rondeau's fondest possessions, even a friend to the hermit. He did not take kindly to Trembley's insults, such as his frequent insistence that, "I could carry more into the woods than that old jackass you have outside."

This always resulted in sharp exchanges between the two, and, eagerly anticipated by the onlookers, sometimes physical threats and blows between them. Rondeau had made out a criminal complaint against Trembley after one roust in the bar, and Trembley was "soo-peeneed" to court. A conviction and criminal record resulted, and the two didn't speak to one another for years.

Eventually, after Rondeau had been in town for a week or two, there would be the inevitable confrontation, and often fisticuffs, with friend or foe. Finally, tired of "socializing," he'd returned to the woods and not be seen again for many months.

Rondeau was a patchwork of local pride and prejudice, like all of us. I was counting on his knowing that when I asked my next question. In bargaining with the hermit, I wanted to be sure I cut a deal that was fair to me, too.

"Rondeau, did Colvin and Trembley talk about the boundary for the state land that Colvin was surveying? Look at this map? Look at what was written?" I pointed to the words about sharing boundary with Longfellow.

Appearing perplexed, he answered, "I do not read well, *eh bien*. I do not know what this says."

My throat tightened and I felt warm and flushed in the face

"Did Colvin tell Trembley that the land he surveyed for the state shared a boundary with Longfellow?"

Rondeau looked me straight in the eye, sensing that his answer would be important to me. His eyes twinkled. "Ah, *oui*, yes."

He paused a moment, then continued, buoyed I am sure by the relief in my face. "Colvin and Trembley try to find state boundary as we go down the east boundary of your land, the land of Longfellow, that is what Colvin say. They can't find it on your land, Durant. They go to hunting path and trace out five miles to mountain top, to mountain we call DeBar."

And then, with perfect timing, Rondeau pointed to my map, which he was ready to interpret. His finger went to the boundary running from DeBar Mountain to the hunting path.

"And there," he said pointing to the marginal note in Colvin's hand, "Colvin call me over and he say, 'This solves the riddle, Rondeau', and he write those words on the side of his map and say, 'Longfellow boundary the one we want,' to me and to Trembley."

I pointed to the words. "Here, Rondeau, these words right here? These are the words Colvin wrote when he said that Longfellow's boundary is shared with the state?"

"Yes, those words he write there on his map. Those words."

"Rondeau," I replied, "you have my word. You may stay here as long as you like. But understand me well, Rondeau, your testimony is required, and the trial for Mr. Aber is coming soon."

I pulled from my pocket a subpoena, which I'd prepared for the occasion, and handed it to him.

"I'll get back to you soon about the date for your testimony. Plan to be at court on May 15th, the first day of the trial term. And enjoy the brookies!"

Rondeau looked uneasy. He had a final question.

"Mr. Durant, Trembley, he is not a witness in your trial is he?"

"No," I said, "it's up to you, Rondeau. I'll see you on the 15th."

The Aber trial date would be set at a May 1st calendar call conducted by Judge Heath. A calendar call to set a date for a jury trial in a civil case was a rarity in these parts. I guessed that Judge Heath had carefully followed the case and wanted to move his calendar, and this case in particular. Ours could be the first case of the spring.

"Are you ready to try the case, counselors?" he asked. "Well, be ready, for yours is first and I'm setting the date for the opening of the term on the 15th."

It seemed that word about the upcoming trial rapidly spread. Bill McGrath's interest in the case, apparent from his almost daily reporting on it for the paper, put more pressure on us to win. He published an editorial, writing that the outcome of the case would be important for our area and for any number of our citizens, and that we all should closely follow it.

I was becoming convinced that Judge Heath's in-court ruling on the admissibility of my Colvin map was likely to determine the case. Hamilton and I both knew that Colvin was no longer a competent witness, and that the state had won a tactical victory in Heath's pretrial ruling on the evidence. We both also knew that the foundation testimony of any witness I might call would be subjected to excruciating scrutiny. But if a jury of North Country peers were to see the Colvin map, I was certain it would be seen as overwhelming proof of our case and tilt things in our favor.

Word came to me secondhand that the state had sent an investigator into the woods to find Rondeau or Trembley or both. I'd assumed that both men's assistance to Colvin would come to the attention of Joseph Hamilton, who left no stone unturned in his trial preparations. So I wasn't surprised. But I didn't know the results of that foray and I was uneasy.

The day set for trial, the 15th, was upon me. Father had decided, despite his earlier assertion that it was his case, that I was ready to try the case. Even so, his pre-trial preparation with me had been intense and arduous.

Sitting across from one another at the law library table, we went over the order of our witnesses: Mr. Aber would likely be first, followed by Rondeau, and finally, if we had to, Doc Wellsprings on his memory that Abers farmed their land for a long time, well before the key 1883 date we had to comply with. We had our subpoenas served, and a trial brief on all points of law and evidence was served on Hamilton and furnished to the court. Trial preparation was subject to change however, and Keene and I knew the order of our witnesses could readily change. We advised the Abers and Rondeau of this fact, not relying on the mail, but sending messengers in to find and inform both of them.

Wellsprings was so upset upon service of the subpoena that he refused to communicate with me, other than a note received in the mail saying that the inconvenience would greatly diminish his spring sales, and he fully intended to set up his loaded buckboard wagon of goods outside the court each and every day of trial. He added that he did remember the Abers farming their parcel "for many years. They still owe me for an implement they bought but never paid in full." So much for a good impression for our case and the Abers' integrity.

True to his word, on the opening day of trial, there in the courthouse square, bright and early and surrounded by the buying public, sat Doc Wellsprings on his wagon of goods. He seemed to be doing a brisk pretrial business, advertising loudly to one and all "a special on all my brooms, and a very special sale price for all my medicinal sacroiliac syrups, from Sam Wellsprings and my staff of seven sons!" A high-pitched whistle accompanied each 's' sound escaping the gap in his dentures. Well, he'd provide entertainment value, if nothing else, I thought, feeling a wince of anxiety for the way the case was stacking up.

Nevertheless, I was ready in every aspect, save for real trial experience and savvy. Hamilton and I quickly but carefully picked a jury of six men, all from the area, all known to me, and all with views I believed would give us a fair hearing. Hamilton didn't show any uneasiness as the court clerk swore in the sixth man, but in my gut I knew I had the jury we wanted. Surely Hamilton was too smart not to sense this, and to know his case would be that much more challenging.

Mr. and Mrs. Aber looked terrified, sitting at the counsel table in the majestic courtroom, with its high ceiling and brass casting of the lady of justice prominently displayed just to the right of the bench. I know that Hamilton sensed their distress in this formal setting. Alone, their humble, scared selves wouldn't be enough to carry the day, and Hamilton and I both knew it.

The state was the plaintiff and so had to open. The burden was upon it to prove its case by a preponderance of evidence. Hamilton's case went in flawlessly. A state surveyor who had succeeded Colvin, a Mr. Andrews, testified clearly about Macomb's Purchase and about the state's, the Abers', and Longfellow's chains of title. He described where the boundary was, using the Colvin map that I felt was erroneous. His testimony, while credible on its face, didn't address the later and more accurate Colvin survey I had as evidence.

I decided not to vigorously challenge Andrew's position, preferring to let his credibility be put at issue if and when I could put in evidence the later Colvin map with its marginal notation. It was a calculated strategy, but one Keene and I adopted after deciding we would get in to evidence our Colvin map through Rondeau. And if Judge Heath ruled against us, we would have grounds for a successful appeal.

Even so, the state's case looked unassailable. Hamilton had got in to evidence everything that he wanted, all the relevant deeds, the Macomb Patent, and most importantly, the early Colvin map. Taken in a vacuum, his evidence led to only one conclusion: that the Abers did not get good title from Pacquette, since the latter had no title, and the state had sole title. Even our friendly jury of Adirondack citizens looked unhappily convinced, shifting uneasily in their seats in the box. They would be hard put to find against the state unless we had a knockout punch to throw.

Hamilton seemed to gloat as he finished his lengthy direct examination of his witness with the ultimate question.

"Mr. Andrews," he asked of his man, "Do you have an opinion to a reasonable degree of certainty, based on the deeds and map in evidence you identified, who owns the Aber parcel?"

"Yes, I do. The State of New York owns the Aber parcel, as well as other parcels around it. The Abers acquired no title from Pacquette."

Silence filled the courtroom. The surveyor's words seemed to amplify and resonate in the cavernous space, and were made all the more dramatic by Hamilton's pause, followed by the rehearsed but convincing look of satisfaction he directed at the jurors. Finally he turned to me in a smug manner, flashed his victory smile, and extended his hand toward his witness, now subject to my cross-examination.

"Your witness, Mr. Durant."

A murmur went through the courtroom when I stood, trying my best to sound nonchalant and said, "No questions of this witness, your Honor."

Hamilton, still on his feet, now even more self-righteous, confidently announced, "Your Honor and gentlemen of the jury, I rest my case."

I had to seize the moment, take momentum away from Hamilton. I spoke immediately, in a clear, even tone.

"Your Honor, gentlemen of the jury, I call my first witness, Moises Rondeau."

Hamilton's face changed from smug to surprise and then concern. He didn't know what Rondeau would say, for Rondeau, as it turned out, had refused to talk to the state investigator who visited him in the woods. Rondeau had ordered him off the land. Hamilton no doubt knew his testimony was important, that it must bear upon the map he knew I would offer.

My witness was escorted into the courtroom by the bailiff. As he walked in, I detected a titter from the spectators, and so did Judge Heath.

"I will have silence and order in the courtroom!"

Total silence followed as the small, wiry man walked

slowly to the bench, appearing old, his shaggy white-streaked beard, high forehead, and long grey hair aging him even more. He wore his old and tattered wool tweed suit, string tie and faded white shirt, an indication of the importance of the occasion and his respect for the court proceeding and his peers. He was sworn in by the court clerk and the judge told him to take his seat in the witness box, next to but below him, and only a few feet from the jurors. The old man looked uneasy, but nodded to the jurors as a group as he took his seat. Several jurors returned the nod. I wanted to put Rondeau at ease for his testimony and get him started so that we could establish a good, confident-sounding pace.

But Hamilton had other ideas, interrupting my attempted start.

"Your Honor," he said, "the purpose for calling an unknown witness, please. I believe I am entitled, especially since it's the first witness and the defense has not provided his identity or its reason for calling Mr.... Rondeau, did he say? May we approach the bench?"

Heath waved us forward for a sidebar conference out of the jury's hearing. Hamilton's tactic was to delay and rattle my witness, and perhaps even prevent him from testifying. I had to think quickly.

"Judge," I said, "Mr. Rondeau is prepared to testify that while employed by Verplanck Colvin, Mr. Colvin uttered in his presence, at the site of the boundary in question in February of 1883, that the Longfellow tract, which shares a boundary and the same title as the Aber parcel in issue, shared a boundary with the state land—that in fact that boundary for the state land was some miles removed, near the location of DeBar Mountain. And further, that Colvin noted his conclusion in the margin of a later map, which

I intend to offer after I establish the foundation for its admissibility, just as stated in your pretrial order."

I'd spoken as clearly and yet succinctly as I could, summarizing what Rondeau would testify to. Heath had listened intently, and with great interest.

"Mr. Hamilton," Heath said, "I have held that the map by itself without explanatory foundation testimony is inadmissible. It appears that counsel is offering that foundation testimony What do you have to say?"

"It's preposterous, Your Honor, that counsel—"

Heath sharply interrupted. "If Mr. Rondeau's testimony is admissible, Mr. Hamilton, the map also comes in for the jury to see, notation and all!"

Hamilton could not restrain a visible gulp.

"This is hearsay of the first order — and unreliable testimony that is not competent to prove counsel's point. It is not the best evidence! The filed map already admitted is the best evidence. This map was never filed with the state! This entire line of testimony and evidence should be kept out!"

We were coming to Heath's in-court ruling, and we both knew it.

"Proceed with the testimony, Mr. Durant. Mr. Hamilton, you may state your exception on the record at the appropriate time."

I turned back to the lectern, buoyed by the go-ahead from the court. But the real test still lay ahead. As I passed by Rondeau sitting in the witness chair we made eye contact, and I saw that he understood what had just transpired. He'd heard the colloquy at the bench. Our turn had come.

"Good morning, Mr. Rondeau," I said.

Rondeau nodded but did not answer, turning his

body in his chair, tense but ready. We quickly established who he was and where he lived. We identified Colvin and the fact that Rondeau had been hired by him as a guide for the 1883 surveying expedition. All this established my reasons for calling him to testify. I noticed that Rondeau spoke in his better English, something he did to show the court that he could speak with some command, if he wanted to.

I moved to the heart of what Rondeau had seen and heard.

"Sir, were you present in the woods in this county, working for Colvin on February 26, 1883, near Baldface Mountain, formerly called Unnamed Mountain?"

"I was there, Mr. Durant. We started there, at Baldface. Back then it was called Unnamed Mountain, and I remember it—all of it."

"Did you see Colvin holding a map in his hands?"

Behind me, Hamilton rose from his chair loudly and with a great flurry. "Objection, Your Honor! In light of the court's prior written ruling, this is improper and inadmissible. The question, indeed the entire subject matter, should not be allowed. I object in the strongest terms!"

"You may have your objection. Proceed, Mr. Durant, with your question."

Proceed I did.

"Mr. Rondeau, please answer the question. Did you see Colvin holding a map?"

"Yes sir, Colvin was holding a map. I clearly remember the map and what he said."

"On that day, what were you doing for Mr. Colvin in the line of your duties?"

"I was working on his survey party to find a boundary there."

I asked him for a description of the boundary. He didn't need prompting, but proceeded to tell his story and I let him have his head. Father had taught me that occasionally, with an eager but good witness, the emotion and stress of the moment takes over, and that was happening now. I recognized it for what it was and made the call to let him continue, despite the danger of a runaway witness over whom I could lose control.

Judge and jury leaned forward in their seats, concentrating on the old hermit, curious to hear his words. It was early in the trial, yet we were going for the jugular.

"I was hired in the woods by Colvin himself the day before I saw him with his map," Rondeau explained. "He said he was surveying state land and needed help, and did I want to help him? I said yes, for pay of course. We agreed. I would be paid to run the lines, clear his courses with the other men, so he could shoot his sextant.

"We were near DeBar Mountain. Colvin worked that day and talked to me as he did his lines, and to another man he'd hired, Trembley. Our reason for being there was to find the state's westerly boundary in a large state-owned piece of land.

"We hadn't found what Colvin was looking for on the unnamed mountain, the one we now call Baldface, a few miles away on the old hunting path, so we'd moved to DeBar. After much work to get there, I helped Colvin set up his sextant to shoot a course at DeBar. We were next to a brook and on a path. I saw Colvin make a line and write something on a map he worked from."

That was far enough. I held up my hand to get Rondeau's attention and quickly moved to counsel's table, where the Abers sat. With a flourish, I grasped in both hands a large rolled up map. As I unfurled it, I caught sight of Father sitting in the front row and looking calm, which I took as a good sign.

All eyes were now on me. Such intense attention was unmatched by anything I'd ever experienced.

"Showing you this map, marked as defendant's exhibit one, Mr. Rondeau, can you identify it for the record?"

"That's the map Colvin worked from that day. I was standing next to him on the path as he held it and studied it. Colvin said he was satis—"

"Objection, your Honor. May I be heard outside the presence of the jury?" shot Hamilton in a thunderous tone, cutting off Rondeau. I assumed that the seasoned trial lawyer now sensed what the witness was ready to say.

Heath agreed, and asked that the jury be shown out of the courtroom. Hamilton remained on his feet.

"There has been no foundation for this line of questioning," he began the moment the last of jurist had filed out the door, "and no proper identification or authentication of this map or anything on the map. This line of questioning should cease and it should be stricken from the record. I cannot call Mr. Colvin as a witness, as you know, and to attribute words to Colvin is placing the state at a great disadvantage. The state's case is greatly prejudiced by this testimony."

Judge Heath looked to me for a response.

"You have ruled, and we agree, that Colvin isn't competent now to testify. This map is his final product and was made after the date of the state's survey, already in evidence. Obviously it's on point to the issue of the Aber-Longfellow boundary. Along with the map already in evidence as part of the state's case, this map's greater details will assist the jury in its deliberation. And finally, it offers some proof that the Aber and Longfellow boundary is shared with the state, as Colvin wrote in his marginal note — and as this witness was about to testify. Even Mr.

Hamilton cannot deny its authenticity and materiality. I ask for the court to proceed with this testimony."

"Counsel, your map, exhibit one, can be identified by this witness and he can testify to his knowledge up to a point that I will have to identify as you proceed. Let us see where this takes us. Bailiff, send the jury back to the courtroom. Your objection is overruled for now, Mr. Hamilton."

When the jury was seated again, I continued. I held the same large, rolled map, and each juror's eyes focused on it as I again unfurled it and approached my witness. My voice gained strength and confidence.

"Mr. Rondeau, is defendant's exhibit one that I now show you the map that you testify Colvin had on the trail of February 26, 1883?"

Rondeau examined the map, which was held in front of him..

"Yes, Mr. Durant, it is and that is what Colvin wrote on his map as I stood there on the trail with him and Trembley." Rondeau pointed with his free hand to the marginal note.

"Right here, sir," I pointed to the note, "where it says 'Longfellow boundary shared with state'?"

"Yes, that's what he wrote as he talked, as he said those words. And he put the date here, February 26, 1883."

I'd set up the response from my witness, I realized, even though he could not read well. But he'd seen those words written and had given a truthful response: that he'd heard Colvin utter the words at the same moment he'd written them on the map. It was admissible evidence, I felt. The judge now had squarely before him a final evidentiary ruling to make.

"Your Honor, I move exhibit one be received in evidence. This is evidence from a man hired by the state's surveyor, and it should be before this jury. I request that it be shown to the jury now."

Hamilton was on his feet. "I renew my objection. This map should not be received in evidence for reasons I have stated on the record." But the tone of his voice suggested he anticipated the court's response.

"Exhibit one is admitted in evidence. Bailiff, pass it among the jurors for their review."

The court was silent; all eyes studied the reaction of the jurors as they looked at the map and then at Colvin's marginal note. Each jurist nodded in the affirmative as he turned to the next juror, nodded at him, and passed the map on, all the way through to juror six. The process took several minutes, and I noticed that Hamilton studied the reaction of each juror and made notes on his pad. He was hard to read and I didn't know what he was thinking.

"Your Honor, I have one final question for this witness," I said, and the judge nodded for me to proceed.

I carefully placed the map into the hands of the court clerk.

"Mr. Rondeau, did another person appear just as you were on the hunting path near DeBar that day in February 1883?"

"Yes, Monsieur," Rondeau said. The excitement in his voice told me he sensed that the momentum was going in our favor.

"Mr. Pacquette. Colvin handed him a paper and said, 'Here, Paquette, your name is on this deed.' That's all he say, nothing more. This was near the land where Abers lived, even then."

"That is quite enough, Monsieur." I spoke in a friendly and composed tone that belied the elation I was feeling. "Thank you. Your witness, Mr. Hamilton." And with that I sat down.

Oddly, Hamilton remained seated, appearing to study the notepad in front of him, or using it for a momentary prop while he thought. Then he rose slowly, paused, and looked around the courtroom for a moment, still deep in thought but with a blank quality to his distinguished features. Finally, he spoke.

"Your Honor, may the state please have a short recess before proceeding with cross-examination?"

"Court will stand in recess for 15 minutes. Bailiff, show the jury out. His gavel came down with a sonorous ring on the wood bench, startling some of the spectators, who'd had sat rapt in attention all morning.

People stood and talked and moved about in animated fashion. There was a jovial and positive feeling in the courtroom that was quite satisfying, considering all Keene and I had worked so hard on for so long.

Once the jury had filed out Hamilton walked over to my side of counsel's table. I was talking to the Abers at the time, explaining how I thought the case was going. I was also watching Rondeau, suddenly surrounded by McGrath and other members of the press, and having all manner of questions thrown at him simultaneously. Hamilton stood over me until I turned my head and saw him.

"Mr. Durant, a word with you in counsel's room, right away," he said, his voice urgent.

He walked out of the courtroom through the side door reserved for attorneys. I excused myself and followed Hamilton into the privacy of an adjoining small counsel's room. He was already seated, studying his notepad, so I sat down across him at the small table.

"Durant, this evidence you've just put might appear to be credible and compelling now, but my cross-examination of Rondeau will make a shambles of his credibility. I'll bring out how he lives out there in the woods, and make clear the personal stake he has in the outcome of this trial. He won't be so smug when I finish with him."

He had my full attention.

"I can perhaps succeed in changing the court's mind about leaving the map in evidence. At the least, I can certainly have an appeal on the evidence ruling by Heath that an appellate court will reverse. Plus I can produce witnesses who will say this map was not the best evidence, is not accurate. I have them ready for my rebuttal. The state can keep this matter in the courts for years and can ultimately prevail."

Hamilton's keen insight on this case was astounding. He'd anticipated Rondeau's testimony and was prepared to press on with his case. And then he casually dropped the name of his rebuttal witness.

"Durant, I am prepared to call the guide, Trembley, who is ready to refute much of what Rondeau has said."

I hoped my shock didn't show on my face.

"Trembley came to us and volunteered to help after he heard his 'old friend,' Rondeau, would take the stand. I have other rebuttal witnesses ready, as well. We'll destroy your case.

"Congratulations on getting your Colvin map into evidence, and the testimony you elicited. But let me suggest to you that it's in your clients' interest, and your interest, to go back into court with me and tell Judge Heath that we agree to discontinue this case. You have my word that you'll never again hear from the state on this boundary, or its claim to ownership. I can lick my wounds and acknowledge that either one of us could win this case."

I wasn't sure where he was going, and so I said nothing.

"But the stipulation cannot state a reason on the substance of the case, or its merits, only that it is with prejudice to bringing this particular claim again. You then can legally preclude future action, and have a strong basis for protecting the same boundary for the great Basin, presumably owned by Longfellow's heirs." The fact that Hamilton avoided my eyes suggested that he was aware of the unresolved title issues regarding the Basin.

I quickly assessed what Hamilton was telling me. The effect would be a win for the Abers. If we made the stipulation Hamilton suggested, it would preclude future action against their parcel, and be a basis for protecting the same boundary for the Great Basin. The latter point Hamilton must have implicitly understood, but it remained unclear whether he knew that the players in the Basin title were Kora, Keene, and me. What was undeniable was Hamilton's concession of the Aber case, and the strong position in which it left any owner of the Basin.

"Durant, what I'm proposing protects your clients, and I hold it open for you until court reconvenes. You should take it and run." Hamilton stood, walked to the window and looked out at the mountain range visible in the distance, his back to me.

I stood to give Hamilton my answer. He turned to face me, looking composed and calm.

"Mr. Hamilton, I agree with much of your analysis and your conclusions about our case. Let me advise my clients to accept this and put it on the record in court with Judge Heath. Today, now!" I said with finality.

It was done. A binding stipulation was made in open court. And with that, in May of 1911, the case ended in a quiet victory. The state had been fended off from a claim to eject the Abers from their land, and it seemed probable that thousands of acres of pristine wilderness had been placed out of its reach.

The Great Basin remained intact for now. The jury looked disappointed as Judge Heath advised them the case had settled, that, as he put it, "the state withdrew its claims in the case with prejudice, and therefore there is nothing for the jury to decide." Heath pounded his gavel with a final resonance and walked from the courtroom, thinking, I later learned, that the jury would have found in the Abers' favor based upon his rulings and Rondeau's testimony. Judge Heath's rulings even today are chewed over by local lawyers wherever they gather to share trial stories. The case became part of Adirondack legal lore.

Keene Durant and I locked eyes at the counsel's table after the stipulation was put on the record. His joy in the outcome was evident as we exchanged greetings, congratulations, and a warm hug. Hamilton offered his congratulations to first Keene and then me, shaking our hands, and then turned and walked from the courtroom.

The Abers, content with the stipulation, went back to a peaceful possession of their small tract. And though they didn't pay us money, they were faithful in their regular deliveries of eggs and hams from their farm.

The townspeople were buzzing with the news as they left amid laughs and slaps to Francis Aber's back. Rondeau was in the group of well-wishers, and he too received congratulations and, later, more than a few drinks at the tavern at the celebration that followed. Doc Wellsprings was rumored to have sold out that day, and he bought round after round for his customers.

Gradually the revelers and well-wishers drifted away to the celebration at the tavern, and after a time I found myself standing alone in the courthouse. Fiddle music, played by traveling minstrels from Quebec, wafted from the tavern across the square. I remained standing in the courthouse, absorbing the day's events and my feelings, which were not celebratory, but melancholy. I missed Kora, and wished she were here to share this moment with me. With the trial over, she instantly moved to the front of my thoughts again.

Walking out of the courtroom, I asked myself again how I could approach her, but I came up with no easy solutions. I wasn't even sure where she was living. Finally I decided I had only one place to start: I would write Janet Longfellow in New York City and ask her to put me in touch with Kora.

I sat on a bench in the square, listing to the music coming from the tavern and the happy voices and loud laughter. I lost track of time, and it was late in the afternoon when I realized I was still in the square in the shade of the giant elm trees, seated at the bench in a kind of trance. Elaine came along and saw me. With a broad grin on her face she said that Keene was planning a celebration at the Basin lodge with a few friends and colleagues that night, that William Kelly would be there, and that I would be the guest of honor. I said I'd be there, and again found myself alone.

I gazed down the village street, slowly emptying, and saw a lone figure standing next to a donkey. It was Rondeau packing up Zeke, already loaded down with every manner of provision. But apparently Rondeau hadn't had his fill of village socializing. He tethered Zeke next to a pail of water and a bucket of oats, then sauntered back to the tavern for more rounds of free drinks and fiddle music, for singing French drinking songs and dancing. Rondeau wore a big grin, perhaps because of pride in his newfound standing as a person who cared about his fellow man after all.

For his part, Zeke seemed to miss the significance of the day. He rested, peed in the dirt road, and snacked on his oats.

George Patte

I heard the crowd singing as one now, the fiddlers going off on a riff as the voices carried the melody:

> *Prend un petit cout c'est doux,*
> *Prend un petit cout c'est doux,*
> *C'est plus que agréable,*
> *Ca rende l'esprit malade,*
> *Prend un petit cout c'est doux.*

Sixteen
Reunited

That night at the Great Basin camp congratulations and toasts were offered all around. Duryea prepared a special dinner for Bill McGrath, William Kelly, Father, and me. Kelly had planned to come up for the trial, but had been late arriving. Nonetheless, he served as our sounding board for our recollections of the trial and settlement. Three lawyers, a newspaper editor, and Duryea made for lively conversation. Our finest wine was broken out of the cellar, a red Bordeaux bottled in 1894 that Father had imported and aged.

"This is a fitting wine to celebrate with," Father said, "since 1894 was the year of the approval of the forever wild provision of the state constitution." He talked about Longfellow, who would have been so pleased with that provision. As Father spoke, I looked out over the magnificent landscape he'd loved so much, and I felt proud of my pledge to protect and keep these lands safe.

"So let us raise our glasses to this place, to the memory of my friend, and to the preservation of this wild landscape." Father gave me a significant glance at the latter part of his toast, which brought quizzical looks from Kelly and McGrath.

Duryea, in typical fashion, moved to the kitchen after a sip of Bordeaux, to check on his cooking. Watching him slip off like that, his humility apparent in his assumption of the role of servant, I thought of our long-ago conversation about his life and mission, and of my promise to him that I would see things through on the Basin.

My thought was interrupted by Keene, who was making another toast, this one, I realized, in my honor.

"And to my son, Jack, a fine lawyer and trusted partner, a treasure to me, and to our good friend, Duryea, and finally, to the French concept of terroir, the precious home soil, which we celebrate tonight.»

For his part, Bill McGrath said he thought justice had been done. He said he would write an editorial about the case and the future of the Adirondacks, along with a proposal for oversight of the entire area within the blue line by some responsible authority.

Bill caught me eye especially as he made his toast. Moments later he found occasion to stand beside me and say, "We must talk about that very thing privately, Jack."

The meal of brook trout, tortiere — a seasoned meat pie of ground pork, onion and diced potato in a fine crust — roasted duck and the buds of fiddlehead ferns served with champagne, was devoured while stories of times past were told and retold by Kelly and Father. But enjoyable as it was, my thoughts kept slipping away to Kora.

After dinner and brandy on the porch with a good cigar, I excused myself and retired to my room upstairs. In time silence came to the great camp and, gathering my thoughts, I sat at my desk and wrote to Janet Longfellow, asking her to deliver the enclosed letter to Kora.

And then I proceeded to compose that letter to Kora. The wine and brandy had induced a euphoric state of mind, one that helped to liberate some of my feelings. The words flowed into my letter, words from my heart to Kora's, words never before written by me. When I'd put down everything I'd wanted to say, I placed the letter in a separate, sealed envelope and tucked that inside the envelope addressed to Janet.

I posted the letter the next day to Janet's New York address. By light of day, reviewing in my mind what I'd written, I hoped I hadn't pushed too hard too fast. I'd told her that we should see each other again, and that the Basin should unite, not divide us. I wrote about the trial in some detail so that she would know that the state's challenge had been defeated, and also to brag a bit about what I'd accomplished. But then I'd concluded my letter to Kora with these words:

> *We should be together, here on the wild lands we have explored since childhood. I love you and need to be with you, to live out my days with you. To make love to you again, as we did in the high ferns along the murmuring brook where nature whispered to us, where God touched us as a man and woman meant to be one, to have a child who would be part of our lives here, as we once were to our parents. These are the longings I now share with you. My love for you, Kora, runs deep and forever. Would you please come home to be with me?*

The date on the letter was May 16, 1911. Janet Longfellow received it May 20 in New York, I later learned. Having read my request, she passed my letter on to Kora a few days later when they met for lunch.

I checked the mail each day for a long time, but nothing came. My life felt on hold.

Finally, a long year later, I received a letter from her, postmarked New York City. Her words held no response to the love I'd expressed for her; there was only a statement about the Basin. She said that, having thought a long time about it, she agreed that title be shared jointly between us. She would send money for taxes as she could. She asked me not to contact her and gave no return address.

Her closing sentence was, "I shall try to contact you, Jack, when I am able to, in the future."

The tone of her letter was profoundly unsettling. Something was wrong. But what? And what did she mean by saying she'd contact me in the future—why couldn't we be in contact now and over the last year? When in the future would she get in touch?

I sat that day in the Basin camp library, alone, the entire afternoon, reading and re-reading the letter and crying. Going for a walk, my pain only grew, shooting through me with each step. My spirit and energy were sapped, and when I returned to camp I was exhausted.

Something told me I'd lost Kora forever, that I would never regain the love and trust that had been between us. And the cause of our failure, for the mistrust that had developed, pitting Kora against Father and me, was the issue of title to, and the future of, the Basin.

I understood that Kora felt edged out by us. She saw Keene's actions as my own, and Father was determined to hold his ground on his duty to William Longfellow and the pact that had been made. I couldn't disagree with him, but I still felt caught in the middle. And I found myself distrusting her offer to share title jointly, sure that in her heart all trust had been lost, and she was just saying that to keep me at bay for a while.

Bitterness overcame me in the ensuing days and weeks. I withdrew into my private thoughts of remorse and grief, not sharing them with Father or Duryea. I ached for things to be different, for the Basin to have united, not divided us.

Time passed slowly. I took to visiting my good-time women-friends more often, traveling to Malone or Plattsburgh or Glens Falls, anything to fight off the loneliness and despair. I discovered that Montreal was a worldly city to enjoy. I drank and caroused, sometimes too much for my own good, not knowing whose bed I would wake up in come morning.

Eventually a woman living near Plattsburgh caught my fancy. Elizabeth was devoted to me, but I less so to her. We grew close in a way, but she had no interest in wilderness, or in paddling, fly-fishing or hiking, and after two years it was apparent to me, if not to Elizabeth, that the relationship was doomed. The points of difference between us were fatal.

I moved on. There was no replacement for Kora.

Duryea and Father both expressed concern about my habits, but I didn't answer. Instead, I'd grab my fly-fishing gear and head off to the stream. I remained devoted to my legal work and the Durant Law Firm, but my general unhappiness was no secret to Father or Duryea.

Then, out of the blue, in June of 1918, a letter from Kora arrived. It was brief, stating only that she would come in July and asking if I would speak to her. She was coming only for a short visit and would stay at the hotel.

June passed so very slowly. I tried to keep myself constantly occupied with fly-fishing forays into the backwoods and brooks, where I found plenty of squaretails to take my mind off things for brief interludes. Each bank of high ferns I came across brought back indelible and passionate memories of Kora and myself. I still didn't have a date for her arrival in July, and I expectantly watched and waited for further word.

One afternoon at the office in mid-July the hotel clerk delivered a note to me from Kora. She had arrived by train the previous evening and wanted to see me the next morning at eight at the hotel veranda for breakfast. My heart raced, aching to catch up on all the news of her life and for a renewal of our relationship. But then I recalled our last early morning meeting on that very same veranda, which had ended in bitter words, and dread crept in. But I didn't share my anxiety with Father, Duryea, or Elaine when I announced that Kora had arrived and I would see her the next day. No one offered advice.

I wanted to arrive at the hotel early and gather my equilibrium, so I was there by 7:45 on a sunny, glorious July morning, a morning that would prove to be either a bellwether day or a disaster. To my great surprise, however, already seated on the hotel's wonderful sunlit porch, looking to the mountains, was Kora. She saw me approaching and rose, smiling wanly, and held out both hands to greet me. She appeared nervous, and when I grasped her hands they shook in small tremors that ran to her fingertips. We said only our hellos, then Kora motioned for me to sit, as she resumed her seat.

I'd decided not to speak first, but to let Kora disclose her purpose for coming here and for wanting to see me. Our eyes met only briefly before she averted her glance. We sat in silence for a minute or more as Kora shifted in her seat, and let her hands rest on the white tablecloth.

Suddenly, my eyes alighting on her white, beautiful hands, the truth struck me with full force and I had to keep myself from leaping up from my chair.

There on her ring finger was a gold wedding band.

I realized I was holding my breath and not daring to look Kora in the eyes. When our eyes did finally meet, Kora's were filled with pain, even guilt, and I felt tears of disbelief and hurt fill my own.

"Jack," she said. Her eyes now stared out to the lake and distant mountain range, "I've been married for more than five years. My husband is in New York. He is a retired physician and businessman there. I didn't want to write this to you this, Jack, especially not after Mother gave me your letter — which, by the way, I didn't open for many months because ... because I couldn't bring myself to read it. I had just been married when it arrived.

"After our last meeting about the Basin and its title, I returned to New York despondent, beside myself with grief over the situation — ours personally, I mean, not just the question of ownership. That's when I met him, Peter Hubreth. He's an older man, Jack. We were married shortly after he proposed. I didn't know what to do — at the time, I honestly didn't think I could ever bear to be around you again — and he was insistent. He takes care of me, Jack. We live our lives, his...ours, mine...." Her voice trailed off, but she offered in a whisper, "He will not grant me a divorce, Jack, this I know."

I sat stunned, unable to say anything. The shock had caused my back and neck to stiffen and my throat was taut as well. I hardly even knew how to comprehend her words. "He takes care of me... He will not grant me a divorce... this I know."

Words would not come, and Kora sat silent with a painful look on her face. I looked to the distant lake and to this beautiful but suddenly wretched July morning. My gut tightened and my chest didn't seem able to draw a full breath. My entire body ached, and a feeling of sickness came over me.

I didn't know if Kora, too, ached. She was talking again now, but I heard only a part of what she said.

"... Yes, he does care for me, Jack. I'm... well, comfortable, if not happy." She looked down, and I studied her for a long moment. Her face began to change to a new look. Our eyes met again, Kora's now brighter.

"How I miss this place, Jack. Do you remember our paddles? Our meeting at John Burroughs' camp? Do you know he's still alive and writing about nature, still concerned, as we are about..."

She stopped, mid-sentence. A tear formed in one beautiful, dark eye, then the other. I sat, suspended in time, unable to fully absorb these events and Kora's mood changes, which were coming too fast for me to understand. She dabbed at one eye with a kerchief. Again, we sat staring at each other, silent.

I found myself inspecting the Adirondack clothes she wore, the lightweight, red-checked flannel shirt over a black silk camisole, set off by a black crocheted vest done in a woven pattern, a brilliant silken cloth showing from a stitched chest pocket on her vest. The red silk reminded me of the babushka she'd worn on her head in the storm many years before. Over her legs she wore a broadcloth cotton skirt on which were embroidered two small canoes sitting in whitecaps driven up by the wind. Kora's shirt fit loosely, but even so her breasts and upper-body strength were apparent and attractive.

The waiter arrived to take our order. Once he was gone again Kora said suddenly, "Jack, I want to ask you to go for a paddle in a canoe with me."

Remaining temporarily speechless, I somehow found a faint smile to offer. Kora and I in a canoe again. The thought made me laugh softly under my breath. A canoe was where our love had been kindled as teens, and where it had grown through many shared paddles that still retained their magic in my memory. We'd never said as much to each other, but it was our unstated truth. Kora was still waiting for my reply.

"Why don't we go now, Kora?" I offered with more ease than my broken heart felt. I'd take the day off, ask Father to watch over things.

I allowed myself to look, really look at her face. It was the face of a 30-year-old woman in the prime of life, no longer a young beauty, but still fresh and vigorous, natural and beautiful. She was more stunning now, really, with the added maturity of her years. Remaining lithe and athletic, her beauty had grown to a mature sensuality.

"The long birch bark canoe — the canvas-covered one — in the boathouse," I said. "Meet me there in 20 minutes. We'll go for a paddle — even if you are a married woman."

That comment hung in the air, having surprised even me. I regretted it immediately, but it was too late to take it back. Kora's eyes gave way to hide her hurt.

"Jack," she said, "you must understand some things about the choices I've made. But let's leave that for later." She rose from her chair on the empty porch and looked directly down at me.

"I'm telling no one here except you that I'm married." She pulled off her wedding ring defiantly and shoved it into her vest pocket, looking all the while at me.

"While I'm here, that remains off. I've come to spend time with you, time that I believe is precious to us both."

I could find nothing to say, and Kora went on. "I need to make you understand me, and then maybe you can forgive me."

I could barely fathom what she was saying about herself, but at least I now understood why she'd remained so distant from me for the past six years. There was some small comfort in at least understanding that much. She'd made a bad decision and had agreed to the union with Hubreth. By now, I gathered, she'd at least grown accustomed to her situation. She was comfortable, she'd said, if not happy.

I stood and put my hand on her shoulder. "I'll meet you in 20 minutes at the boat house."

I walked from the porch, glancing back once. But Kora had already left and was nowhere to be seen. Our waiter, however, was just delivering our coffee.

Hurrying into the office, I announced to Elaine that I was taking the day off and asked her to tell Father as much. I went into another room and grabbed the lunch Duryea had packed for me that morning. My heart raced, despite all the remaining hurt. Kora wanted to spend time with me, and that was all that mattered.

Just before dashing back out of the office, I called to Elaine, "Get word to Father and Duryea that I'd appreciate having the camp to myself this afternoon. Tell them I'll explain why later."

Why had I said such a thing? I wondered as I pulled the office door closed behind me. Why in the world did I think Kora would go to the camp alone with me? She was married, she was now Kora... what was her last name now?

I quickly decided I didn't care what it was, and I walked deliberately to the boathouse with my lunch stored in a pack basket.

As I neared the boathouse I saw her sunlit figure standing by the water. An eye-catching red babushka was upon her hair, and over her beautiful face, a wonderful broad smile.

Light air makes a canoe slide easier, go faster, somehow infusing lightness and speed into the hull of the boat as it moves across water. I felt this in our canoe as we stroked away from the boathouse. The old canoe responded to my paddle in the stern and to Kora's in the bow as though it were responding to my charged feelings.

The lake was calm and reflected the highly varnished hull back into my eyes. Kora was silent, but vigorous with her stroke, as if brimming with energy and thought in the quiet of the morning. The air was perfect, still brisk from a cool Adirondack evening. It felt right to be in the boat under our own power, with my partner of many such passages across North Country flows.

It felt as if we could keep paddling forever in our heightened state. We didn't speak, preferring instead to enjoy the pace, which began to vary with our whim. Every few strokes Kora turned her head to the side, glancing back at me with a smile. Then she'd face forward and return to paddling hard. Her stroke was just in front of my mine, firing the boat an instant before I fired with mine. Just like old times.

We went well down the lake in this fashion, silent, and warming to a sweat. My shirt grew damp in the warming air, and, Kora's back was soon spotted in moisture.

In mid-lake, the pace changed. Kora went to a longer, smoother stroke, the one used to cover distances over an extended period. In a few minutes she went to the slow, even pace suited for making observations on shore, or in the distance. Soon that gave way to the lollygag, barely a paddle at all, the lost-in-thought stroke, the stroke of choice for being together and exchanging glances and quiet words; for enjoying silence and the sounds of water gently rolling by. At each change of Kora's pace, I adjusted too, as we went on our little voyage down the lake in the general direction of the Basin camp, hidden away in the next bay.

So it went on our junket down the long and indented Adirondack lake until suddenly, Kora stopped. She shipped her paddle and pivoted in her seat on her rump, her legs raised. She faced me, now. Her agile move had startled me.

"Jack, paddle me to the Basin camp. I want to see it again. I want to see the oval window again."

I renewed my stroke, heading now for the camp.

"Jack," Kora said, still facing me. Her eyes were riveted on mine, and there was a tone in her voice that I'd not heard. I held my stroke, and waited in silence.

"I love you, Jack Durant."

I felt my whole face and my insides enflame with joy.

"Kora, I've loved you for so long! You're the one woman in this world I need to be with. We have to find a way!" I couldn't let it rest there.

"You say this man will not give you a divorce, and I can't simply forget that you're married — we have to deal with that somehow. I'm still in love with you, Kora. I'll do anything to see us together."

"For today, and this visit, we should forget that I'm married. I meant it when I took the ring off my finger." A look of uncertainty came over her. "I love you, so… you help me decide how to behave, Jack. Do you understand me? You do, I can see it in that handsome face of yours. Get us to your camp. I'm not taking my eyes off you until we're there!" And she didn't.

The hull of the canoe squished softly on the sandy beach next to the finger dock. Still facing me, Kora deftly moved from the canoe to a sitting position on the low dock. I lifted the canoe to stow it, and felt Kora's warmth pressed against my back. I turned to her. Neither of us held anything back as we embraced and kissed, rekindling passions that returned so naturally because they had never left either of us.

"Inside," she said, and we moved toward the camp, our arms around each other's hips. I grabbed a grape from the pack basket, intending to feed it to Kora, but she tossed it over her shoulder. "Time enough for that," she said. "Come with me."

Inside, Kora stopped to face me and pressed against my body. "Show me the oval mosaic now, Monsieur Durant." She took my hand and led me to the stairs and to the mosaic, not far from my bed. We stood before the window for a moment, holding on to each other and gazing at our mountains. The sun drenched us in its warmth; the lapping waters at the beach brought us a unique harmony.

Kora pushed back from me, then slowly took off her vest and unbuttoned her shirt, revealing her breasts and dark, taut nipples. Slowly, she took off her pants and underthings. I kissed her first on her deep-pink lips, then on her neck and her firm breasts. Our passion grew with each stroke and caress.

The unrequited love of years was released. If there was some small hesitance at first, it was quickly replaced by full and then unrestrained hunger. Finally bodies and souls were fulfilled. Kora fell asleep in my arms on the feather bed, and I followed fast behind her, falling into a deep sleep and a recurring dream.

I saw myself with a sad Kora who had not given her love to me. We weren't even in love. Each scene took place somewhere other than in the Adirondacks, in some unfamiliar city. The time, strangely, was in the future. I always seemed to realize that I was dreaming, and yet dreamed that I kept waking and finding Kora not at my side, but ready to leave for New York without saying anything further to me, and absent any understanding between us.

But I awoke and Kora was there still. Our naked bodies still moved as one. Kora rebuked my bad dream when I told her about it.

"I do love you, Jack, and I'll get here to see you as I can. I can't say more, since I know I won't be given a divorce, and I don't have grounds for filing, myself."

We lay quietly, twining our fingers together in different patterns.

"Tell your father to complete the deed to you and me for this property. We can work it out some way. Somehow we'll preserve both this place and our love." She pushed up on her elbows so that she was looking directly into my eyes. "I refuse to feel guilt about our love. I've loved you since I was a child, and I always will. Don't ever forget that, no matter what might come between us."

Her words left sickening unease in my gut. I didn't doubt our love, but I still didn't fully know this woman at her core, did not fully understand her. I pulled her back into my arms. Burying my nose in the fresh scent of her hair, I stroked her back. This day had been different from any other in our lives. We weren't youngsters anymore; we'd come together in a mature, experienced union that would have been impossible before.

But our union was incomplete, of course; Kora's marriage stood between us. Yet what our lovemaking had just forged was a union of body and mind that I didn't think anything could break. Something sacred had come from that day's love.

Kora would be in town only for a few days, and we were determined to make the most of our time. Father remained in town at his house there, and Duryea stayed with him. No questions were asked, a kindness for which I'll always be grateful.

Kora and I spent most of our time in front of the oval mosaic, wrapped in sheets and blankets, talking, reading, making love, watching the sun set and rise, and sleeping cozily but briefly, too taken by each other's company to sleep more than necessary.

I'll never forget Kora reading me her favorite love poem from Shelley, "The Indian Serenade". I still even remember the last lines:

> *My heart beats loud and fast*
>
> *O press it to thine own again*
>
> *Where it will break at last!*

We'd fallen fast asleep in each other's arms again, but awoke toward dawn. Lying in bed we talked about our love, and of wilderness and our love for it, our need to be in it. We made love again as the sun came up over the high peak in the east, and the first shaft of light penetrated our nested space. We talked of the wonderful morning light coming in, and felt the sun's warmth on our skin. I'd been reading from John Muir's journal and letters that both Duryea and Father gave to me, and it came to my mind to read Kora his description of dawn in the high Sierras.

"Kora, let me get Muir's journal and read to you how he saw the new day in his mountains." I held the journal and read aloud:

> *Morning light rayless, beamless, unbodied of all its purple and gold. No outgushing of solar glory pouring in torrents among mountain peaks, baptizing them; but each pervaded with the soul of light, boundless, tideless, newborn from the sun ere it has received a hint of good or bad from our star.... The trees, the mountains are not near or far; they are made one, unseparate, unclothed, open to the Divine Soul, dissolved in the mysterious incomparable Spirit of holy light!*

Kora lay silently against my chest for several moments. "It's beautiful, Jack," she said. "Read some more."

"Listen to this man's love for a woman he could not be physically with, a woman who was married to another man, even though she loved Muir deeply."

Her mouth formed an "o" of surprise at the parallel of Muir's situation and ours. I turned the pages of his journal to a letter set I'd marked in pencil.

> *In all my wanderings through Nature's beauty, whether it be among the ferns at my cabin door, or in high meadows and peaks, or amid the spray and music of waterfalls, you are the first to meet me, and I often speak to you as verily present in the flesh.*

Kora did not hesitate to answer Muir's muse.

"It is us, Jack! We both think it." She paused, snuggled further under the sheets, and a twinkle came to her eye. "And I like Muir's reference to the ferns!"

We laughed, reaching out to hold hands as we shared our little remembrance of love along Otter Brook.

I turned another page and read on.

Oftentimes, when I am free in the wilds I discover some rare beauty in lake or cataract or mountain form, and instantly seek to sketch it with my pencil, but drawing it is always enormously unlike reality. So also in word sketches of the same beauties that are so living, so loving, so filled with warm God, there is the same infinite shortcoming. The few hard words make but a skeleton, fleshless, heartless, and when you read, the dead bony words rattle in one's teeth.

"He brings Thoreau and Emerson to mind, as you've said."

And by then, on that glorious morning, it was time to have breakfast and go outside to enjoy nature. We went for a long walk in the woods along the brook, holding hands as we went, not once letting go of our grasp, save for leapfrogging over the brook to go deeper and higher into our north woods wilderness.

On our return, Kora gathered up Muir's journal and climbed to the loft.

Passionate and wonderful, our two days together came to an end.

I took Kora to the train station. We said our good-byes without so much as an embrace, just a long gaze with no words. Kora seemed uncomfortable in public, as if she didn't want to be seen with me, though she didn't say as much.

She turned and boarded the train, and then she was gone again from my life, for how long this time, I had no idea.

I returned to work with the weight of the world on my shoulders. Father asked how our time went, well aware of Kora's brief visit. I told him that she was the same lovely woman, that she lived in New York, and would return to see me again.

"When, Jack?" Keene asked.

I shrugged my shoulders, not saying anything. I didn't tell Father that Kora now wanted the Basin deed transferred to her and me jointly. I still didn't trust her not to change her mind. But the subject of the title was on Keene's mind.

He simply said, "I'm not getting any younger, son, and it would be nice to have a better understanding of things, do you hear?"

I needed time to think on these matters. And time I had plenty of. I threw myself back in to my legal work, which thankfully I loved. Kora didn't contact me, except for a brief letter giving me her address and telling me she was "getting along and missed me." She asked me not to write her at her return address, but to use her mother's address. She ended by saying she would remain in contact with me.

I was left to struggle with the questions remaining in my mind: who was Kora Longfellow Hubreth, and just what, exactly, was her plan?

But her plan, had I been more perceptive, was already in place.

Seventeen
Kora's Design

Kora astounded me, once more, by waiting an entire year to contact me again. When she did, it was in the form of two letters, both postmarked from London, England. The first described in some detail her life in New York and her barren marriage to Peter Hubreth, 20 years her senior and extremely wealthy. For Hubreth, she wrote, the marriage was satisfactory because Kora was young and beautiful and came from money. She was also sufficiently alienated from him that she made no demands on his time or loyalties. In fact, she lived a life quite separate from his, except for those times when societal demands required that he have a wife of polished social skills on his arm.

For her part, her needs and wants were met, even extravagantly. She did little but what she wanted to do, when she wanted to do it. She admitted, however, that she'd entered the marriage too hastily following our argument at camp that stormy morning when we'd exchanged sharp words and she'd threatened legal action over the Basin.

Her decision to marry was a mistake, and she'd known it almost immediately. And, with the passage of several years, apparently Hubreth had come to regret the marriage as well. By then, however, they were quite established as an international couple and Kora had become indispensable to his business and social life.

Her second letter made me shake as I read it, so much did it confound me. She wrote more about her life with Hubreth, her situation with him, and about her son. When I could read further, I began to see that, our undeniable passion notwithstanding, I had been an unwitting player in a very clever plan.

In her sixth month she'd gone to Hubreth and announced she was with child. Blame and accusations had been thrown about, and their acrimony and anger resulted in a hidden truth being brought into the light: Hubreth announced to Kora that he was sterile; his physician had the proof.

Only weeks earlier, an argument over Kora's spending had erupted into a bitter exchange of words. The battle escalated until each one's years' of complaints boiled over and spilled out in many unkind words. What Kora and Hubreth had been left with — the environment into which Kora brought her revelation — was a fragile shell upon which her announcement was essentially its last straw.

Kora consulted with her lawyers and was told just how nasty Hubreth could get and yet stay within the bounds of the law. She sensed how miserable he was about to make her life.

At his age and under this cloud, Hubreth did not want the social smear of a divorce, and announced that none would be granted. After a period of ugliness, Hubreth decided Kora was to be sent to London, where she would remain until the birth of the child. The baby, however, was not to return to New York with her.

The boy was born in March of 1919 in London. Kora stayed on there longer than Hubreth desired, unable to give up her child, and trying to figure a way to deal with her circumstances.

I let her letter fall to my lap for a moment while I stopped to catch my breath and reflect on what had happened to her. Under the state's domestic law, I knew, Kora had been reduced to fodder for Hubreth and his lawyers. The only ground for divorce in New York at that time was adultery, and Kora did not have that against him. She had almost no rights in this situation; Hubreth was in control of her life. If his demand were met and Kora adopted the child out, he would keep Kora in a small apartment in New York, out of sight.

This was not uncommon, then, in high society when a man "had the goods" on his wife and had no desire to re-marry; those in the know simply kept a tight lip about things. Such was domestic life among the wealthy in 1919, and though society's views on such things seemed to be changing somewhat, the law had not.

I was not sure if Kora understood her circumstances, or how vulnerable she was to Hubreth's power and control over her.

But now, as Kora explained in her letter, a decision had to be made. Hubreth was demanding that she return from London, but without the child, who was to be put up for adoption. If she left Hubreth, she would descend into something very like destitution.

"I am compelled to seek guidance from you about the infant and his well-being, since you have provided guidance for me before. Truly, I prefer to be with you, if things can work out regarding my son and about coming to an understanding regarding the Basin."

I could read no further. Realizing that I might be father to a boy created from our union stunned me to the core. I had no idea how to feel. Kora was holding something back from me, and I could not rest until I understood and addressed whatever it was. Of course I saw my quandary: I couldn't claim a wife or fatherhood publicly because of Kora's plan, as egocentrically conceived as our child, I surmised. And yet there was our child.

Kora had obviously plotted her visit to the Basin, and our time together, to form a union with me of a different nature than I had understood in the moment. She'd cast her lot with a marriage that had failed, and now she wanted a way back into my life — and, I further surmised, she wanted to make it plain that her son was an additional factor in resolving the Basin title in her favor.

Although she'd offered to resolve things by sharing title equally with me, no deed had yet been presented to her for her signature. Father and I had discussed it briefly, but thereafter Kora had virtually disappeared. But she'd surfaced now with a story so incredulous that it left doubt in my mind, and in Father's, as to whether we should proceed with finishing the deed. Father pointed out that if Kora was in dire financial condition, judgments for debt and any resulting liens would be filed against her and what she owned, including the Basin deed, if it included her.

I thought hard and long, and tended to view the situation in the darkest possible light. Father and I made no decisions. We decided to wait and see.

Her way back into my life through a child fathered by me, but raised in New York by her, had gone bust. Hubreth's sterility, and his insistence on adoption, had been her big miscalculations. Father's concern, and mine, was that now she might fight hard for a greater stake in the Basin because her economic well-being and social status were now being taken away by Hubreth. He controlled her legal status as a married woman and worse yet, he controlled her life.

My dismay with Kora grew, but now there was a third person, a child, to consider. I wrote back saying that there were more questions than answers, but that I would help her if she came to see me. I didn't tell her this, but though I still loved Kora, I no longer trusted her unquestioningly. It was certainly possible that I could be the father of this boy, but that was a determination I would make only if and when I saw the child with my own eyes.

But then another year came and went with no word from her.

Then in June, a short note announced that she and the child were coming from London. She had made no decision yet regarding her son, whom she called Will, and I couldn't fathom how she could survive such uncertainty about the fate of her son, combined with such a dismal marriage.

The visit promised to bring with it far more questions and stress than anything else, given how much there was to consider: how Kora would emerge from her miserable marriage; what her financial condition would be if she did divorce Hubreth; what her plans were for her son. All this portended great challenges — for me and for the future of the Basin lands. The equation among Keene, Kora, and me had now changed.

She would arrive in just a few days, and I grew itchy in the office. I stewed and ruminated, thinking of various aspects of the problem and various possible resolutions. I was trying to put together all the pieces of her story, including her whereabouts over the last two years.

Trout fishing was my answer. It would rejuvenate my spirit to wander and walk the stream. My problems with Kora would disappear, surrounded by moving water, and, hopefully, as often happened in a stream, a new thought, some new perspective, would bubble to the surface of my mind.

And so, intending to catch a trout and a new view of life, I announced to Elaine, the day after Kora's letter came, that I was heading for parts unknown on some wilderness piece of woods and water. I closed up my office and headed out.

The brookies would be hungry and I'd need to match the late spring hatch of Hendrickson mayflies with the Ausable pattern I used with some luck. Once on the stream and rigged, my tactics worked, and before long I was cooking a late lunch of small brookies on the Otter Creek bank. Sitting on a sandy spot where the sun penetrated and warmed me, I felt like a bear coming out of hibernation to soak up the warming spring sun after a long Adirondack winter.

Kora was coming to town with "her baby." Something in my bones told me that this child was mine—and not the result of an unplanned dalliance, but of Kora's deliberate plan to conceive our child and then show up to make certain demands in her own interest. Her husband, needing to avoid humiliation, was insisting on placing the child for adoption. Kora said she needed my guidance through this, but I sensed there was more to her visit than that. I was caught up in her design, and I was angry and felt extremely manipulated and vulnerable. Yet I loved her; she owned my soul, and I still hoped to figure out a way for us to be together.

The relaxation of fishing dimmed quickly with these thoughts. Dousing my campfire, I headed back downstream to the mouth where I had left the canoe, feeling no more resolved than when I'd left the office. It brought me great pain to think such uncharitable thoughts of Kora, and yet I feared I was reading her plan correctly.

Pushing off, my fly line played out as I trolled aimlessly across the lake, thinking more about becoming a father than about landing a fish. I wasn't even aware that I'd picked up my stroke to a speed most trout would find alarming. The only thing I could feel certain about was that, if the child was mine, then he should be reared where I knew he'd be properly raised and provided for, here in the Adirondacks. What Kora had in mind I didn't know, but I feared I'd find out soon enough.

As I continued paddling back to the Basin camp I made myself acknowledge that there weren't any quick answers in sight. I decided my next step was to return to camp and read Kora's long explanation in full.

She'd written at length sharing how keenly aware she was of her precarious circumstances; she knew her options were narrowing and described steps she had taken. As a last resort, she went to the Hopewell Foundation for Orphans, recommended by her closest friend in London, Mrs. Stockwell. There she had talked to its director, Mrs. Elizabeth Raintree.

Having put the entire story before her, Kora looked the woman straight in the eye. "Mrs. Raintree, should I give my son up for adoption? What are my options? What can I do?"

The woman had advised her, "Go to this man in the Adirondacks. Tell him your husband is insisting you give up the boy. Hubreth can refuse you a divorce and leave you without support, you know. He has the power and the money to go to court to enforce the laws surrounding divorce in your state. He probably wouldn't even have to pay child support under these circumstances, and he certainly doesn't have to pay you spousal support. So you must make the best decisions for yourself and your son — which may mean being separated from your child, if you can find a home for him." Mrs. Raintree no doubt knew her next words would be difficult for Kora to hear.

"This agency is ready to arrange the adoption of your baby. But to do so, we will need the consent of both mother and father." She advised Kora to go to the father and get his consent, at which point the agency could proceed.

"I know it isn't easy," Florence Raintree said, "but I advise you to think of your own life, too, Kora. Try to put it back in order in a way you can live with, both for yourself and for your future relationship with your son and the child's father. Please promise me you'll go home and think about this some more, that you'll give the decision the time and attention it deserves."

I couldn't help but notice, reading Kora's letter, how at every step she avoided coming right out and naming me as the boy's father.

She'd responded to Mrs. Raintree by promising to take her advice.

At first, Kora didn't even notice when Mrs. Raintree rose and walked into the next room; she was too deep in thought about approaching me for my advice, about the adoption. She began to cry. She wasn't sure she could go through giving up her son Will, but she knew she couldn't consign herself to the poor house. And Hubreth had made clear in a letter that if she got rid of the child, she could return to New York and that she would be restored to her prior status. If she didn't, her future would not be bright.

Mrs. Raintree busied herself in the other room and Kora sat in the office for a long time, thinking. Finally, she knew what she would do. She went and found Mrs. Raintree.

"I am going to see Jack Durant, my friend in the Adirondacks, to get this resolved and make some decisions. Thank you for your help."

By the time she'd left the Hopewell Foundation, no doubt she had nearly perfected the plan of action she was certain she could make work, a plan that required my direct involvement.

When I finished reading Kora's letter, I was more miserable than ever. I surmised that her hope was to turn her son over to me, then return to New York and live on the meager stipend her husband would provide her. I couldn't free my mind from the sinister thought that the Basin had become in Kora's mind an "asset" on her balance sheet, something she could use for her personal gain. One she now intended to employ to settle the Basin title issue, and even our relationship.

Kora was due at the train station in the morning, on the early arrival, and she would be carrying a bundle in her arms. I hadn't seen her since our liaison in June of 1918. The calendar had turned now to 1920, and her most recent letters were dated in June.

The evening was long, and too quiet and lonely, as Father and Duryea were spending the night in the village. Finally, having thought all I could stand to, I set down Kora's letter and prepared for bed. But sleep came only after the third brandy, which I downed propped in the featherbed in front of the high oval mosaic looking out on the lake and distant range. My last thought was the memory of making love with Kora in this very bed. But the passion had now waned, replaced by the knowledge that hard decisions loomed before me.

Eighteen
The Visit

Not knowing what answers, if any, might emerge to clarify the situation, I arose early that spring morning in 1920, and went out to meet Kora and the baby. Given the certainty of extra cargo, I chose the double-ended church boat, our longest and most seaworthy of the oar-driven crafts, at nineteen-feet-six-inches.

Having traveled all night with her small companion, Kora was the last person off the sleeper car. The child, almost two now, was asleep in his mother's arms, wrapped in a Hudson Bay eight-point blanket and looking angelic and peaceful.

"This baby didn't sleep until we hit the blue line," Kora offered with a warm smile and a roll of her dark eyes. "It must be the wilderness that quieted him." Motherhood appeared to agree with her. "I slept very little myself, and I'm exhausted. Even so, it's so good to see you. You look wonderful, as always, Jack."

"Thank you. You do, too, Kora."

"This is William; I call him Will."

I could feel her eyes on me as I studied the little boy. He was carefully bundled, but I was able to see his small nose and closed eyes with prominent dark lashes and brows. His little pink lips curved just as Kora's did at the corners of her mouth, and a wisp of dark hair was visible by his ear. Despite myself, I couldn't help but smile at him.

"He's a wonderful boy, Jack. And I warn you, he grows on you real quick!"

An awkward silence set in and I'll admit I enjoyed Kora's discomfort. But I couldn't keep from looking at her and the sleeping child. Kora's beauty, matured since last I saw her, still caught me, but her eyes weren't as welcoming, which I must say unsettled me. Despite my anxiety about what her visit portended, I found myself thinking about what the last two years must have been for her.

"Well, Jack? Has the devil got your tongue?" She stopped and looked nervously up at me.

I smiled, but I honestly couldn't put words together yet.

"What arrangements do you think we can make… I mean, for Will and me? I was rather hoping to spend time at the Basin camp so that Will could play on the beach. Perhaps he could stay there with you."

"Well …"

"It would be fun if you got to know Will. Heaven knows my husband doesn't pay him the least little attention."

We still hadn't moved from our spot on the loading platform. Looking about, I realized there was a considerable stack of luggage to get aboard the church boat. Among other things, we'd be transporting a variety of toys, including one small child-sized fishing pole. Something for the future, I thought, and an indication of Kora's planning.

I noted it was not a fly rod, but the intent to get the boy thinking like a fisherman was still admirable.

Still without answering her, I began picking up as much of their belongings as possible. Kora added, as if I'd made a full response to what she'd already said, "And let's save the conversation about Mr. Hubreth for later, shall we?"

Duryea arrived, as if on cue, with the horse-drawn carriage. He tipped his hat politely to Kora, and looked pleased to receive a hug and kiss in return. He immediately began helping me load the cargo into the carriage.

"Isn't this a real Adirondack spring morning!" Kora said brightly, now looking at me uncertainly, as if wondering if she could get any response from me at all. I smiled in return, but let Duryea give her fitting verbal responses. For myself, I sat perfectly still as we rode toward the dock, hoping that my silence would drain her of pretenses, would prevent her from thinking she could slap a free and easy veneer over this difficult situation. I hoped, by not speaking, to make her speak what I assumed was the truth about little Will.

But Duryea shot me a disciplinary glance, telling me, I knew, to mind my manners.

"It's an Adirondacker's day, indeed," I finally said. "Maybe we can find something to do back at camp. All three of us, I mean, even little Will here."

Kora turned toward me then in the bright morning sun. Our eyes met. As if propelled by something greater than my desire to punish her, I found myself leaning toward her and holding out my hand. To my further surprise, I put my arms around her briefly, and gave her a kiss on the cheek.

Struggling to compose myself I said, "I'm wondering if the three of us plus all your luggage will fit into the church boat. Maybe we should use the one-lunger and go out to camp under power. It's a little broader."

"That's a good idea," she said. "I assume the old one-lunger will putt us out to camp."

And so we went to the boathouse, got the launch ready, and loaded up. Will continued to sleep as the single cylinder inboard sang out its melodious ka-putt ka-putt ka-putt. We made the passage and Duryea unloaded while Kora, Will, and I went inside. "He'll be hungry soon and will wake up." Kora pulled at my elbow. "While he sleeps, I need to talk to you." Leading the way into the great room, she placed Will in a secure place on a love seat, and turned to meet my eye.

"Please sit down, Jack."

She motioned to me and sat herself in a matched stuffed chair five feet away and facing her. I noticed then that she held a brooch in her hands, which she worked back and forth through her fingers as though she were kneading dough. Her fists were white from holding the brooch so tightly.

"I've been talking with a woman friend about Will, Jack, and I must talk to you about him now." She looked down and away. Her spirit felt so heavy, I couldn't help feeling tenderly towards her.

"As difficult as this is to say, Jack, I'm now considering, along with Mr. Hubreth, putting Will up for adoption in New York. We think, given our circumstances, that it may be best. I've told you of our relationship and, well ... you hopefully appreciate what—"

My anger exploded. "Know what you mean, Kora? I know you've led me to believe you were in a barren marriage that would produce no children. So you owe me an explanation!" I got hold of myself and added in a softer voice, "Please."

When she flushed and looked away, I went on but in a more even tone. "You wrote me and dissembled at length, Kora. So now let me come right to the point, Kora. Is this our child?"

The words echoed in the large room. When I stopped, Kora's head dropped to her chest. She took a deep breath, fighting back a sob.

"Jack, I did not literally mean that my husband could not father our child. I'm simply telling you what we're intending, so you know. Mr. Hubreth has told me in no uncertain terms that he will support me and only me, that he is shocked at this turn of events and that as long as the adoption occurs and it is kept from New York society, we can go on. He will not grant a divorce — he insists I remain his wife for convenience, but only under his terms. Do you now understand, Jack? Do you see what a hold this man has on me?"

So this was it. Kora intended to play out the threat of adoption, and ask me to step in as a parent so that she could then she return to New York. How could she, when what was at stake was a small child she'd brought into the world?

"Then why did you come here to me, Kora? You said you needed my guidance, but it sounds as if you and Hubreth have everything figured out. You've decided your lives will be much less inconvenienced if you just get rid of the boy."

The cry that escaped her was a sound I'll remember the rest of my life. I was ashamed of myself for my cruelty.

When she could collect herself to go on, she wiped her eyes and forced herself to look at me. "I came here because, before Hubreth and I do anything, I want to ask if you'd be willing to take this child and raise him." She sat straighter, as if calling on all her mettle to get through the conversation. "You have the means, and it would allow me to see my son as he grows. He'd be good company for you, Jack, especially as he gets older. I know it is unusual. But... but I make this offer to you and your father as part of a plan to resolve things on the Basin between us."

I could barely understand her. What was she really proposing — to settle the Basin issue in exchange for my taking Will?

"Jack, this plan for Will—it must include a provision that he become owner of the Basin lands on your death, or sooner, if you want. That will fulfill what my father promised me and my right of inheritance from him. It will be a fair outcome, all things considered. I realize you need to think about all this, and I know you must talk to Keene."

Shocked and speechless, I threw my arms to the air and stood up. My body felt taut, and my face hot. My brows were deeply furrowed. Who was this woman who would barter her child for property? And who did she think she was, coming to my home and proposing this outrageous scheme! She still hadn't even answered my question about Will's paternity. I tried to regain my composure, but it was a while before I could speak.

"Kora," I finally said, "you and Will may stay here a few days, but then I want you to leave. I don't have any response to your crazy plan. It doesn't even merit a response." I was surprised to sound so relatively composed, given the rage battering my insides.

"You and Will take the room on the north side on the second floor. Duryea can help you settle in, if you like. I'm going out for a walk."

I stayed out of camp most of the day, not wanting to face Kora. Her proposal was vintage Kora, an outrageous plan she concocted and announced as a fait accompli. She hadn't specifically stated that Will was our son, yet she had the audacity to insist on special treatment for him as heir to the Basin. And I was to raise the boy, to boot! How convenient, I fumed. I vowed to call her bluff and insist she go ahead with the adoption.

And yet, when I stopped long enough to think of the consequences, I paused. I believed Kora's husband would force the issue, given his prominence in New York's society and his shock at being presented with a child so late in life — especially given his uncertainty of his own paternity. Kora obviously knew that too, and must have assumed I'd never stand for an adoption, that in the end, I would agree to raise the boy. Was her assumption based on her certainty that I was the father? Or on her knowledge that she owned me, heart and soul, and that I could never resist any request of hers?

Father appeared around dinnertime. I heard him on the porch, calling out that he would enjoy visiting with Kora and a young boy he'd heard had arrived with her. I stepped out to the porch, intending to talk to Keene about Kora's plan, but she arrived at that same moment with an awake Will in her arms. She strode with confidence across the porch. Keene's eyes were glued to the baby, and finally, as Kora arrived in front of him, on Kora herself.

"Keene Durant, it's been too long," Kora said with some excitement in her voice. She extended her left hand to Keene's right hand, and then surprised him with a quick hug and kiss to his cheek, with Will fitted snugly between them. The child, looking squeezed, nonetheless looked with interest at the new face presented to him. There was no denying that Will's eyes bore a distinct resemblance to Keene's in both the intensity of their blue color and in their almond shape.

"Is this your son, Kora?" Keene asked.

"Yes, this is Will!"

We sat on the porch, and soon the evening shadows began to set in. Will toddled about, learning his new surroundings. The light moved to dusk as Duryea rattled his pots in the kitchen.

In a while, Father went to read in the library. Glancing in through the screen door and into the library, I saw that he was writing intently, pen to paper, and then studying his work. I was curious as to what he could be working on, given that there was company in the camp. It was unlike him to do legal work while others besides me were present. I needed a chance to talk with him before things went any further.

I excused myself from Kora's company, encouraging her to enjoy the porch a while longer with Will, and went inside. As I walked deliberately past the library door, Father motioned me in. He looked up from his writing as I approached and stood over him.

"Jack, let me tell you something." His voice was quite serious. "You have some decisions to make because that boy, I'm certain, is your son. You don't have to explain anything to me, but you must plan for your future, young man. Kora is a married woman, Jack, and we should decide together what to do, which, I assume, you've thought about long and hard. You're 30-some years old now. What are you going to do about your son, my grandson? He's a Durant and he should be raised where Durants are always raised—here in the Adirondacks, and not in New York City.

"Now, I'd almost bet there's a demand coming, something to the effect that Will is heir to the Basin lands and should get the deed, probably as sole titleholder. Kora knows of the escrow deed I still hold. But here, Jack is the third generation. There may be the chance to resolve things within the family. And Jack, I think this boy is family."

I was more speechless now than when Kora had
announced her plan. Keene Durant had it all figured out.
When I could, I proposed to him that we take things one
step at a time and see what happened. I thought we needed
to talk further about Will with Kora

"Maybe you're right about my paternity, but she
hasn't been at all candid with me."

Duryea called out for dinner.

"Let's the two of us go sit and talk with Kora and
Duryea," I said. "Who knows what we might be able to
come up with. But for now Father, please, let's keep this
conversation to ourselves."

"Perhaps, for a while. I feel pressed to get something
done, though. You never know how much time you may
have in this life to do what needs finishing." Keene paused
and looked up at me, and something about his words made
me uncomfortable. "We shall have to make decisions,
perhaps even faster than you think. I have a feeling this Mr.
Hubreth may force the issue, and we must be ready to do
the right thing."

Keene turned and walked resolutely toward Kora,
who was now seating herself at the dining table.

I didn't have time, as I followed Keene to the table,
to ask what he'd meant about making decisions, but a
trepidation gripped me, even as I managed a small grin
toward Will, who was just falling asleep again against Kora's
chest.

Blessedly, Father began a lengthy monologue about
his life in the Adirondacks and the Basin, about how it and
our country had changed over the years. The others of us
merely nodded as we ate, acknowledging what he said. By
dessert, he'd covered the years from before his birth up
through the present. He told stories of being snowbound
where even a horse-drawn snow sleigh could not be used;

of the first photographs he ever saw; of the abolitionist John Brown and Gerrit Smith's freedmen who got their deeds the day Keene was in the courthouse; of the night of the flash fire in the forest in 1894, specifically mentioning the words William Longfellow had spoken to him about preserving the Basin lands; of Teddy Roosevelt's careening down Mount Marcy to be sworn in as president after the assassination of McKinley; of the coming of reforms and labor unions demanded by the Populists, Ignatius Donnelly and William Jennings Bryan; of John Muir and John Burroughs, both of whom understood wilderness yet were philosophically diverse about man's relationship to it; about baseball coming to the North Country, where it was played by many stars to large crowds of fans; of the newly arriving horseless carriages to the area which, he was certain, would change the Adirondacks forever; of going to see Buffalo Bill and Annie Oakley perform and spin tales of the fast-fading Wild West; and finally, of the invention of the typewriter, which he had learned to use, he was proud to say, noting that he kept an L.C. Smith machine both at the camp and his office. The stories poured forth, covering the past seventy years, right to the year we lived and breathed in, 1920.

"Some progress is wonderful, and the typewriter changes everything, does it not!" Keene seemed at last to be at his ending, a look of satisfaction and relief on his face that he had got us all safely through a pleasant dinner. He took another drink of the fine red Bordeaux.

Kora had been so thoroughly engrossed throughout the meal, she'd looked as innocent and young as I sometimes still thought of her. She thanked Keene for sharing all those stories, and especially for reminding her about John Muir's huge contribution to the wilderness. As she said that she gave me a knowing glance, which I pretended not to notice.

Dinner seemed to be winding down without any mention of the Basin title or Kora's stake in it. Kora had earlier placed Will in a rocking cradle she'd pulled up next to the table, and just as we were all finishing off Duryea's dessert, Will's eyes opened. Keene went and picked him up, very gently, an equally gentle smile on his face.

"Will, you have to get to know the Adirondacks better. After all, your family comes from here."

Keene looked directly at Kora and then at me. Kora managed an uncomfortable smile, and I excused myself and walked to the kitchen with dinner plates, both to help Duryea and to distance myself from the table. Duryea, aging now, with stooped shoulders, went ahead of me to his kitchen, but he came to a stop when he heard Keene addressing Will. Then, smiling, he continued on his way.

From the kitchen, I could hear Keene's continuing conversation with Kora.

"Well, Kora, what do you think of your son, Will, here? He is a fine young boy, don't you think?"

Kora headed directly into the matter at hand just as I returned to gather more things from the table.

"He should have his rights to these Basin lands — this wonderful wilderness you refer to — as my father's heir. That's what I'm thinking about at this moment, Keene. You know of my longstanding love for this land. But you haven't heeded the words of my father or my mother, have you?" Kora gave Keene a hard look.

"That's not quite what I was talking about, Kora," Keene shot back immediately, at the same time setting Will back in his rocking bed. The veins in Keene's neck and forehead rose to the surface as his tone grew serious and pointed. "I was talking about his living here in the north woods, getting to know the forest and stream—just as you did, as Jack did." Keene plunged deeper into the intensifying exchange.

"Remember, young lady, I still hold the deed, with your father's instructions written to me the day he died—which I will follow through with at the right time. As you know, there is no mention of you in that letter to me. Young Will here adds another factor for me to consider, another person who is part of this equation."

Keene raised his voice to a loud but controlled pitch. "The time is approaching when I shall have to make a decision."

Father walked around the table toward the stairs. "Now I think I shall get some rest. I have many serious matters to think about. Goodnight, Kora. I hope Will and you will have a pleasant night at Basin camp and that I can visit with you more tomorrow. Goodnight, Jack, and my friend, Duryea. You cooked another unforgettable supper!" And with that, Keene began ascending the steps to his room.

As he neared the top step, still in view, he patted his chest coat pocket and pulled out a paper, something that looked like an old legal document folded in quarters. This reminded me that he'd seemed to be doing some legal work in his office before dinner, and how unusual it was for him to be carrying legal papers at camp.

That's when it hit me, full force. My God! He'd brought the escrow deed to camp!

Kora moved to the rocker and picked up Will, who for the first time all day cried out loudly, as if for attention and love from his mother.

Will soon calmed and, as I sat in the library, I thought I heard the faint tap-tap-tap of the L.C. Smith typewriter coming from upstairs in Father's room. There were pauses, then the typing would resume for perhaps five minutes before another period of silence.

I wasn't sure if Kora or Duryea realized what in all likelihood had just occurred. Kora and I remained within view of each other in the open rooms, but I avoided eye contact with her. She sat by the open fire Duryea had lit, the flames crackling. Kora began to read a child's book to Will. I was struck by how ironically peaceful everything looked, in the very moment that the things were in fact just beginning to roll to a full boil.

Needing to get away for a bit, I said I was going for a walk before total darkness descended, and left the camp. The sparks of Kora's sharp exchange with Keene seemed oddly far away. Yet as I walked the beach in the chill night air, the lack of agreement among us continued to haunt me.

I returned to a silent sleeping Basin camp and collapsed into a deep sleep.

"Kora, each of us takes a pathway through this world. Sometime, it's winding and mysterious and takes us in directions we didn't intend to go. But it remains the path we've chosen. I realize you're on your path, trying to find your way with young Will. You'll find the right path, I believe, but it may take some time. The loss of your father's guidance, so many years ago, is something that can't be made up for, and I understand that. Your mother once told me things about you and your father, how close you were, and how you hiked the Basin with him and …. Well, I'll leave that for later."

I lay in my bed, early the next morning, easily overhearing Keene talking to Kora in the library downstairs.

My heart raced, mindful of the earlier confrontation between them.

"Keene, you know me better than I thought, better than many people, including your son, Jack."

Someone began fussing with the fire burning in the fireplace, and no one spoke for a moment or two. As quietly as I could, I got out of bed and moved to the top of the stairs.

"Jack is distant at times," Kora went on. "He doesn't often let me know what he's thinking. Keene, you know that he and I have always been fond of each other. And you know that I'm married. But Jack's and my relationship … goes beyond … fondness. I love your son and I believe he loves me. Unfortunately, our two paths have taken us in separate directions, and … well … that's … all." Kora's voice trailed away to a whisper, and silence filled the room.

I stayed frozen in my furtive position at the top of the stairs. After a few moments, Keene responded.

"'All', Kora? That's quite a bit! Especially when I know that Will's father is Jack. I know this in my heart, Kora, you don't even need to confirm or deny it."

She didn't reply. The only sound was that of embers in the fire as someone continued shuffling and working at them with a fire iron. Keene's next words hit me like a lightning bolt.

"Last night, Kora, I took your father's escrow deed for these Basin lands—took it and put it in the L.C. Smith typewriter and typed in the names of the new titleholders, the grantees who should own the wilderness. I know what you proposed to Jack, and I think you and Jack can live with it, and that your father would be pleased. I'm not going to show it to you or Jack just yet, but I will, soon enough."

No sound came from the library, only a silence that lasted a full minute. Then, Keene elected to speak again.

"I shall take your silence as acquiescence, Kora."

Kora spoke, but all she said was, "The coffee's ready, Keene."

I heard the sound of coffee being poured and the delicious aroma drifted up the stairs.

"I'm going for a walk on the beach for a while," Kora said. "Would you please listen for Will ... and pick him up if he cries?"

I heard her move across the room to the front door.

"Certainly, I'll do that for you, Kora—and for Will." Keene's voice rose, as if a surge of energy had shot through him. His voice was more vibrant than I'd heard it in years.

I threw water on my face, dressed quickly, and went to Keene, still in the library. Saying only good morning, I poured myself a cup of coffee. Keene nodded at me, but was preoccupied. Angled rays of the early sun streamed through the high oval and down through the open mezzanine area, lighting his face. He sipped his coffee from a mug.

"Kora has gone for a walk, Jack." He rose from his chair and moved closer to me.

"You've made me proud as your father — the way you've done things in your life. Our law office has done well, Jack, in large part because of you and the way we've worked together. You've done things in your own style, and often on your terms.

"Now you have a wonderful son. And a relationship with Kora that I hope you somehow work out, even with all the difficulties, since I understand she's the one for you. It seems she always has been, doesn't it. Well, enough said. You're a man I admire and respect and ...love a great deal. Our time together has been a gift." Keene started to turn away, then stopped to face me.

"And, yes, I have completed the escrow deed. I believe you are protected and that Kora accepts it. The time has come for me to say and do these things, Jack."

He came to me and we met in an embrace, father and son, man to man.

He drew back and looked me in the eye, not wanting any other response from me but to reflect on what he'd said, as had been his practice with me since my youth. A look of satisfaction flooded his face, filling in the age lines around his eyes and mouth.

"And now, son, my grandson is still asleep and I need to leave early for the office—there's something I must complete. So you watch Will. I'll take the Austin guide boat."

Patting the chest pocket of his suit jacket with one hand, Father said, "On my way to work, I'll stop at the county clerk's. Anything you need there?

I shook my head.

"I'll see you later at the office, then. Take your time. You might want to visit more with Kora. You never know what the two of you might work out."

I laughed out loud at the magnificent twinkle that filled his blue eyes. He turned and walked out to the boathouse.

A minute later I heard the faint squeak of the pinned guide boat oars pivoting in their locks as Keene Durant powered the Austin double-ender toward the point. I stepped to the window just as his boat cleared the point and disappeared into the early morning mist.

Nineteen
New Fate

The memory is seared in my mind forever.

It was almost noon of that same morning, June 10, 1920, and I'd decided to stay at camp to get to know Will and to visit with Kora. We were down by the boat launch and I was dangling Will in the water. His squeals of excitement rang out over the water.

Suddenly Duryea came into view at the point. He was in the Austin double-ender — the boat Father had rowed to the village that morning.

It was clearly Duryea, not Father, at the oars, and for an old man he was moving at a frantic pace. As he rounded the point he began yelling something, his head turned toward his destination where I was standing. I couldn't hear him. He waved his brimmed hat frantically as if in distress, then took to his oars again.

As he came closer and I could finally hear him, I realized he was shouting, "Jack, stay right there so I can talk to you this minute! *Venez, Jack, c'est important!*" His voice carried a piercing tone of urgency, and he'd broken into his dialect. I knew immediately that something was very wrong.

Duryea's boat came in to the dock.

"Jack, it is your father. He was in the village, *je lui vois et j'aide, mais... mais* — He was not feeling well, *il me dit*—after he rowed from camp. He had just been to the courthouse, and we stood and talked, but I could see he was not comfortable, not well. Then, Jack, he grabbed his chest. His color turned white, ashen. He went down, Jack. His face was in great pain."

My jaws had tensed at his first words. He continued just as Kora came closer to see about the commotion.

"I shouted for help. Bill McGrath was nearby, *je pense*, and we got Keene to the Dr. Trudeau's office. I stayed only a few minutes — *je ne sais pas*—I do not know what happened — before the doctor said to come and get you."

I felt like stone, unable to move.

"Jack," Duryea said, "I saw the priest come to the office as I left."

With that I said to Duryea, "Get us to the village. Come, get in the boat!"

"We're coming with you, Jack!" Kora cried out. She climbed into the double-ender with Will, and Duryea and I pushed off from the dock. We each manned a set of oars as hard as we could, Duryea in the bow and I in the stern, with Kora and Will in between in the middle seat. A good breeze came off our stern, and the usual twenty minute oar was narrowed to about fifteen minutes to the village. We didn't talk as we went.

Father O'Brien was waiting at our boathouse.

"Jack, I'm sorry. I administered the last rites to your father, and Dr. Trudeau has pronounced him dead. He said there was nothing he could do, that it must have been his heart. You should come with me to Dr. Trudeau's to say your good-byes."

I could not believe my priest's words. I could not grasp that Father was gone. As I walked numbly beside, Father O'Brien toward the doctor's, the priest spoke again.

"Your father was able to get out — he whispered to me during last rites — that you must go to the county clerk's office soon, that you would know what to do and where to look. And just at the end he sat up and cried, 'Jack,' and then collapsed. It was his last word."

Dr. Trudeau was waiting for us. After offering his condolences, he took me aside.

"Jack, your father wanted no one to know of his heart condition, which has been quite serious over the last few years. He tried to be careful, as I advised him, but … this moment was inevitable. I thought you would want to know this now. I am sorry."

I said nothing as he walked away, but understood that it was like Keene to keep his problems to himself. Father had said it right: none of us knows how much time we have here.

But we had a good and valued life together.

Not knowing what else to do, feeling unmoored and emptied, I followed Father O'Brien on to the stone chapel. Duryea went with me, and Kora, too. She never left my side the whole day. Will was uncannily quiet and still. Bill McGrath, who accompanied us, held the child, freeing Kora to provide comfort to me and Duryea, who was silent with shock.

We knelt at the front pew and prayed silently together. The stone chapel was a place in which I'd prayed often over my lifetime to my wildnerness God, and it was of some solace to be in its peaceful quietude on the edge of the village where it met the wild forest. The brass dedication plaque was dated 1915. Our parish had commissioned a young local stonemason named Covey to design it in a simple country style, and Duryea to build it. Father had written the dedication plaque and its words echoed the beauty, goodness, and truth of nature, life, and God:

> *This chapel is erected to the memory of all our people, young and old, who have passed through this world and gained God by so doing. It stands for freedom of thought, prayer, and action. It is built in a place of peace and solitude, in a land of wilderness that we must come to understand and honor for all its inhabitants, animal and plant. May the the Lord bless all of these, and may this always remain a place of spiritual and mental renewal.*

Duryea and Covey's creation was laid up with local fieldstone of granite, and designed with a transept on each side of the main nave. A stone fireplace stood behind the raised altar, its matching stone chimney rising to a high peak. The nave was finished with five massive stone pews on either side of the aisle; the transepts were left open, flanked at the outside wall by 15-foot high stained glass windows. At the top of each, clear glass was installed so that the tops of mountain peaks could be seen in the distance. I studied the distant purple peaks for many long minutes, praying for a reserve of strength to carry on without Father.

Friends from throughout the region attended Father's funeral the next day at the chapel. His burial was at the plot next to Mother on the Basin lands at a rise in view of the Basin camp.

The obituary printed in the Albany Times Union on June 11, 1920, was in the same issue that announced that the New York Yankees were in negotiations for George Ruth, a Boston pitcher of some renown who could also hit.

The '20s roared in for me on a low note and an empty place in my life. My partner, my mentor, my father, and the great protector of the wilderness, was gone.

It was a few days later that I summoned the resolve to go to the county clerk's office in the courthouse. I knew what to ask for in the recorded documents docketed there. The clerk, Peter Grinnell, was charged with completing the document, as it was left in escrow with Keene by William West Longfellow. Now, however, it had the language added by my father, and I still didn't know precisely what Keene had put in the grantee clause of the deed.

As soon as I walked in, Grinnell spotted me, picked up a document on his desk and walked to me.

"This is what you are looking for, Jack. Here, sit down and take your time. I've already put it on record."

He handed me the deed that was escrowed no longer, and was now subject to public scrutiny. I sat at the large oak table. It was quiet in the clerk's office this early summer morning.

"Thank you, Peter."

I took the deed, drew a deep breath, and sat for a moment, not reading but pressing the document in my fingers. Thinking of my father and our last conversation, I didn't want to rush my reading. I still knew the deed from memory, despite its length, due to my preparations for the Aber trial. But what I hadn't seen, what I was about to read, was the grantee clause.

I opened the folded deed slowly and my eyes moved down the page. It read:

Tᕼᓮꙅ ꙆᴎꙎᴇᴎ꓄ᴜꙄᴇ
made this twentieth day of November, 1894, by and between WILLIAM WEST LONGFELLOW, of Franklin County, New York

Party of the first part,
and KEENE DURANT, of Essex County, New York, AS TRUSTEE, TO HOLD IN TRUST, FOR JACK K. DURANT, and any grandchild or grandchildren of the grantor hereafter born to my beloved daughter, KORA LONGFELLOW, until his or her eighteenth birthday, and thereafter, outright, as equal tenants in common,

Parties of the second part,
WITNESSETH that the party of the first part, in consideration of the love and affection between the parties, does hereby grant and release unto the parties of the second part,

A LIFE ESTATE for their respective lives, and upon the death of the survivor, does grant and release unto THE STATE OF NEW YORK forever and in perpetuity the sole remainder interest on the condition that the Basin lands conveyed herein remain wilderness for use as such by the people, in conformity with the forever wild state forests created in the State of New York Constitution for the great Adirondack Park, and further, on the condition that the Basin camp built on the premises remain intact and be preserved by the state. Title shall revert to the holders of the Life Estate, or their heirs or distributes, in the event of any breach of such conditions. Any trust created herein shall terminate on the eighteenth birthday of any grantee, and his or her life estate at such date shall then be in his or her own right.

Mr. Longfellow had signed the deed, and it was acknowledged by the local justice of the peace, under date of November 20, 1894. The land conveyed was all 400,000 acres Longfellow owned. The clerk had officially recorded the deed, placing his seal upon it the day Keene died. The second time through, I became aware that the typing on the grantee clause was obviously more recent than the rest of the document.

By so completing it, Father had fulfilled Longfellow's intent to preserve the Basin lands. I sat in silence in the quiet room, thinking of Father and the demons that had played on his mind for over twenty five years before he'd come to complete the transfer. He had not mentioned Kora, but had made an entreaty to her by conveying to any child she might have. On this, Kora might choose to make an issue, and assert her claim to title.

Father's last words to me, you never know what you two might work out, still rang in my ears. Keene Durant had a way of making people work together, or fail if they would not. On my way out of the clerk's office, I handed the deed back to a curious Grinnell.

"The name on the grantee clause looks like it was typed the day Keene walked in here and handed it to me for recording," he said.

I shrugged my shoulders, said nothing except thank you, and walked out. Returning to camp, I told Kora the deed had been recorded, that the grantee clause had been completed, that it named me and any grandchild of her father's as life tenants, and the state got the remainder interest in perpetuity after we were both gone. I didn't mention Will by name.

"I knew your father would do something like this!" Kora cried out. "It's just like him! Will is William Longfellow's grandson." She spoke each word slowly, defiantly, holding my eyes as she did so.

"As you can see, Jack, this ties us together through our son."

I sat down, surprised, but pleased at the same time by Kora's admission in plain terms, and without qualification, that Will was our child.

I still said nothing, and she went on. "I'm returning to New York soon, Jack. You keep Will here, where he belongs," she said in her usual direct manner. "I'll get you legal papers for custody and paternity. I'm sure Mr. Hubreth will see that this is done. As for us, there must be a way we can … ." Kora stopped and a tear rolled down her cheek.

"I need more time to think things through, but there must be a way for us to reunite, and maybe now is the time to approach my husband on this point. Your father has spoken now through this deed, so we shall have to see what we can work out."

Kora stood, still in the middle of thought.

"I'm terribly hurt that it is not your and my names on the deed. My mother told Keene years ago of the conversations my father and I had about the future of the Basin and his promise to me."

When she said this, I remembered Father's discomfort in his office when I mentioned that Janet Longfellow might not be happy to see Will and me named as the grantees.

"But there's nothing in writing, nothing I can prove, and I can perhaps accept what Keene has chosen to do, though I do think my father would strongly object. But the state will protect the lands, won't it, Jack, under the constitution, as my father said in his letter to Keene? That at least is of some solace."

Kora had said so much that I didn't know where to start. But then it struck like a punch that I was to take custody and raise a boy two years old!

Groping for responses, I grabbed hold of the easiest thing to address.

"Yes, the state is obligated at the right time to take over and honor its commitment. If it didn't, we'd have rights to go to court on this and ask for the transfer to be declared void. We can designate someone for the future, for after we're all gone, to watch over this."

We stood looking at each other, knowing we were talking around the greater issue, here.

"And ... I will honor your request and raise our son here on the Basin, where he does belong." It was said, and in that moment I knew it was right. "But Kora, you must try to get back here to be with us as soon as you're able. We both need you, Kora!" When she made to reply, I hurriedly went on. "But don't worry about my needing help here. Don't forget Duryea, he knows children! He just about raised me. It was a long time ago, but we'll get along."

"Jack, listen. I'm not going to say good-bye to Will. I can't." Her face was strained with a grief I couldn't begin to imagine. "I don't know what else to say or do. Now I must prepare to leave here."

Kora and I clutched in an embrace, our tears mingling. She looked a last time into my eyes. Kissing my cheek, she turned and walked from the room to prepare for her return to New York and Mr. Hubreth.

For my part, I turned my thoughts to the serious matter of rearing a young child. My stomach knotted as I thought of the challenge ahead.

I still needed to search the office for any last instructions Keene may have left for me. I would do so, however, only after I got Will situated, or at least to a point of beginning to settle in at his new home. This was to be a new start for me, and a sad good-bye to my life with Keene Durant, whose spirit lived on with his last words and acts. Sitting in the sand watching Will, I thought back to 1912 when Kora visited—when I intended to propose marriage to her but was shocked by news of her marriage to Hubreth. In a way I regretted my inaction in that moment, my failure to insist that she get divorced at any cost. Now, in 1920, it might be too late. Was there any way, now, that I could marry her and we could bring our son up in a good and loving family?

Six long years of the prime of my life had passed from 1912 to 1918, during which time I'd heard almost nothing from Kora. She'd gone away, mad at Father and mad at me over the Basin ownership, then she'd reappeared for our romantic interlude. She'd disappeared again, and now she was back, following the birth of our son.

In Kora's letter after she'd first left the Basin, she'd described herself as zealous in protecting her self-interest. Her words had certainly proved apt. It was clear that any further complications in her life, or in my own, would doom any chance of reconciliation now even if Hubreth were to concede a divorce, which he showed no sign of doing.

For now, I must take stock in my life. I was 35; I had just become a father and custodian of my two-year-old son; I had no woman to help me raise the boy day to day, just an old, kind, and gentle soul in Duryea. No wife with whom to share love and comfort, and the return of the woman I loved was uncertain at best. I'd lost my father who'd been my voice of reason, my mentor; I'd lost my law partner. Doubtless, I would draw the opprobrium of the community for raising a boy I called my own, though his mother was not present.

To top it all off, the mother of my son had just informed me that she was the rightful heir to her father's property, that he had promised her the Basin lands. But title to those lands had been recorded just before my father died, leaving me with great authority over the future of the Basin, and over my son.

And finally, I mused, I had acquired a potential new fishing partner in little Will, though only time would tell for sure. And I had a thriving law office to keep going.

I'd been dealt my cards, and now I must play out my hand.

Twenty
Kora's Reprise

How could Will be twelve years old? I watched him in wonder as he moved ahead of me on Otter Brook fishing the pools with the new fly rod I'd just built for him. It was his first official new fly rod, not a hand-me-down, and it seemed to have caught his attention. I'd waited a long time for his interest in fly fishing to develop and it had been slow in coming.

It was August 15, 1931, and I had privately marked eleven years since the passing of Keene Durant. I still sorely missed his company and good advice. But glancing up at Will I had to grin, for my boy was the embodiment of Keene Durant, from his blue, almond-shaped eyes and his perfect posture. I'd raised a fine young boy, and largely on my own. Kora had visited us as often as she could over these years, but she'd remained married to Mr. Hubreth and living in New York. Our relationship had withered, from my perspective, though she claimed that wasn't so for her.

Hubreth continued refusing to grant a divorce. By law Kora and I were a nullity, yet by agreement as lovers we had conceived a son. I began to think of us in those terms — as lovers by agreement — after Kora compared our love to Muir's for a married woman from whom he was separated. She copied out some of the passage from Muir's journal — the same one I'd read to her in June of 1918:

> ...*in the high meadows and peaks* ...
> ...*you are the first to meet me, and I often*
> *speak to you as verily in the flesh.*

Under it she'd penned, "This is how I have come to see us — as lovers separated, but not truly apart." Inside the envelope she'd tucked her best-tied streamer imitation, one of which always showed up when I least expected it.

I still have that letter, which I carry with me every day in my pocket diary. 'I've employed her streamer to good use catching, but releasing, many a fine trout.

But it was day-to-day life and bringing up Will that now dominated my life, with only an occasional respite in a letter or visit from Kora. Father had left an estate with enough to keep Will and me comfortable, even without the law office operation. I still carried a caseload, but I'd trimmed my work down in scope to give Will the time he deserved

Recently I'd had to admit that real property taxes had become a burden. The only income generated from the Basin land came from small annual fees paid by Dunning and Rondeau. But rumor had it that each man would soon have to come out of the woods, no longer able to continue the rugged existence of his younger years. It had been some time since I'd seen either of them, but I knew the passage of time took its toll on woodsmen and lawyers alike.

Economic news was also glum. The stock market had crashed on Wall Street two years before, and I was concerned that investments made by Keene and me were now worth a lot less. I worried as well about the stock market losses' effects on Kora and her well-being.

Keene's instructions to see what I could work out with her came to me often, but there seemed to be, in the main, only glum news coming from her, as well. She still occasionally referred to her unexercised claim to title of the Basin by virtue of being William Longfellow's sole heir. The deed Keene had recorded, in effect conveying title to Will and me for our lives, seemed like only a stopgap measure, something Will and I would need to act on during our lives. My interest in the wilderness was still strong, but for the first time it was tempered by the reality that I couldn't go on indefinitely owning the land and paying taxes with no return.

But on this day, out in the wilderness on the stream with fly rod in hand, my thoughts were focused on Will. His springy step of earlier in the day was now absent, causing me concern that he might be losing interest and not learning patience.

"Father, your speckles aren't home, are they!"

"It's early, Will. The rises should start. Have patience. Your mother's coming tomorrow, and you know how she likes fresh brook trout. We can't give up yet."

We sat on an old hemlock stump, listening to the stream's gurgles and looking out over the pool at the next bend. It was there the hatch of hexegenia would occur, if it happened at all this day. And all the conditions appeared right for it.

"E-P-T," I said in chant like style, putting the emphasis on my E. I wanted to get Will's attention.

"What did you say father, E-T-T?"

"E-P-T," I chanted again. "It's something old Duryea taught me, Will. When you want a hatch, you chant their calling card. E is for ephemeroptera, P is for plecoptera, and T is for trichoptera — mayflies, stoneflies and caddisflies! Our chant is to rev them up, get them going. Right now our emphasis should be on the mayfly hatch I think is coming. So chant the hardest for ephemeroptera, like this: E-P-T — with the emphasis on the E! E-P-T, E-P-T!"

Will joined in and we had a time with our chant — E-P-T, E-P-T — getting in unison and hitting each E with emphasis. In a while I held up my hand and we stopped to wait and watch the surface of the pool.

"Duryea taught you that?"

"He did. He was my finest teacher on insect life. A self-taught entomologist."

"But Father, the chant really should be hex-hex-hex!" Will insisted, expressing his view of things. I sensed that I finally I his interest in the hatch.

"Duryea taught me that the hex mayfly we're looking for hatches on an August evening just like this one. He wasn't often wrong. I'm sure you remember Duryea talking about things like mayfly hatches right, Will?"

Will nodded, as I'd known he would.

Duryea had died in 1928, and life had not been the same for Will or me. I'd come downstairs early in the morning and found him sitting at his reading chair, slumped over. Muir's journal was resting on his chest and there was a peaceful, comforting look on his wonderfully lined old face.

I shut his eyes to the world for the last time, there, and in that moment, turning off his gas lamp in the dim early morning light of dawn, I felt a light in my own life flicker to a close. I'd lifted the book from his chest and glanced at the page he'd been reading. In the margin, Duryea had written in his own hand:

A few places remain free and wild—and God can be found there.

I was glad, at least, that Duryea had died surrounded by his books, and by his sketches of various things he'd designed and built. One of those drawings hangs now on the camp wall, framed and under glass, as a tribute to him. It's his sketch of the Basin camp, dated by him in 1893, the year before he built it On the back side, out of view from the world, is a penciled notation, not in Duryea's hand, which reads, "Plan is good and your conditions are acceptable." I believe the unsigned note to be in the hand of William West Longfellow. And Duryea's diary, which I later read, confirms that he and Longfellow had an agreement about the Basin and the camp he built here. A journal entry from 1894 reads, Mr. Longfellow now understands about wilderness. He is in agreement with me on preservation.

The great mentor proved again he was a man of his word.

Will and I buried Duryea in his favorite clearing, a meadow not far from camp with a view of the mountain peaks in the distance. Will didn't talk a lot about Duryea for quite a while. He'd always been one to think his own thoughts and share them only in his own time.

But now, of late, it seemed he wanted to know everything I could share about Duryea's life and about things Duryea had done with me when I was a boy. I used those occasions to tell stories of fishing trips and what Duryea had taught me on them. I shared with him my promise to keep the Basin wild, and told him what men like Muir had thought about the value to the soul of unspoiled wilderness — that the hand of God was here to be seen. I showed him Duryea's entry in the margin of the Muir journal he'd died holding. Will seemed to appreciate this. I knew he missed our companion as much as I did.

This great camp, which he went to his death questioning as an intrusion on the wilderness, remained only one of his many legacies.

I maintained my resolve to carry on where he had left off. His lessons were always with me, resurfacing in new forms, especially any time I was on the stream. His knowledge of insect life and fly tying was well ahead of his time, and what Will and I were about to see on the surface of this pool did not surprise me. Duryea's mentoring proved right again!

As the evening progressed the brook trout began to arouse with interest. The hex moved from the gravel beds in the riff above the hole, their wing covers and gill plates still intact. One and then another, first males and then females, wriggled free of the detritus of the stream bed where they had lived.

Tiny bubbles rose straight to the surface and released the hex, and there they got caught in the current and washed into the pool below. Each brownish hex wriggled in the surface film of clear water in newfound freedom. Wing covers previously hidden under a wing pad revealed emerging wings as the hex worked, twitched and floated. They were no longer nymphs living under the water, reliant on gills. They were on the move. Some primordial force, an inner clock and thermometer, told them it was time to transform into now-breathing insects whose gill plates had transformed to tiny lungs capable of sustaining them in their new environment.

Emerging wings dried in the gentle breeze rippling across the surface. Dimples began to appear on the surface caused by curious and hungry speckles, now attuned to the feeding orgy presented to them.

"Look, Father, dimples on the surface! I see hex there, Father! Quick, grab your fly rod! Put something on to match. Do you have something to match?"

Now was the time to teach him, as Duryea had taught me.

"Here, Will, tie this on your tippet!" I handed him the hex pattern Duryea had perfected and shown me how to tie. It was a first rate imitation, down to the dome-shaped projection between its antennae on its head.

In the next hour, Will set the hook and landed speckle after speckle, all hard fighting ravenous trout. He lost a fair number, too. His hex pattern started to look chewed up, and I told him he didn't have to keep every fish he brought in. He slowly accepted that, and released many with a sense of pride. But we kept ten large and full fish, each over fifteen inches, and one measuring twenty one inches, all gorged on hex, each caught on the fraud we presented to them in the form of our imitation hex.

The feeding came to a sudden end as the last light disappeared. We gutted the haloed beauties, revealing deep pink flesh, and headed back to camp across the dark lake, paddling and talking as we went. Will was proud of his catch, and his release. It had proved to be an unforgettable night of fly-fishing with my best fishing companion.

Over time, Will and I would form an indissoluble union with the wilderness, and a deep respect for it, talking often of Duryea and his teachings.

"When can we go again, Father?"

Soon, Will, but let's not forget your mother is to arrive tomorrow. You need to spend time with her. And ...so do I, Will."

Of Kora's many visits in the eleven years since Keene's death, some had been foreboding, some unforgettable, and all had been interesting. To me, Kora's brief visits were always magical; to Will they were a source of delight, concern, and frustration, in that order.

We always made the best of our time together, touring on the rugged but recently constructed Adirondack roads in my newly purchased Ford. The car carried us to trailheads where we hiked, and to other venues, where we paddled.

Kora's and my favorite places remained the remote reaches of the Basin, and the featherbed in front of the oval mosaic. In all those years, I broke silence on the subject of her divorce and remarriage only twice. On the first occasion, as we lay together in the featherbed, I'd asked about it directly. Kora had grown somber and looked away.

"Jack, I want to marry you. But Mr. Hubreth won't ever grant a divorce — if for no other reason than that it would make me happy."

The second time, I told her I would approach Hubreth to negotiate a divorce on his terms. But she used the same words exactly to explain that there was no hope for my success in that.

After that, I didn't bring it up again.

"Who is Mr. Hubreth, and why is he able to control Mother?" Will had recently demanded. "Why can he do this to us? I don't understand, Father."

It was difficult to explain, but as he matured, I told him that his mother and I had a relationship long before her marriage to Hubreth, and that we loved each other very much, and him. I said nothing about being unable to marry his mother, or about the possibility of her living with us some time in the future. Will still accepted what I said, but as he grew older the full truth would have to be told to him. I sensed that that time was rapidly approaching.

But more pressing events put all other issues aside. When we returned to camp, a Western Union envelope was posted on the door, left by a courier from the village. I opened it and found a telegram from Kora. It read:

New York City August 15, 1931

Peter Hubreth died today STOP Chaos here since crash, when he lost everything STOP Will be delayed in arrival STOP Hope to be there before fall STOP Love to you both STOP Kora

I read the news to Will.

"Let me see it, Father," he said.

Will read it again and again, then put it down. We ate dinner in a contemplative silence; neither of us had much appetite. I put the trout on ice, hoping they'd keep for Kora's arrival, but uncertain when that might be.

The disappointment was obvious in Will's face. As he washed up the supper dishes, he said he was going to bed early. I too felt drained by disappointment and concern for the future. What ate at me unceasingly that night was a sense that my life with Will might soon change, that forces coming to bear upon Kora, and that would impact directly on Will and me, were beyond my control.

How cruelly ironic that Hubreth's death should, but did not, bring Kora freedom to marry me. Instead, the financial condition in which he left her had become her curse. I could not bring up marriage under the circumstances.

But time would tell. Father's words — about getting together with Kora, that we really didn't know what we might work be able to work out — reverberated in my mind. But what could we work out if Hubreth had gone bust with a mountain of debt — debt Kora could be held responsible for, and that could drain every asset she might inherit from him, leaving her destitute? Her remaining asset would be the Basin lands.

She would have to be careful in her moves with creditors, too, something she knew little about, for they could attach even an expectant or equitable interest in real property. And that reality had to be heeded well by me.

At every life turn, it seemed, Kora's and my relationship was to be defined by conflict.

I gave Will a hug before he went to his room for the night.

"Things will work out, Will, don't you worry."

Whatever was coming, it wasn't coming fast. Kora was not heard from for some time, except for occasional letters to Will, which contained little information about her life or circumstances.

My fears for Kora's financial and emotional well-being were borne out over the ensuing years. We heard from her about one difficult circumstance after another, as creditors pursued her for debt on which they said she had liability. We saw each other only once or twice a year, though Will visited his mother once in New York, only to return and say he would never do so again. Her apartment, Will said, was quite dark and unwelcoming.

Kora walked in to my office unannounced on September 3, 1937. She looked ashen and shaken.

She apologized for having stayed away so long, explaining her absence as a result of Peter Hubreth's disastrous financial situation, just as I had supposed. Hubreth had had Kora sign with him on at least one obligation, and she'd been sued by that creditor, and advised that she might be responsible for other debts as well. It was possible, she'd been told, that every asset would be consumed.

Finally, she got to her real concern.

"The major creditor is aware of my claim to ownership of the Basin," she said. "I may file bankruptcy, which could hang over me for the rest of my life, Jack. I'm sick over this!" Kora broke down and sobbed. I came around from my desk and pulled her from her chair to hold her. Her body shook uncontrollably.

"I couldn't bring myself to tell you or Will in a letter, so I said little and kept away. It's been so hard for me." In a while she dabbed at her eyes to stop the tears. "I'm a single woman, Jack, but I feel like I am in shackles. Is there any way out of this? Can you help me?"

"I'm sure there's something we can do, Kora. And of course I'll help you."

But I didn't really know a way out, and I didn't know what real help I could be, especially if things were as bad as she said.

"One thought, Kora, is not to file bankruptcy if you have any inkling that the Basin could be at stake. There's a legal theory by which a creditor could attach your interest, and ...."

Kora had never looked so forlorn. I returned to my desk chair, and she lowered herself back into hers. We sat and looked at each other for a long time.

"This ruins just about any hopes we've had for marriage, doesn't it, Jack?"

Suddenly her face changed, as rapidly as the sun can be obscured by clouds. She sat bolt upright in her chair, nodding angrily at me. "Oh, I understand, now! You think my interest in this matter should be to keep the Basin free and clear for you and Will. You don't want me to cause any problems with that — do you! I've never felt so awful or so vulnerable, and you're only thinking of yourself! I shall file bankruptcy to get out from underneath this, and you cannot stop it!"

As angry as her accusations made me, I couldn't respond, knowing there was truth in what she'd said.

I'd never wanted my overarching plan to stand in the way of our marriage, but there it was, directly in our path. Not for the first time, I reviewed Kora's situation. She could sign off and release any interest she had in the Basin, but even that wouldn't prevent the bankruptcy court from claiming her underlying interest in the land. And if we married, that could drag Will and me into court to explain the full circumstances.

I thought better of sharing those thoughts with Kora at that moment. I changed the subject.

"Kora, let's go see our Will. He's at the camp today and will be so excited to see you."

Kora recovered herself quickly enough with this suggestion, smiled slightly and nodded in agreement. We left the office together.

On our way to the landing, I said, "Since we want to get right out to Will, let's motor out."

"Motor out, Jack? You don't mean to use one of these new outboard motors, do you? They disturb the wilderness and pollute the water!" Her words were shrill, and she came to a stop, demanding my answer.

"Yes, exactly that, Kora. It cuts down on my time to camp and really doesn't seem to disturb a thing."

She began spitting conservation theories at me, threatening to fight me on this, despite her financial situation. We continued walking down the dusty village street as we talked.

"Do you remember our talk with John Burroughs at his camp" I said. "You know that he became well respected by conservationists, and he told us the wilderness is here to be used by all of us. Respected, to be sure, and treated right, too, but enjoyed. My boat with its new little motor doesn't hurt a thing."

We'd arrived at the boathouse, and I hopped into the craft with the shiny new Johnson outboard. I quickly wound the starting line into its position on the engine head, and. It answered with a purr, not missing a stroke. I turned to smile at Kora, to show her that the motor was harmless. But following her eyes, I saw something I'd never noticed before: a film on the water beside the purring engine. It was an oil slick, and it colored the surface as it floated there, forming a small plume as it spread outward. Kora remained standing on the landing.

"That's not what Mr. Burroughs had in mind for our lakes, Jack. Lots of families are refusing to buy these things—because they pollute, as you can see."

At least I'd got her mind off her financial problems to one she liked better. But I had to admit that her comments rang true. An invasion into clean water was right in front of me in an oily film on the surface of the water. My first thought was about what would happen if everyone used these new inventions. My second was to wonder why I'd been so willing to buy one.

I choked the engine to a stop, oil still pluming from the engine, smoke still coming off the engine head. I shoved it to an upright position, out of the water.

"Come on board, Kora. Let's go to see our lovely Will." I reached for the oars, putting each into its locks, then held Kora's hand as she stepped lightly into the old wooden boat. She had a look of satisfaction on her face, without a trace of spite.

There in the boat, on the water, the warmth and beauty of her once-young face surfaced, as it always had in natural light. I studied her features as I sat waiting for her to arrange herself in the boat. She was a remarkable woman. Despite her years of pressure and unhappiness, she'd maintained her physical health and vitality. Her manner of dress, an Adirondack style with a hint of New York, was eye-catching. I couldn't help but notice, however, that her clothing was a bit worn, despite the money I'd been sending her on a regular basis for a couple of years now.

She gave me a faint smile.

Returning hers with my own, I began to row to the Basin camp. We traveled in silence across the water, enjoying the familiar wilderness. As always, my thoughts turned to preserving it for Will, for generations of descendants and others to enjoy. I was now more uncertain that ever of Kora's intentions, and knew I would need to remain circumspect of her chameleon-like behavior and the effect on her of her poor financial condition.

Stroking hard and looking at her face across from me, I thought again about her self-description in that letter written years ago as she went off on her own. She'd said she was zealous in her own interest and did not trust others to act on her behalf, including Keene — and now probably including me, as well.

At camp, Will greeted his mother with a small hug. He was now 18, and showing his independence. Now taller than I, Will had his mother's good features, including her wonderful smile, but he had almond-shaped eyes like Father and me. His thick shock of wavy dark brown hair seemed to bee a combination of Kora's hairline and Keene's full and prominent hair. His height, I presumed, came from William West Longfellow.

"Look at you, Will!" Kora stood back and looked up at him admiringly.

"Where, where have you been, Mother?"

I'd never heard him speak so harshly. Kora's answer surprised me. "I wrote you, Will! I explained my difficulties and told you something of my plans to ... you know. I haven't been able to get here any earlier, son. I'm sorry!"

Will walked in one direction and Kora in the other, leaving me to stand alone to wonder and think the worst.

Twenty One
Show Cause

I was able to piece together, from people in the village and other evidence left behind, Keene Durant's movements on June 10, 1920, the day of his death.

He didn't go directly to the courthouse in the last hours of his life. Carrying the deed, he walked to the office, in a sweat from his row in, and sat at his desk alone in the silence of early morning. He rested quietly there for a time, and I can imagine that he felt an odd grief, holding the soon-to-be-recorded document, under his total control for the last time.

From his bottom desk drawer he drew out the dram of Canadian whiskey, poured a half glass, and sat at his L. C. Smith to type a letter to his grandson, Will, and me. Keene probably let the whiskey take its first effect before typing, so that as he wrote he felt relaxed, almost euphoric about his life and the Basin wilderness. He knew the time had come to write the letter that had long been on his mind. It's easy to imagine him pecking away with two fingers.

June 10, 1920
Dearest Jack and grandson Will,

I am about to record the deed for the Basin lands, which I have long held under instructions from William West Longfellow. The deed leaves each of you a life estate, then the remainder interest to the State of New York.

I want you to understand that if either of you at any time in the future feels that Kora Longfellow Hubreth might attempt to revoke the deed or transfer her interest — if any — you should step in and stop her.

I have never shared with anyone but Duryea that years ago, when Kora was a little girl, Janet Longfellow told me about William's promise that one day the Basin would be hers. He never said this to me, however, although Kora has more recently done so.

As time went along, William's views changed, as evidenced by the agreement he came to with Duryea and me to preserve the Basin as wilderness. Apparently he never brought himself to tell Kora of his change of heart. It is my decision that his written instructions in 1894, and his statements to me to keep the Basin forever wild, must be the factors determining the outcome. William Longfellow wanted the land preserved forever wild, as the state constitution guarantees for the state forest. The deed I record today accomplishes this.

However, I'm especially concerned that if Kora has financial setbacks, you will need to be alert and be prepared against any legal action she might attempt. I authorize either of you to notify the state, holding the remainder interest, of any such action by Kora, as her plan could destroy the *intent that the remainder interest to the state shall preserve this land forever. I am notifying the state of this possibility by sending Mr. Joseph Hamilton, Esquire, a letter and a copy of the recorded deed.*

I fear also that upon your death, Jack, if Kora survives you, she will have the greatest temptation to act in her own self-interest by selling the land at a time she may be under financial duress, or facing some other emergency. I hope I am wrong.

To you, Jack, my beloved son, my utmost love and respect. You have been a wonderful partner in my life.

To my grandson, Will, whom I have just met, I trust that as you grow older and know of my efforts, and your father's, you will understand my concern, and at the same time, my admiration, for your mother, Kora.

Finally, Jack, I know you will not forget our gratitude to Rondeau, now an old man. For his loyalty, he must be permitted to stay on the land as long as he likes

I am now going to the courthouse to record the escrow deed that I have long and faithfully held under my duty to my client, and under what I have come to believe is my moral duty to preserve this wilderness in perpetuity.

Keene Durant

And so Father summarized his knowledge of Kora and William and the Basin. He left the letter on his desk, where I found it the day after his funeral. It became, in my mind, the operative document for Will or me to act upon.

Suspiciously enough, it was the letter I'd discovered was missing from my desk during Kora's visit in 1937.

Will alerted me to some disturbing facts during Kora's visit in early September of 1937. It troubled me that our son was caught in the middle of Kora's and my purposes, but I was very grateful to him for his willingness to fill me in. His information was that, due to the stock market crash, and some continuing losses and claims against her and her deceased husband's estate, Kora was under intense financial pressure. She'd come to the Basin this time intending to consummate a secret and devastating transaction.

She was set to sell her interest in the Basin to Thornwood, a New York City developer and the principal creditor of Peter Hubreth. Hubreth owed him $120,000, and Kora had unknowingly signed onto the debt some time before, when Hubreth and his banker insisted she do so; now she had the liability. Thornwood agreed to release her if he got title to the Basin.

She'd gone through my desk to determine as much as she could about the Basin and its legal status, and that's when she'd found Keene's last letter, there amongst my papers. She'd also found the deed I'd prepared, surrendering Will's and my life estates and giving the full fee interest to the state. I hadn't decided yet if that was the best route to go, but I'd prepared it to review with Will now that he was of age. I'd also shown him Keene's letter to the two of us. Until then, he'd been too young to understand all the complexities of the title, his mother, and our relationship. But Will had turned 18 in March of 1937, and he was ready to hear it all.

"Father," Will had said, after reading Keene's letter as we sat in the Basin camp library, "Grandfather Keene foresaw the exact situation we're now in. Look, he writes in 1920 that 'we must be alert and take quick legal action,' and he authorizes either of us 'to notify the state holding the remainder interest' of Mother's actions—the very actions I fear she intends to take now!"

He grew quiet for a moment before going on. "I've told you about Mother's letters to me stating that she's desperate. And her view on things is changing—because she's desperate. I'm pretty sure she means to go through with things and sell her interest." He looked out through the open porch door for a moment. "Let me think about things, Father. I understand what you, and Duryea when he was here, have had in mind for this place."

Then he walked away, reminding me of Keene Durant telling me of William Longfellow's failure to complete his escrow deed. Will had spoken in the same tone of voice, sounding ominous and rightfully concerned.

When I'd realized she'd found Keene's letter and my proposed deed, I knew with certainty Kora would be infuriated, and more determined than ever to go through with her sale. She would conjecture what Will knew about my proposed, but unsigned, deed giving our interest to the state. And finally, the day's events convinced me that she was ready to carry out her plan. Bitterness and years of pressure had taken their toll on Kora, and to a great extent, on me.

The sound of a boat motor approaching at the Basin camp dock brought me wide awake at dawn. Stabs of anxiety went through me as a man's voice called out, "Mrs. Hubreth, are you here?"

Kora didn't answer or go out, but I heard her stirring in her room, the space that opened to the magnificent oval mosaic on the third level.

Listening to these early morning sounds I thought back to the conversation we'd had a night or so ago after I'd decided not to confront Kora directly about her plans. Still, I'd told her in no uncertain terms that I knew that her situation was not good, and that before she took action of any kind regarding the Basin and her finances, she must consult with me.

I'd got little satisfaction that that would occur. Kora had given me a blank look, as if she was incapable of understanding me, and I'd realized then, with a certainty I'd never felt before, that I was unable to help her. More disturbing yet, I knew our relationship was all but destroyed.

Lying in bed that night I'd thought hard and had come to realize just how lost and confused, and how mad, Kora was. She had no choice but to sell her interest, in her mind, and she was bitter over her perception that Keene and I had cheated her. I learned from Will that she'd arranged for the boat to come to camp that morning to come and take her into town. There she would complete her transaction by delivering her interest in the deed, as Longfellow's heir, in exchange for release from liability

After I'd tried to talk to her that night, hoping to convince her she must consult with me before she took any action at all involving the Basin, Kora had gone to Will on the porch and told him parts of her plan, disguising them as theoretical possibilities. They'd talked there, under a dark sky backlit by a waning quarter moon, and she'd finally confessed her intentions. Will repeated to me Kora's exact words: "There may be no other way. I have to do this. Forgive me, Will. You're my flesh and blood, and I wonder how I can do this to you, to me, to Jack and to the Basin. But I don't have any other way out, Will. Please try to understand that!"

He said Kora had paused, that her body had begun to shake and that she'd lost control and wept. He tried to comfort her, but it was in that moment that Will decided it was time to take action.

Only the night before, I'd dreamed of a sobbing Kora in a nightmare. I'd awakened myself by crying out, "No, it can't be!" and bolting upright in a full sweat. Sleep didn't return for many hours, as I tossed and turned over the question of whether Kora was capable of revoking the life estates Keene had given, and passing title to some creditor to resurrect her own financial condition. I took a whiskey at three a.m. to soften the dream's portent, but even that didn't help.

I got out of bed again at four to read from the diary I'd kept intermittently for some years. I leafed back through several years, letting my life reflected on those pages take hold of me, and losing track of time.

Flipping pages, I came to rest on the account of the day I was caught on the trail between the sow and her cubs, and the hunters guided by Dunning. As I read, I felt the sow's warm breath as she rushed past me, followed by the cubs. I put my hand to my chest, where the imprint of the paw was still faintly visible. I recalled Trembley's rage at the violation of the north woods ethic, and I thought again about how hard Father and I had worked to win the Aber trial. My thoughts went all the way back to Kora befriending the Aber children, Etienne and Susie, to all of us picking blueberries, and Kora's loyalty to her friends that stormy winter day.

Father's face came to me, a gentleness to it in the light of a late day as we worked on the Aber case in the library. The patina of honey-colored tones from the wood walls cast a warm glow; Father's face was intense with concentration. Perhaps I drifted back toward sleep keeping company with that vision of Father; all I know is that he seemed to speak directly to me.

Look what we have left of the wilderness, Jack. In my lifetime I saw entire species of animals wiped out —the big cats and little cats — the panther and the lynx — along with elk and moose. Now the virgin forests are almost gone. The brook trout are fading fast—they're no longer what they were just a few short years ago. Hunted out, fished out, and the forest cut down. The water in your favorite Otter Brook is not as pure as it was. The air doesn't seem the same. And no one thought it could happen here. Yet how many Adirondackers seem truly concerned?

It was as if I heard his very words.

You know my wishes for the Basin—and you know that I left it in your trust, along with Will's, to see that it happens, that the waters and forest and the air are preserved, even if Kora has other problems and other plans.

Keene began to fade away, or I began to reawaken, as he said, *You take it from here and do your best. God is found here in this wilderness.*

And then he was gone, vanished like the wind, which came up just then and moved through the Basin camp. I remained on my bed, alone with my diary and my thoughts.

A sense of having been with Father, close to him, stayed with me for a long time. But in time my image of Father was replaced by a vision of Kora, and I awoke again. I took pen in hand and made an entry in my journal, perhaps a talisman, for what was to come.

I wrote of my love for Kora, but also of the pressure of life forces upon her, which kept coming back to a resolution satisfactory only to her surrounding her claim to the Basin. I wrote out my fears for what would become of the wilderness, and our love.

"I place my love for you, Kora, in limbo, in a lock box, and I am going to store it in safe keeping for some time, or perhaps forever. I hope our love will survive even this, though for the first time in my life, I'm not certain that it will." And then I said a prayer and closed my journal.

The only two things I was certain of, just then, were that Kora was going to act, and that Will and I would be forced to do what was necessary.

Kora could succumb to developers who would rape these lands for their timber — put railroads through, erect hotels on unspoiled shores, bring in tourists and new residents, changing it forever — unless the Basin became part of the state forest, protected by the covenant the state had made with us, the people, to preserve it.

Her debt, inherited from the husband she had never loved, controlled her destiny. I didn't see a way to help her that wouldn't disclose to the entire world that she could claim the Basin. If I did that, I would only insure that her interest could be claimed by Thornwood and other creditors, and that would make meaningless any forever wild provision.

I poured myself a whiskey. The spirits soon gained full hold, and my mellow mood was replaced soon by rancor. My thoughts turned to Will. Will, my son by Kora, would have to choose between his parents. He'd see things my way; he'd see things through, wouldn't he? Difficult as his choice was, I expected him to join me and rise to the task of protecting the Basin—thus placing himself squarely between his mother and me.

Sobbing.

Somehow I'd fallen back to sleep, but I was reawakened by a sobbing Kora in the room just above mine. I heard the rustle of paper, and heard what I thought was scribbling, like a person writing with a quill pen on parchment, something Kora often did.

"There. Done," she said, in a half-aloud whisper, her last word coming from deep within, an almost guttural sound. It certainly sounded, from her odd voice, that Kora was under the hold of her whiskey.

I knew she'd just put her plan into action.

The soft staccato of the one-lung packet boat came to my ear again as I continued listening to Kora stirring in the room she'd occupied this visit. It was the first time she'd been in camp that we hadn't slept together.

The boat had come for her and for the paper she had just signed. Her way out had arrived, courtesy of Mr. Thornwood of New York City, on this early morning of September 4, 1937.

"Mrs. Hubreth," a voice called out. "We're ready, are you there? Come. Now."

I heard Kora step out of her room into the light from the high oval window and move down the steps, through the great room and across the porch to the waiting launch. She moved quickly and quietly. In the morning mist I could make out the figure of two men in the boat, who cast off as soon as Kora arrived and headed with their cargo and a signed paper for the village landing. I knew there was nothing I could do to stop her, short of physically restraining her, which, of course, was out of the question. So I went to her room and saw there an envelope with my name on it. I opened it, already knowing its content.

Jack Durant, we have lived our lives, sometimes together, but more often apart. As Keene said, we each have a life path, and this is mine. Don't you see? It's my only way out. I have a plan, you must know. Mr. Thornwood of the development company, who is acquiring my interest in the Basin, will take great care for its preservation. He will not desecrate it with many houses or hotels ...."

There the note stopped, mid-sentence. Kora perhaps realized the lie of what she'd put on paper, and could not go on with the charade. She'd probably flung her quill to the bed, where it now lay, and hurried to leave the Basin camp.

I stood at my window listening as the launch headed toward the village landing. I imagined the scene as it would probably unfold: a dark figure lurking at the village dock steps to the launch with hand outstretched for the delivery of an executed paper giving the Thornwood Company valuable rights to the Basin, and enabling Thornwood's company to prevent my plan for delivery of a deed to the state under the forever wild clause.

This vision was not a dream; this was reality. And Will and I would have to take action immediately if we were to save the title and protect the trust placed with us by Keene Durant.

Pushing through the door to the law office the next morning, I found Will up early and hard at work with two men, the elder of whom I once knew: the now-retired Joseph Alexander Hamilton from the Attorney General's office. Hamilton was an old man now, but he was in the company of a young lawyer, Alexander Russell, who was now in charge of Adirondack land holdings for the state. They meant to protect the state's interest in the Basin, with our help, and had arrived at my office before me to get a head start.

Together, we worked purposefully and completed an order to stop any transfer by Kora. That afternoon we presented the paper to a court. The judge signed it, and the order was ready for service on Kora, requiring her immediate court appearance to show cause why the relief requested, to temporarily prevent her attempted transfer of any interest in the Basin, should not be granted.

The papers, drawn by young Russell under Hamilton's direction, spelled out that the title that rested in Will's and my names, with the remainder interest to the state. Will had heeded well Keene's and my advice to take action in a timely way. He'd recounted in the papers only enough facts to reveal that the deed from Longfellow was to me, and to him as the sole grandson of Longfellow, that it had been recorded in 1920, and that Kora did not have an interest in the Basin property under that document.

Neither he nor I revealed Kora's possible claim to title as Longfellow's heir, since the deed by Longfellow, if given effect, would control the title. We asked for that 1920 deed to be given presumptive effect as the controlling title document. It wasn't revealed that Keene had held the deed in escrow for twenty six years. Will swore to the facts about Kora: that he'd spoken to his mother and she'd admitted her need to get relief from her creditors in any way she could; that she'd been hounded by them and robbed of any peace of mind for the past many years. Will testified that he'd become aware that Thornwood had put the greatest pressure on her through a debt collection law firm that had dogged her, even putting her through depositions and court procedures designed to get at her assets; that Kora was threatened with jail if she didn't reveal all that she owned or had an interest in, and that she'd gone on record in those proceedings as having no interest in any land in the Adirondacks.

Our papers filed with the court consisted of the deed document from Longfellow to Will and me; the letter of instructions from Longfellow to Keene, and from Keene to Will and me; and supporting affidavits from Will and Hamilton. Those should be legally sufficient papers to submit to the judge in Elizabethtown, requesting him to issue the temporary order making it clear that any conveyance Kora made without court approval would be treated as null and void.

"I remember well my commitment to you, Jack," Hamilton said, "that I'd make sure there were no challenges from the state to the title proven in the Aber trial."

But, he said, just before the papers were filed, there was one more urgent need: Hamilton wasn't convinced the state could take any action until Will and I were ready to surrender our life interest in it. I told him that both of us were prepared to do so in order to put the property out of harm's way. Supplemental affidavits were then prepared and sworn to by Will and me.

Our affidavits, stating we would sign off, were filed as part of the court application. The judge realized irreparable harm could be done to the Basin title, and immediately signed the temporary order requiring Kora's appearance to explain herself.

Hamilton walked to the village landing, knowing from his sources in the village that Kora would appear there soon to meet Thornwood's courier. She'd already had a meeting with the agent that morning to review the document that would result in her release from debt in exchange for her deed to the Basin.

She was smart enough to insist that the release of her liability, signed by Thornwoood, be placed in her hand first. That worked to delay things, as the agent wasn't sure about doing that, and had to go in search of Thornwood for approval. Kora was told to meet the courier at the dock in two hours for the final exchange. That was all Hamilton's contacts knew about the situation, but it was enough.

He and I went to the landing later that morning, arriving in time to see her hired launch approach, and the man waiting for her step abruptly forward with hand outstretched for Kora's signed document.

Hamilton went into action while I stayed in the background.

As Kora handed her paper over, Hamilton stepped forward with his order to show cause. "Mrs. Kora Longfellow Hubreth, here is a court order that requires you to be in court tomorrow. It states that you must not transfer any interest in the Basin lands to anyone without court approval. I suggest you take back the paper you just handed this gentleman—it's worthless and in violation of the court order!"

Kora looked at the order and shouted, "What is this? Why is 'any transfer by Kora Longfellow Hubreth of an interest in the lands herein' prohibited pending a court hearing? Just who do you think you are, sir, to hand me these papers? This is an outrage!"

"Read on, Mrs. Hubreth. The paper also states that upon your failure to appear and satisfactorily explain, any transfer by you of the Basin lands shall be treated as null and void. It says that the deed recorded from William West Longfellow gives Jack Durant and Longfellow's only grandson, William Durant, the title for their lives, and the remainder to the State of New York. The order is returnable in court this afternoon, madam."

Kora didn't appear that afternoon in court. After Hamilton's confrontation with her there at the dock, she'd ripped the signed deed out of the courier's hands and shredded it. The courier quickly disappeared in the rising mist, and the agent quickly left town.

"Damn you, Jack! Go to hell!" she'd glowered at me. It was the only time in her life she'd sworn at me.

Our quick action that day had succeeded, but it left Kora with her financial problems. She left for New York on the waiting train, the Thornwood debt still a dead weight on her.

Six weeks later, I contacted her by telephone to talk things over. Subsequent to leaving town, she'd learned that the court order had been entered when she defaulted in appearing. Soon afterwards, Thornwood and other creditors lost interest in the Basin lands, raising Kora's hopes that ultimately they'd give up on trying to collect from what they saw as a lost cause. That, at least, provided her some relief.

But at the time of that phone call, our personal future looked very uncertain. We decided to leave well enough alone: we'd visit occasionally, but we wouldn't discuss either marriage or ownership of the Basin, ever again, in direct conversation. This understanding proved a good one.

Hamilton and Alex Russell, along with my friend Bill McGrath and Will, all joined me back at the office. We congratulated ourselves for succeeding in getting the

Judge to sign the final order, which remains in effect today, restraining Kora from any transfer of the Basin lands. But the victory had been won at great personal cost to Will and me.

"In my mind, Father," Will said, "this leaves only one important loose end. We should in fact deliver title to the state soon by surrendering our life estates — on the condition that the state abides by the language and keeps the land forever wild."

Will had heard about a new Adirondack Agency that, together with the new state Conservation Department, would have responsibility for the preserved lands. Sitting around the office library table, Bill McGrath, recently retired from the *Adirondack Daily Enterprise*, told Will that finishing the deed and giving title to the state would honor Keene Durant.

He added, "And it would honor your father, as well."

McGrath, always the savvy native with a built-in distrust of the state, surprised me with the following.

"You fellas know I am older now, and I've had time to think on things. I see what's happening to the character of the Park, and I don't like the new Park Agency proposal we keep hearing about out of Albany." There was a long silence as Bill looked down, then around table.

"But as long as they do their job, I don't know any better way to preserve the Adirondacks for all the people— now and for generations to come." McGrath shook his head, as if surprised to hear the words coming from his mouth. "And with that said, I say we adjourn to the hotel for a bourbon on me! You gentlemen look in need."

"We'll be right along, Bill, but I want a private word with Jack, first."

McGrath and his young colleague left, and Will and I faced each other.

"Will, you went into right action and we didn't even have a chance to talk it over. But you instinctively knew what to do if the Basin was to be preserved. And yet I think you're right. Maybe it's time to put the deed over to the state now. I suppose they'll let us have use of the camp for a while. Rondeau's use can be written in and we can enjoy the land along with all the people. As for the Abers, they're safe and sound under their deed from Paquette. Just think. This land as part of the public domain! And it'll stay that way for all future generations. So, Will, are you ready to sign off?"

He nodded. "From now on, the state will defend title and preserve the land. Right?"

"Yes. I'll set up the arrangements. But for now, let's join our friends at the hotel for a drink. This isn't really a celebration, though, is it, son. It's the end of an era." Looking at him, I was sure I read his thoughts. "And we'll do everything we can to reconstruct things with your mother, if that's possible."

I didn't tell Will, of course, that my love for his mother had shifted to some other, but still important, part of my being.

"Mother will have to find her own way out without involving these lands," he said, surprising and deeply pleasing me. "I'm prepared to live with that reality. But I'll always maintain contact with her."

He led the way out of the office. The boy had his grandfathers' iron will and prescience, despite his youth. It appeared to me that Kora was finding her way out of her financial morass. Our court action against her had led Thornwood to lay off, and Kora told me that Hubreth's estate had been successfully closed in New York. She was free of harassment and could now move on, though she understood that she had to wait out the judgment against her, filed in New York, for many years until it expired finally in 1952.

I let out a sigh of relief. The court action had placed Will and me in a difficult position in which we'd used what leverage we had to gain a measure of power over Kora. But we would lose control over the Basin to the state when its remainder interest took hold. Kora knew this too, but made her peace with it, she said.

The entire North Country talked about the news of the order served on Kora to show cause. And it seemed that everyone was waiting for the other shoe to drop, too.

Will and I had extended talks, with each other and with state officials, about signing over the deed to the state on condition that the land and lodge be kept forever wild. But as we talked between ourselves, I began to urge caution about signing our estates over immediately. We clearly had the state officials on our side, finally, and we had breathing room in which to consider our options. Will agreed, after thinking about it, and so time went by. In fact, years moved on to decades of waiting and watching.

I would occasionally hear from the state officials on the intended transfer. There were discussions about a fair price, the status of the title, Kora's possible remaining stake in the title as an heir of Longfellow, the effect of the Thornwood judgment against her, and a host of other things. As it turned out, the state was not in a hurry to take title, as long as it knew it would ultimately do so.

And so the question of whether Kora would sign off her interest as William West Longfellow's sole heir at law remained unanswered for years to come.

I honored Kora's wish that we never again discuss it.

For many years, in the forties and fifties, she and I planned a summer paddle in our canoe. We paddled to reaches of the Basin, where we talked and loved. We continued to exchange letters. With each visit, my love was let out of storage, and each time she left, it went back in. True to our agreement, we hadn't talked of marriage in years, even when it was clear that Hubreth's creditors no longer pursued her and her assets.

On a hot afternoon in August of 1958, Kora and I paddled silently on the lake. It was our lollygag stroke —nice and easy. The familiar motion felt good to me, but Kora seemed preoccupied.

"Jack, let's paddle to the stone chapel for a visit!"

I was surprised by her request, but responded by ruddering toward the chapel on the edge of the village on the far shore. Kora turned briefly from the bow and gave me a faint smile.

The chapel had remained a place of refuge for us; we'd spent many hours here over the years. We pulled our canoe ashore and walked into its quiet. Muted sunlight came from the high arched stained glass windows, and distant mountain peaks were visible in the high clear glass of the transept windows.

Standing hand in hand, we let the place take us in. I found myself thinking about Keene's final conversation with me at dinner, the last night of his life — about events, people, and the wilderness; about the great challenges he saw in the years to come, and the risk of losing the wilderness. It comforted me to think that this place, at least, might remain unchanged.

When Kora stirred beside me, I looked down and found her face fully on mine.

"I wanted us to come here, Jack, to be here together with… with God as our witness."

She looked at me expectantly, but I didn't yet

understand what she was leading up to. Seeing my uncertainty, she chewed at her lower lip. I shook her hand gently.

"Go on," I said. "Tell me what it is you want."

She drew a breath and said, "Let's exchange private vows of love—as husband and wife."

When I still didn't respond, she said, "Why don't we have it between us that way, Jack? It's our truth."

I stared at her wonderful half smile as she pulled me gently toward the altar. I felt my life flashing before me, all the ups and downs with this woman I'd loved all my life. The woman who'd brought both intense pain and profound gratification, who'd brought me our son Will, the grandson of Keene and William — and three of whom I sensed were there, joining me for this moment of ceremony. Each of them had in his own way, I realized, wanted this moment.

We moved close to the altar and stopped there, both our hands joined.

"Jack Durant," Kora said, looking into my eyes, "I declare you as my husband and lover in the eyes of our Maker." Her eyes searched mine intently. "For the ages."

"Kora Longfellow, I declare you as my wife and lover—in the eyes of our Lord and for all time."

We kissed gently. I held Kora in my arms as she looked directly into my eyes with a smile of genuine satisfaction. I felt the deepest sense of relief and happiness I'd ever experienced.

In a few moments Kora led me out the aisle, toward the sunlight. On the way, we paused to read Keene's words on the plaque, dated 1915. I read silently at first, but then aloud to Kora that this chapel was "a place of peace and solitude in a land of wilderness that we must come to understand and honor for all its inhabitants, animal and plant. May the Lord bless all of these, and may this always remain a place of spiritual and mental renewal."

I stopped there and looked at Kora.

"How fitting," she said, "that we've exchanged our vows in this place."

And so, between us, we became husband and wife and chose to tell no person. Outwardly, we carried on as usual, living apart for months at a time, but in our hearts our bond, though private, brought us a sense of well-being. After all the years, there seemed no reason to publicly state what we wished to remain a private matter of our devotion; we had no need for any official sanction. Bill McGrath, smiling happily, said it was just nice to see us together, and that was enough for us. Will just shook his head and carried on with his life, telling us he was happy to have his father and mother on good terms.

Whenever she came from New York we spent time together. She always left some of her well-tied flies in some place for me to find and delight in. Every year on March 15th, Will's birthday, he received from his mother a bouquet of roses mixed with North Country ferns and silver moss. Every June 10th, at Father and Mother's grave in the lovely clearing with a view of the Otter and distant peaks, we placed fresh alpine flowers to mark the date of his passing. My mentor, Duryea, lay close by in a clearing looking to the other side of the Basin, and there I paused each year to remember this man of unequalled ability and warmth. Every year I seemed to have an even deeper appreciation for his wisdom and the way it had guided me in every aspect of my life. There was a deep comfort in the knowledge that I had passed on his wisdom and guidance to Will, who would, in his own way and in his own time, come to terms with his heritage.

For his part, Will seemed willing to wait and watch

the Adirondack scene, with its slow, insistent changes, and to think about the future of the Basin. He matured and his views changed, I noticed, about the state's ability to care for the property as wilderness. But he said he didn't see any better alternative, in the final analysis. In the family tradition, he'd gone on to law school and joined the Durant Law Firm in the same office Keene and I had occupied. The same lettered sign, now with new gold leaf lettering, hung outside above the door, and Will moved into Keene's space.

Will's avocations were two: trout fishing with me, and his newer interest in running. He ran to any place he could in the Adirondacks and beyond. Natives of the area looked forward to an unexpected visit from Will when he stopped for a drink of water and a rest. One day he ran to Elizabethtown along the state route, and another time as far as Saranac Lake.

He'd return to report to Kora and me how far he'd run, what he'd seen of our fellow Adirondackers and of wildlife, and of his concern that the area was starting to feel and look crowded. Will kept a journal of his observations, which ran from the 1940's and all the way through the 50's. He was an athlete and a journalist, it seemed, as well as a good lawyer and person. He did not marry, but had girlfriends all over the North Country.

As for me, the decades marking my passage through my forties and fifties rushed past. I was feeling like an older man, but the time Kora and I spent together still brought me deep satisfaction.

By 1958, Will was 39 and still a single man, and I was 73. We resolved to complete the Basin transaction by the summer of 1960, when I would be 75. The state conceded that it was ready for the transaction, even without Kora's sign-off, but it would pay us only a fraction of its real value since we held only a life estate. Also, if Kora would not join in the deed, there was a possible cloud on the title, despite the court order. Even with our private vows, I still had not come to terms with Kora on a plan for the Basin wilderness. I chose to wait and see and not bring it up until she was ready.

So it was with some consternation that I received from Kora a letter addressed to both Will and me. It was the first time she had written us a joint letter. It was dated June 10, 1960.

> *Dearest Will and Jack,*
>
> *I now urge you, Will, and your father, my beloved Jack Durant, to complete the transaction to the state, and to do so in the name of Keene, Will's paternal grandfather, a man possessed of uncommon foresight and love for these lands. And do so in the name of your maternal grandfather, William West Longfellow, who loved these lands as much as anyone. He told me, when I was a young girl, that one day he wanted me to have the Basin. But he also insisted that it be left forever wild, for all to behold.*
>
> *Will, your father understands that I cannot bring myself to join in the transaction, but I want you both to know that I now understand that its completion is best for all concerned.*
>
> *Will, you must know that your father and I have loved each other forever, even though we have lived apart. Your grandfather, Keene, told me that your father and I were on separate life paths, and he was right. But that has not held us back, and I wanted you to know that we have for years shared the sentiments of John Muir, who observed of his relationship with the woman he loved:*

'In all my wanderings through Nature's beauty, whether it be among the ferns at my cabin door, or in the high meadows and peaks, or amid the spray and music of waterfalls, you are the first to meet me, and I often speak to you as verily present in the flesh.'

I shall hope to see you both soon and love you both very much.

Kora

Will read the letter after I did and from his nods, I gathered that it helped him understand some things. His life had been spent deciphering our relationship.

But reading Kora's words had left me drained and emotionally spent. For the first time in my life I wept in front of Will.

"I love your mother dearly, Will."

He comforted me.

Kora was the only woman I wanted to lie with in my camp, by our oval mosaic that opened to our shared wilderness. The time apart, I tolerated. This was our lot as lovers in our Adirondack wilderness, a place of lands and love, set aside, reserved, forever wild under the law of man or God. It was our notion of things, as they had come to be. Some would say that ours was an incomplete love, but I would not. My Kora and I have been on seperate life paths, all right, but we've shared as much in our lives as each path allowed.

I didn't know Will's thoughts as he finished reading Kora's letter, only my own. I left it to our son to draw his own conclusion. But in our own way, we remained our own close-knit family of the Adirondacks.

Will and I have agreed to meet at the basin camp today. September 10, 1960, with state officials to sign over the title. It will not be an easy thing to do, we know, but it shall be accomplished this afternoon, God willing. The locals are saying that the moment the deed is presented for recording, the county clerk is to call the Adirondack Daily Enterprise, which plans to run a prominent story, with the following headline:

STATE NOW OWNS HALF OF COUNTY AFTER DURANTS GIVE DEED

Bill McGrath has promised to write a letter to the editor in support of our deed, which will keep the Basin forever wild, so at least there will be one voice of support. All the talk in the North Country is about the transfer, about how things will never be the same in these parts. It's a long talk, with many sides to it, and the debate goes on and won't soon end.

Will and I noted the other day that more people are coming here to get away from their daily lives, to camp and paddle in a place that's peaceful. Kora predicts that the Adirondacks will become a salvation for future generations.

And so I sit here on the grand porch of the Great Basin camp, waiting to meet Will and take action on our intention, agreed to so long ago.

I hear his vehicle driving in now.

Epilogue
July 4, 1968

A young man and woman paddle their canoe across the Basin lake to the mouth of Otter Brook. Their eighteen-month-old daughter naps, snuggled in the canoe in the warming morning sun. They're exploring the lands the state had finally opened to the public, the lands from Macomb's Purchase along the ancient path of the natives. They're enjoying the Basin lands deeded to the state by Will and me years before.

"Look at that wonderful brook, Neil! It looks like it's coming off the mountainside! Let's paddle up it a ways."

"Sure, let's do it!"

As they go, the brook narrows and they put in to shore and find the trail. No one else is around and the silence can often be unnerving, at first, to the city dwellers who visit the wilderness.

Neil backpacks his daughter up the trail, ascending toward a granite face he sees in the distance. He talks happily to his wife, Sara, he calls her, and to the child. He carries his fly rod, hoping to catch some fish – speckled trout, as he's heard the locals call them.

He ties on his favorite mayfly, a hex pattern, and casts out to a riff that settles below in a pool. Letting the fly drift to the quiet water, he stands patiently, perched on a large boulder. A speckle rises and sips in, leaving a ring on the surface. Neil sets his hook, and the fight is on.

Sara and their daughter watch. The baby is alert now and looking about as her father engages the large brookie. Neil surprises himself with his skill, and brings the trout in. He lands the speckle and holds it up for his daughter to see. Her eyes grow big as she looks at the brilliant blue halos, red spots, and streamlined shape. She squeals, delighted, and her parents laugh.

Then, as often happens here, Sara seems to sense my presence in the woods behind them, on the bank of Otter Brook. She senses my smile, I think, my happiness for them.

She hesitates, then smiles back. But she says nothing to Neil. She'd feel foolish, I suppose.

My memories of a lifetime spent on this brook pass before me, and I remain silent, content just to observe and remember.

Now all three are facing me, as I remain shrouded by the spruce that overhangs the bank of the brook. It's hard, here in the wilderness, not to sense the joy and peace of those who've lived and loved here, and gone on.

They return to their activities and I think about being raised in this Basin, of spending my best days casting my fly to the rising trout on this water; of walking these lands. The trail that leads up to here comes to mind, and I hope this family has taken it, with a stunning view of the Basin one can never forget; a trail from which you can hear the wind and the brook talking to you, if conditions are just right.

Sara is looking at her state map of the Basin, sensing the possibilities, as if she's reading. I wished I could speak to her.

Neil looks at the trout and, seeing its wild beauty, releases him to the cold, clean waters.

"Come on Sara, we've got a beautiful day and we have to see the wilderness ahead at the source of this brook."

I move ahead, searching for signs of trout in the brook, looking to see if the hex hatch is ready, just as Father and Duryea taught me, and I passed on to Will. When Neil and Sara and their baby move on, I silently wish them well, happy to have spent some time with them.

As a glorious evening falls I return to the oval mosaic where I sometimes reside. I'm feeling refreshed, renewed by the day in the wilderness, by the visitors— new friends— and a rise to the hatch that the wilderness brook has known forever.

I come here often, alone, on the wind, in search of Kora.

The End

Keene's Law is George Patte's first novel. The author's interest in the Adirondacks is life-long. In between the demands of raising a family and running his law office over three decades, he continues to frequent all parts of the North Country, savoring its rich history and its people. You might find him on any brook or stream from Forrestport to Onchiota, or in his hometown of Ithaca, NY.